The Fireflight Initiative

Book 2 in the Dodecarchy series

KL Skinner

*"Courage is the first of all human qualities,
because it is the quality which guarantees the others."*
Aristotle

First published 2022
Copyright © KL Skinner

KL Skinner asserts the moral right to be identified as the author
of this work

ISBN: 978-1-9162902-4-2

Set in Goudy Old Style by Ken Boyter
Cover and book design, typeset by Ken Boyter www.kenboyter.co.uk
Cover illustration by Toby Rigby

Acknowledgments

Thanks to editor, Kate Miller, for your critical eye and encouragement throughout, Ken Boyter, for the design and typesetting and Toby Rigby for the beautiful cover illustration.

Thanks to the Hertford Writers' Circle (www.hertfordwriterscircle.org.uk) for your constructive feedback through many readings and thank you to the volunteer readers, especially Ron and Chloe, who picked up on the bloopers I left behind.

Thank you to Sarah and Richie Beck in Anafiotika, for showing me your life in Greece. I can't wait to get there.

Thanks also to the sexy and mysterious Elena (not her real name), for explaining how legal prostitution works in Athens. You answered my questions with honesty and candour. But I'm not trying that.

Love as well as thanks is owed to Fiona Crawford and Diana Wicks, two amazing ladies. You've been incredibly generous with your time, explaining what life is like living with OCD and anxiety. Thanks also for describing what OCD is not.

Grateful thanks to university friends, Mia, Steven and Hugo. Thank you for explaining serology, genetics and foetal development in words I could understand. Thanks also for describing the amazing possibilities. Any impossibilities are my own creation.

And thank you to Shaun as always, just because.

PART 1

Chapter 1

'Athena, this is Gaia. I really need to see you. Can we meet?' It had been at least ten months since anyone had called me by that name. I swallowed hard.

The phone had rung twice the night before. The first time we were out; Nick and I had been invited over to a friend's house for drinks, and the second time Nick was asleep in front of the TV and I was already upstairs getting ready for bed. They hadn't left a message but were obviously keen to get hold of me.

'Do you know the coffee shop on the corner of Connor Street?' she continued nervously. 'Meet me there tomorrow at 2 o'clock. Look, I can't really talk, I'm sure I'm being watched. Please Athena,' she begged. 'I really need you.'

I had said nothing during that call, but replaced the receiver wishing I'd been able to say no. I wished I'd been able to cry out, shout, scream, anything. But my mouth had gone dry and my mind had raced too fast for me to get a grip on what I was thinking.

My hands were trembling as I pressed 1471. Unsurprisingly, she'd withheld her number.

I walked slowly into the living room, sat on the arm of Nick's chair and stared at the TV. He was watching the motor racing and cursing that our bloke was too slow and losing points. The image blurred before my eyes as I realised that The Company had another scheme in progress. I started to cry when I understood that I was going to get pulled back into that horrible, sordid world and that because someone needed me, I would go.

Nick's arm rested comfortably on my leg and received a light splash, making him look up and stare at me, concerned.

'Kim? What is it?'

'I'm going to need a lift into town tomorrow lunchtime,' I said, but I couldn't tell him why, as emotion overcame me and I sobbed with my head buried in his shoulder.

Nick managed to get the whole story out of me before we went to bed that night and he was furious.

'Jesus, Kim!' he yelled. 'I thought we'd left that bloody mess behind. She's got a cheek phoning you and where'd she get our number from? You should've just hung up.'

'I put a notice in the local paper, remember? We did that together to provoke a response. They've responded.'

'Well, if you're so sure you're going, I am too. I want to be there when she turns up.'

'No, Nick!' I was suddenly afraid. If Gaia was in trouble, as she believed she was, she probably wouldn't come in to talk to me if she saw a stranger there. Although, to be honest I was a stranger too; we'd never actually met.

Nick sat on the edge of the bed with his back to me.

'I'm coming,' he said. We didn't spoon that night.

Ten months ago I'd been sent on a simple errand by my

manager and while out of the office had been kidnapped and taken to a deserted house. I had been made to reveal account codes that released huge sums of money to finance an illegal fertility drug and innocent women, believing that they had signed up for a legitimate drug trial, had their lives put at risk. The company I'd worked for had been a front for a mysterious organisation called Fireflight and everything I'd done for them, the professional relationships I'd formed and the dedication I had shown was wasted. It was all a lie and I'd been a fool. When I'd found out the truth, my biggest concern had been for the welfare of the female volunteers. Gaia was one.

I lay still in the dark with my eyes open. At that moment, there were only two things I could be sure of. I was definitely keeping my appointment with Gaia and, come hell or high water, I was going to find out what Fireflight was up to.

The following day, I was pacing the house like a restless tiger. I'd scrubbed the bathroom to within an inch of its life and, unable to eat anything, was threatening to do the same to the kitchen cupboards. I'd been glancing at the clock every fifteen minutes and had already drunk my weight in tea when Nick returned from work at one thirty.

'Come on, then,' he shrugged, keeping his hands in his jacket pockets. 'Let's hear what she's got to say.'

The coffee shop was still busy with the lunchtime trade when we arrived. Harassed office workers ordered extra strong espresso and calorific snacks to take away while those who could afford to spare a whole hour, lounged in leather chairs as they read the newspapers or browsed their phones. I chose a low table with a sofa facing the door so that I could people watch. I had no idea how I'd recognise Gaia when I saw her.

I bit my nails and ignored a fast cooling cappuccino as Nick sipped black coffee until a quiet voice said, 'Hello Athena.'

She was slightly older than I expected; early to mid-forties with shoulder length light brown hair and blue eyes. She was pushing a modern-looking pram with a baby boy, about two months old, who was wearing clothes that looked more expensive than those she was wearing herself. His serious dark eyes observed me curiously. There was no mistaking who his father was. I would have known Hephaestus' child anywhere.

I involuntarily shivered as I remembered that psychopathic drug developer. He had tried to attack me and enrol me into their plans. I had been lucky to escape him. I wasn't sure I wanted to know what had happened to Gaia.

Gaia sat down opposite me, leaving the pram near Nick who offered the boy his keys to slobber over.

She smiled at me and looked relieved.

'You came. I'm so glad. I read your notice in the paper.'

'I've been waiting for a response.'

'But that was months ago,' said Nick. 'Why wait so long?'

Gaia glanced at the windows. 'Who's watching us? Eyes are everywhere. I was released about the same time you were.' She smiled at the little boy. 'At least I was able to have Eric at home.'

'Who released you?'

'Hermes. When I read 'Athena wishes to thank,' it gave me hope that there was a life outside the clinic. I was surprised you hadn't left the area.'

Nick and I had briefly considered it, but I decided I was going to brazen it out. It was my crazy way of sticking two fingers up at everyone. If we were going to move house, it would be because we wanted to, not because we thought we had to.

I quickly glanced at Nick, wondering if I should introduce him, but Gaia pre-empted me.

'I'm glad you came too, Nick. This will involve both of you.'

I was immediately suspicious. 'How do know who Nick is?'

'The Company has files on everyone. I used my home computer to find you. They probably know that by now.' She glanced at her watch. 'I'm fairly sure I'm being followed, so I'll get straight to the point.' Gaia leaned forward with her elbows on her knees to talk confidentially, but I could see Nick was having trouble taking this seriously. I wasn't sure if all this cloak and dagger was necessary either. If The Company had wanted us dead, we'd be dead already.

'I'm pretty sure that I'll be sacrificed in the next Company project and I want to know if you'll agree to care for Eric and raise him as your own.'

There was a moment's silence as Nick and I glanced at

each other before staring back at Gaia.

'Sacrificed,' Nick snorted. 'Don't you think that's being a bit melodramatic?'

At one point, not so long ago, I thought I was going to be sacrificed too. I threw Nick a shut-up-and-listen look and hoped that Gaia would continue. She fiddled with the packets of sugar and sweetener on the table, arranging them in order.

'After Hephaestus's mistakes became known, we had to move to a different location. We were bussed for miles during the night. When we arrived, I saw that the place we'd been brought to was an abandoned hospital. It wasn't as nice as the clinic, but it was clean. It had obviously been prepared in advance.'

I was unsurprised. The first clinic probably looked lovely, to project a professional image. The hospital was on standby.

'I asked what was to become of me and they said I was a heroine, my baby was destined for great things and I wasn't to worry, they'd take care of me.' She looked towards the pram and I saw a tear overspill, but Gaia quickly brushed it away and glanced up towards the other customers, embarrassed.

'Later, I was told that if I wanted to keep my baby, I had to work to earn the things he'd need. I thought that meant prostitution, but when they found out that I used to be a lab assistant, they had another idea.' She'd finished with the sugar and was now neatening the serviettes in the tray. 'I examined ovarian tissue for its suitability for cryogenic preservation.'

I reached over and gripped her hand to stop her and the touch seemed to startle her, as if physical human contact was strange and unexpected.

'What are they doing, Gaia?'

I hadn't meant for my voice to sound as harsh and demanding as it did. Gaia looked like a rabbit caught in headlights and I could clearly feel her pulse throbbing in her wrist.

'I'm not sure,' she whispered. 'We didn't know where the tissue had come from or where it was going and we didn't ask.'

'How many samples are there?'

Gaia closed her eyes and dropped her chin onto her chest. 'Thousands.'

Chapter 2

I held Gaia's hands tightly and nodded towards the pram.

'And what about Eric?'

Gaia's voice trembled and she couldn't hide her tears this time.

'His every need is catered for, his education assured and the greatness of his future awaits him.'

Nick nodded his understanding.

'Be careful what you wish for,' he quoted.

'Hermes came to the clinic and told me that Zeus wanted to talk to me.' Gaia clasped her hands together tightly. 'But he drove me to the town centre and left me there.'

'What are they up to Gaia? What happens to these samples?'

Gaia glanced towards the windows before she answered.

'The Company has discovered that if they inject a particular compound into a participant before freezing the sample, the resulting embryo has the possibility of becoming a child with unusually advanced intelligence.'

'What?! So now they're trying to create some sort of super race? That's been tried before and it failed.'

'Only because the attempt was too big. Think about it. When these children grow up, they could be company managers or CEOs, running major international operations or high ranking politicians, and doing this in their late teens or early twenties. They could have left school, college and university all before their eighteenth birthday. Who will be running the country then? The regular guys who have had to slog their way to the top? Or the people mentoring these kids, slipping them unseen into the general population?'

I didn't believe it.

'This is ridiculous,' I scoffed. 'It's sci-fi.'

'It's possible.'

'Is Eric....?'

'I don't know, maybe. Maybe he's just a little advanced.'

'Oh, Gaia...'

'Well, nature or nurture, it'll all depend on how he's raised, won't it?' She looked at me directly, still expecting an answer.

'What about your family?' asked Nick. 'Couldn't they look after Eric?'

'I don't have any family. My parents died years ago and I never married. The Company chooses its employees very well.'

'You could have turned down the job,' I insisted. 'You must have known what you were getting into.'

'Nobody leaves The Company,' she said. 'It's not as if I had much of a choice. And besides, until just recently, I believed everything they'd said; they were saving the world and I could do that too.'

'But these tests, all the women they've conned. You were

one of those women. These experiments sound positively Frankenstein. It's just not right.'

Gaia was angry.

'Who the bloody hell are you to say what's right or wrong? We all make decisions, choices; what makes them the right one is the outcome.'

'How can you say that? How could you help them? Didn't you stop to think about the social implications? Don't try and tell me you were assimilated into the mind of the Borg!'

'Don't you dare look down your nose at me!' she whispered harshly. A woman close by pretended she hadn't heard and turned away. 'I wasn't rash and I'm not stupid. I just said yes to the wrong organisation.'

'Well, they're hardly likely to bump you off,' I retorted, 'seeing as how you're such a wonderful asset.'

'What would you say to someone who offered you such an opportunity? I was a perfect candidate for their fertility drug and had the promise of a great career at the cutting edge of science.'

'I'd say, 'so long and thanks for all the fish'.'
Gaia raised her eyebrows and gave one of the looks my father used whenever I back-chatted him as a child. 'So now you're cracking jokes about comic science fiction?'

'Actually sweetie, for a minute there, I thought you were.' Gaia closed her eyes again and bit her lip.

'Have you ever heard of Gaia Hypothesis?'
I shook my head. 'What's that got to do with this?'

'Your body responds to changes, like heat and cold, to keep it working well. If you get too hot, you'll sweat, if you get too cold, you'll shiver. The hypothesis suggests that the Earth can make similar adjustments. Some say it can regulate itself very successfully as long as humans don't interfere. Well, I believe that everything in nature is connected; all natural occurrences, like volcanoes or glaciers can be considered as alive because they are part of the Earth and the Earth can be thought of as a single living organism.'

I shrugged. I didn't really have a particular faith and this sounded a bit too 'new age religion' for me, but hey, each to their own.

'Fireflight have adopted the idea that the human race can be thought of in the same way; as a single living entity. Imagine a shoal of fish, turning and twisting. Moving together, they have a better chance of avoiding a shark. The Olympians are researching newer and more powerful compounds, designed to create stronger and more intelligent children, and they think that the key to discovering them is me.'

I remembered my own experience of the Olympians. They were the committee of twelve controlling members who made decisions about what scheme they would pursue next. They didn't care whom they trod on, either.

They named themselves after Greek gods and Zeus was the unseen Mr. Big of the operation. I wondered if Hermes still worked for Fireflight. Tony Brownlow had been my manager and had freed me against Company wishes and no one leaves The Company.

'So, they want you to be a heroine again. How nice.'

'You don't understand.' Gaia pointed to herself. 'It's me. I am the key. My blood, my body and probably also, my son. They're most interested in a reproductive theory. If they can influence how people have children, where in the world and with whom, they'd control everything.'

'I still don't understand. What has that control got to do with you?'

Gaia sighed and rubbed two fingers and a thumb across her forehead as if she had a headache. 'Look, imagine for one moment, a bulb, like an onion or a whole head of garlic. If you cut it in two or even into pieces and then plant the pieces, they can redevelop and grow into new plants. What if people could face destruction and regenerate in the same way?'

Nick frowned.

'That's horrific – it could change the way we think about war, disease and even life. If they want to save the world by taking it over, why would they destroy people?'

Gaia looked at Nick sadly. 'They won't. They'll just destroy me.'

Nick still didn't believe her. 'Are you really trying to tell us that there's a crazy megalomaniac out there?'

'Yes. And I think he plans to kill me and redeploy component parts of my body like a broken-up car.'

'Are you talking about illegal transplantation?'

'I think that's the most likely possibility. I don't exactly know what they have planned for my body, but I do know that I responded to their trials differently than the other women and they want to explore additional options.'

I'd already lost interest in this theoretical mumbo jumbo and was watching the traffic outside the front of the shop.

A man was helping a smartly dressed woman out from a car and I was impressed by this wonderfully old fashioned gesture. He lifted a heavy and expensive looking coat on to her shoulders and she shook her fair curls over the top of the collar. Somehow this seemed strange. It was a warm day; that was the wrong coat for weather like this.

'That's the wrong coat.'

'What?' Nick was trying to retrieve his wet keys from the baby's mouth and received an indignant squawk.

Already the couple was at the door of the coffee shop.

'Take the pram and get out of here,' I instructed, moving my phone from my bag to my jacket pocket. 'Do it now.'

Nick didn't understand and tried to argue, but the woman was now inside the door, looking directly at Gaia's back. She reached her arm across her body to the inside lining of her coat.

Gaia didn't bother to turn around. She looked back at my husband.

'Please Nick,' she said quietly. 'Save my son.'
The woman was now less than six feet away and paused for a second as she pulled a small handgun from her coat and pointed it at Gaia.

Nick jumped up and grabbed for the pram. Gaia looked

at me.

'Time to say goodbye,' she said. 'Use my name. Say 'goodbye...'' She blinked as her body jerked. 'Say 'goodbye''

I ran around the table and held her to me like a fretful child and we both collapsed to our knees as staff and patrons ran screaming past us towards the exits, jostling the pram. Nick was carried along on the wave of people as panic kicked in.

I pressed my hand to the space between her shoulder blades and felt the blood ooze between my fingers. I pressed harder, thinking that maybe I could stem the flow, but in my heart of hearts, I knew it was already too late. I didn't realise I was crying until I saw that I was making her shirt wet.

'Tell me your name,' I whispered, desperate to grant her last wish.

Gaia rested her head on my shoulder like a sleeping baby. I blinked several times as tears streamed down my face and my throat tightened. I had to cough before I could talk.

'Please,' I begged. 'Tell me your name.'

I could smell her blood and knew that we'd never get to say goodbye; it was that disgusting, sweet, cloying smell that sticks to the inside of your nose.

I placed my other hand behind her head to look at her, but her eyes were now unseeing, unblinking.

The woman's high heels tapped across the floor as she came near to observe the scene, the gun held casually by her side. She tutted as she noticed the spilt coffee on her shoes. Peters looked over her shoulder at the two of us on the floor.

'Ooh, two for the price of one,' he said.

The woman stared at me with pale blue eyes and lifted the gun slightly from her side to point it at my chest.

'You're coming with us,' she said.

Chapter 3

The woman grabbed the back of my collar pulling me to my feet and Gaia slipped from my arms like a pillow on to the floor. Digging the handgun into my side, she marched me towards the main doors and out on to the busy street. Passers-by dodged around us, annoyed that we were in their way.

'Don't say a word,' whispered the woman. I looked down at my hands, to see if they were shaking. They were smeared with Gaia's blood and I started to cry. 'Shut up,' she demanded and gave me sharp poke in the ribs.

Peters was right behind us and had Gaia in his arms, wrapped in his jacket, as if she weighed no more than a naked shop mannequin. He stretched out the hand under her knees and pressed a button on the car key. The boot opened and he laid Gaia inside while the woman ushered me into the back seat. Peters slipped in behind the wheel and drove us North, up Conner Street and away from the town. I tried to calm my breathing and clear my head.

'Don't panic,' I thought, 'Nick made it out of there. He'll be phoning people, calling the police. A search will be underway.'

'Sit still and be quiet,' ordered the woman. 'Do as you're told, or you'll be sharing the boot with Gaia.'

'You don't have to worry too much about her,' commented Peters over his shoulder, 'she's been here before.'

The woman's cold eyes registered a degree of surprise.

'Ares, meet Athena. Athena, this is Ares.' I stared at the woman and the handgun she had pointed at my ribs.

'Isn't that your user name? This could make The Company's plans a little complicated. Didn't you and Aphrodite have a child together?'

Peters laughed. 'Now, now, Kim. Don't be sexist. You know The Company always has more than one plan.' This was true. I could only wonder in which one I was to be included.

'How's your little girl, Peters?' I asked, looking for a weak spot. 'She must be about three months old, now.'

I saw Peters' jaw flex. He kept his eyes on the road and didn't answer my question.

'Don't call me that,' he hissed. 'David Peters doesn't exist. He never did.'

I wasn't too surprised. Everything I had believed in before my first kidnap had been a fabrication. His name was just another part of it.

'What am I supposed to call you, then?' I asked.

'Hermes,' he said.

'Promotion. Congratulations. What happened to the other Hermes?'

New Hermes shrugged. 'Probably dead. He disobeyed the Elite when he set you free.'

'But you don't know for sure?' I pressed, 'You didn't see

a body?'

'He disobeyed them. He isn't around. And nobody...'

'And nobody leaves The Company,' I finished for him. Tony Brownlow had been my boss for over four years before my kidnapping and we had shared a close professional relationship, which had developed into a flirtation. Forming any kind of relationship has always been difficult for me, so it had been a shocking betrayal to discover his position as Hermes in Fireflight.

The car crossed a roundabout and entered a narrow country road. The sound of a police siren made me turn my head, but Ares poked me with the gun.

'Time to take cover,' instructed Hermes.

Ares pulled me down behind the front seats where we crouched for the next fifteen minutes. I slipped my hand into my jacket pocket and pressed the side button on my phone. This time, I stayed calm and counted 900 seconds.

When the car stopped, Ares lifted her head to peek out the car windows. 'Get up,' she instructed. 'We're here.'

Hermes led us across an area of damaged tarmac being used as a car park towards a square concrete building. Ares kept a tight grip on my arm as I was pushed through a small fire door, held open by a latch.

She made sure the door closed fully behind us and I noticed that there was a keypad by the side of the door. There would be a number I would have to learn to get out.

As soon as Ares turned around, her gun was levelled at me once again. I was led along a short corridor and through another fire door into a small, square outside space. Here, a redundant water fountain sat silently, while the water within slowly turned green. The grass pathways around it were now overgrown and seeping into the gravel, joining the weeds as nature tried to reclaim what was hers.

'Where am I going? What about Gaia?'

'You're going straight to processing,' said Hermes. 'Don't you remember? You were destined to be the heroine of the new procedure.'

'I remember. Hera told me that my name had been dropped from the reproduction programme.'

'It had. But The Company has more than one programme and you will be the heroine of this one. Zeus does not forget his promises.'

Ares was incredulous. 'You have met Hera?'

'Yes. In Crete last year.' I had asked to speak to the Olympians and Hera had been chosen to meet me. She was a black-haired woman in her fifties; proud and arrogant with a spiteful streak. I shuddered at the memory of her.

Hermes pulled open a door that had a downward concrete stairway behind. 'Hera has still not forgiven you for your actions back then.'

Ares led me down the steps and into a long basement level corridor, with large pipes running along the ceiling. We stopped at a door about a third of the way along. Reaching into a pocket, Ares pulled out a card attached to a lanyard and held it against a red flashing light on the door frame. The light turned green and the door clicked open.

Hermes pushed against the door and all heads turned in our direction as we entered. There were three women in the large and harshly lit room. Two of them walked to the left of the room, to sit at a Formica table and observe the newcomer.

'I'll leave you ladies to it, then,' Hermes said and turned to go.

Ares pointed to an attractive, older woman wearing a white lab coat; the only one still standing. 'This is Eileithyia,' she said.

'What?'

'Eye-lee-thee-eye-a,' said the woman speaking phonetically.

'Goddess of childbirth and midwifery.' She held out her hand to me. I didn't take it. 'I'm very pleased to meet you, Athena.'

'You're American?'

'Yes. From New York. I had an OB-GYN practice there for many years. I'm also a specialist in ante natal and child health. I promise, you'll be very well taken care of.'

'Get on with it,' demanded Ares.
Eileithyia indicated a reclining chair that looked like it had been stolen from a dentist's surgery.

'Sit there, please.'

'What are you going to do?' I could hear a quiver in my voice and tried taking deep breaths through my nose.

'I'm going to take your temperature, blood pressure and a blood sample.'

'And I'm going to take your jacket,' said Ares.

My heart sank as I realised she'd be taking my phone as well.

'You can keep your jewellery,' said Eileithyia.

I slipped off my coat and felt all the women watching me as I sat. No one other than Ares and Eileithyia had spoken to me since I entered the room.

Next to the chair was a small, glass-topped table, with all the implements of torture I would have expected in a doctor's surgery. Eileithyia took my temperature with an ear thermometer and recorded the result on a clipboard. She wrapped a black cloth around my arm and took my blood pressure with an old fashioned bulb and stethoscope. Next, she reached for the kidney dish.

'What do you need these tests for? Athena didn't have a child.' Already I could hear myself counting in my head, like I used to when panic overwhelmed me as a child.

Ares lifted her gun once again. 'We don't need your children. We only need you. Shut up and do as you're told.'

Eileithyia tied a strap around my upper arm and rubbed the inside of my elbow with a cotton wool ball. I saw the faintest flicker in her eyes as she moved her head just a fraction. Don't.

She gave the filled vial and the top sheet from her clipboard to Ares who took them without thanks and finally left. The whole room collectively breathed out.

'I'm Dr Helen Markham,' said the woman, unwrapping a plaster for me. 'These are Natalie and Sarah.'

I nodded at the women who smiled and nodded back.

'Are you injured?' asked Dr Helen, taking in the blood on my hands.

'No. Ares killed her.' My throat tightened and I had to cough to get the words out. 'She killed her.'

'Killed who?'

'Gaia. She killed Gaia.'

The blonde woman gasped. 'Bitch. If she wasn't armed, I'd kill her myself.'

'Natalie, don't,' said the brunette. 'You know how dangerous she can be.'

Helen ran a hand through her hair and I saw silver blended with the gold. 'Ares is dangerous because she's unpredictable. You'll have to remember that in case you see her again. There's a sink in the corner behind Sarah, but I'm afraid you'll have to wait until this evening before you'll be allowed a shower.'

The brunette moved to the side to allow me access to the sink. A dispenser of anti-bacterial soap was attached to the wall on the right. I scrubbed hard, desperate to rid myself of what I had witnessed, but I started to cry as I watched Gaia's blood disappear down the plughole. Natalie came to stand beside me and placed her hand on my arm.

'I think her name was Marie.'

'Who the hell is Ares?' I yelled.

'I've no idea,' said Helen, joining the others at the table. 'I've not been able to discover her real name. We're not supposed to be using ours, but that's our little rebellion, for what it's worth.'

'But you're working for The Company.'

'Honey, we're all working for The Company. I'm here to look for my daughter, Omorfia.' Helen fiddled with the gold locket at her throat. 'She was one of the participants in the last trial.'

I turned from the sink and rubbed the tears from my face. I shook my head. 'I've not heard that name. It's quite unusual.'

'It means Beauty in Greek,' said Helen.

'Did she have another name? I asked.'

Helen shrugged and looked down at her hands. 'Most likely.'

'So how long have you been here?'

'I've only been here a few months,' said Helen. 'Natalie and Sarah were already here when I arrived.'

I pointed to the badge on her lab coat. 'Do you get to leave this room?'

'Yes. I can get as far as the end of this corridor, but I set off the alarms if I venture any further.' Helen turned over the badge to let me see the reverse. 'You see that silver chip under the laminate? It opens this room, the dining room and the examination room. Sometimes I'm called to the lab, but I can't go in there on my own. My pass doesn't open that door.'

'Don't you ever wonder what would happen if you dug out that chip and made a run for it?'

'Every day.'

'So where do you sleep?'

'Here with you.' Helen walked to the furthest wall and pressed against the right hand side. A panel moved inwards, and what I thought was a partition wall, concertinaed to reveal a bedroom behind. Four beds were neatly lined up side by side, each with a lamp above and a small bedside table to the left.

'This used to be a hospital,' explained Helen as I joined her to view the beds. 'This room was once a contamination ward. This section was created in case one of the patients had to be separated.'

'Eileithyia, report to the Central Lab.'

The voice on the address system made us all jump and I felt the hairs on my arms stand up as I recognised the voice.

'Oh my God! Hephaestus is here!'

Chapter 4

Helen raised her eyebrows. 'You know Hephaestus?'

'We've met.'

'Don't worry. He doesn't come to this unit.' She patted my arm. 'I have to go. There'll be an enforcer on the other side of the door. We'll talk later.'

As the door clicked shut behind her, the brunette came over to talk to me.

'I'm surprised you're not screaming,' she commented, sitting on the bed. 'I couldn't stop screaming the first day I was brought here.'

I sat down next to her. 'That sounds terrifying. How did you get here?'

'I found an advertisement online looking for volunteers for a fertility drugs trial. I wasn't sure I wanted a baby at the time, but mum was upset when I told her I was gay. She took it bad. Every time I saw her, she said how sad it was that she'd never have grandchildren. The advertisement looked really professional and promised generous compensation for our time, so I talked it over with Ashley and she said to go for it.' Sarah paused to look down at her bitten fingernails. 'I don't even know if she'll still be there when I get out of here. If I get out of here.'

'You will.' I tried to smile reassuringly. 'We all will.'

'And what makes you so sure?' asked Sarah.

'Oh, didn't you know? I'm an old hand at this.'

'So I heard. Helen called you Athena.'

'That's right.'

'Hermes said his predecessor freed other women at the same time as you. Gaia, Herse and Aphrodite.'

'Aphrodite was freed? I didn't know that. But why did he free us four? What made him choose us?'

'I don't know, but it must have been a personal decision. Helen told us that the Olympians had selected him for assassination soon after. I think Marie was freed because she was pregnant. Helen said that Laura – Herse - had a miscarriage. She had a bit of a breakdown after that. I don't know about you and Aphrodite.'

'Aphrodite was pregnant. Maybe that's how he chose us. He freed the women who were most likely to have babies on the programme. Luckily, I escaped that.'

The woman nodded. 'I guess so, but why? He was working for them, right? Why let you go?'

'All I can tell you is that no one is what they seem. He was two different people to me, Hermes and Tony.'

'The same might be said of Helen. She dodges every question I try and put to her. She does seem to love her daughter, though. She said she was working in the US and flew to England to find her.'

'How did she get tied up with Fireflight, then?'

'That's what she can't explain. She told me that when she

was an OB-GYN in New York, she worked for a company called Troy.'

'Who are they? Another dodgy outfit?'

'Helen swears they're legit. They finance many different businesses, including healthcare. She asked them to transfer her to the UK so she could look for her daughter.'

'So how did she switch from Troy to Fireflight?'

'She says she doesn't know. When she landed in the UK, she was brought here.'

'You don't believe her?'

'Let's just say I have my doubts. I think you do, too.'

I frowned, but she was right. 'What makes you think so?'

'You didn't tell her your real name.'

I smiled then. 'Kim,' I said holding out my hand. 'My name's Kim.'

'Sarah,' she said taking it firmly. 'Welcome to Hades.'

'So what else can you tell me about this place? Are there other women here apart from you two?'

'I know there used to be,' said Sarah, looking thoughtful, 'but I'm not so sure, now. I think if there were, they've probably been moved. Natalie signed up to the same drugs trial as me. There was a terrible incident a few weeks ago. We're told nothing, but it was really scary.'

'What happened?'

'Well, Natalie and I guessed that other women were also kept here in small groups and were probably separated depending on the procedures they were undergoing. Hera came over from Greece to visit a woman who had just given birth to a little boy. We know this because one of the enforcers hid the baby in here.'

'Who was that?'

'I don't know. The enforcers don't speak. Not to us, anyway.'

'Why would he hide the baby? From whom?'

'We think he was hiding the baby from Hera. Sometimes we see other women in the dining room or bathrooms. We never saw Simone again. Now we're worried the same could happen to us.'

'Have you asked Helen about her?'

'Of course. She says she doesn't know what happened, but I think she knows more than she's saying.'

I thought back to my discussion with Gaia in the coffee shop.

'Gaia, I mean Marie, said that she knew she responded to the tests differently than other women. Do you know what those were?'

'No, but she and Simone were in the same group, so maybe they were the same tests. All I know is that Simone was a willing participant.'

'What?'

Our conversation was interrupted when the door clicked open.

Helen walked in slowly, closed the door and sat down at the table. She closed her eyes and let her head drop into her hands.

'What is it?' asked Natalie. 'Helen?'

'It's true,' said Helen, finally lifting her head. 'Marie.

Single gunshot wound to the back. I just identified her body.'

Natalie frowned. 'Why would Ares shoot her in the back?'

'I don't know, but she wasn't supposed to. Hephaestus told me that she'll appear before the Archon tomorrow.'

'What the hell is an Archon?' said Natalie.

'It's a judge in a private court,' I replied, walking over to the table. Sarah followed. 'Ares will be formally accused of her crime and they will discuss a possible solution. I witnessed a similar situation when Fireflight kidnapped me.'

Natalie looked at me. 'What did Marie say? What could have caused this?'

'I don't know,' I said, my throat starting to tighten again.

'She must have said something. What did you talk about?'

'She said she responded differently to the tests. She was worried about her son. She wanted to know that he'd be looked after if anything happened to her.'

'What did she think would happen?' persisted Natalie.

'She said she thought The Company would redeploy parts of her body like a broken up car.'

'Oh dear God.' Helen dropped her face into her hands again. 'I told her that.' She held her hands in front of her like she was praying. 'Cryogenic Fertility Transplantation. I was trying to send her a warning.'

Natalie narrowed her eyes at Helen. 'You sent her a warning? How?'

Helen looked at the floor. 'If they can hear our conversations,' she whispered, 'we could all end up like Marie.'

'I think it's a bit late for caution, now,' I said. 'You should tell us. How did you communicate with Marie?'

'I found a discarded burner phone and sent her a text. Gaia's private number was already logged in it. I only turned it on once to send the text and then I destroyed it.'

Natalie's voice was low and mean. 'You did what?!' She looked ready to strangle Helen at any minute. 'You had the means to make a call and tell people where we are and you sent one pissy little text?!'

'I don't know where we are! And if I had been found with that phone, I could have been assassinated, too.'

'I'd rather it was you than Marie.'

'Natalie!'

'Oh, shut up Sarah. And where the hell did you get Marie's number anyway?'

'I told you, it was already in the phone. We have our personal belongings taken from us when we arrive. It wouldn't have been hard for them to steal it.'

'Is that what happened to Simone, too?' continued Natalie. 'Was she freed and assassinated?'

'No. Absolutely not. Simone was assassinated here. I'm sure of that.'

We were silent for a moment while we looked at each other.

'And the baby?' I asked. What happened to him?'
Helen looked at me. 'I don't know, but I believe he is safe.'

'What makes you think so?'

'Do you know what one of the enforcers said when Hera

asked him about Dion, Simone's baby? He said, 'who?' That was an act of kindness. Simone told everybody that Dion was Zeus's child. She thought that if she told the Olympians about Dion, she could replace Hera.'

'Really?' I wasn't sure I could believe what Helen was saying. 'Would Zeus simply swap one jealous and spiteful wife for another?'

'Well, I don't know.' Helen looked up and shrugged. 'But that was what she wanted.'

'How did Simone die?'

'That's not my area, but I believe it was a myocardial infarction.'

'A heart attack?' I looked up at Natalie. 'So, she wasn't assassinated. Hers was a natural death.'

Helen shook her head. 'There was nothing natural about it. Simone had regular health checks. I conducted them myself. She was a perfectly healthy young woman. There was absolutely no reason why she should have had a heart attack.'

'No underlying condition?'

'None. I believe she was murdered. She was made to have a heart attack.'

'Who could have done that?'

'There are any number of people who could have done that, but only one who would have ordered it. Hera.'

Chapter 5

'Who is Zeus?' I asked. 'Couldn't he have ordered Simone's assassination?'

Helen shook her head. 'Zeus has a couple of enforcers who act as his personal bodyguards. They know who he is, Hera too. No one outside his immediate circle is supposed to know his identity. Our best guess is that he's a high level businessman, but we don't know. And it's safer for us to keep it that way.'

'So what happened?'

'Zeus paid us a visit. He does that from time to time, to check up on his investments. Anyway, soon afterwards, we discovered that Simone was pregnant. We assumed that the procedure had been successful and Fireflight decided to continue with the programme. But when Simone had the second scan, she discovered she was expecting a boy and I put two and two together. I didn't report the sex of the baby, but Simone was telling everyone that he was Zeus' son. When the baby was born Hera came to congratulate the new mother. The day after, I found Simone collapsed in her unit.'

'When did Hera come here?' I asked.

'A couple of weeks ago,' said Helen. 'I have to email the fertility reports to Hera in Greece. She would have already known that Simone was pregnant, but there were no details about the sperm donor in the report. That's confidential, even from her.'

'But if Simone was boasting that it was Zeus,' said Natalie, 'Hera could have ordered additional tests to confirm that.'

Helen looked startled. 'Well, if she did, she didn't go through me.'

'Where is Hera now?' I asked. 'Still in the UK?'

'No. As far as I know, she was only here to see Simone and ask about Dion. Tony said she was flying back to Athens.'

I was surprised. 'Tony who?'

'The enforcer. I asked him who he was. He told me his name was Tony Bridges.'

My heart beat a little faster as a wondered if this Tony Bridges could be the Tony Brownlow, Hermes, as was, that I once knew.

'And where was he taking Dion?'

'I asked him, but he wouldn't say.'

'Smart move,' said Natalie. 'Trust nobody. That's my motto.'

'But why would he take such risks to rescue this child?' I asked. 'What's so special about Dion?'

'If he really is Zeus's child,' answered Helen, 'He would be valuable to Fireflight. I don't know how, but there would be something unique about him. Hera is vengeful and malicious. If she had Simone killed, there's no telling what she could do to an innocent little baby.'

Sarah started biting her thumbnail. 'Is there any chance she might come back?'

Helen shrugged but I shook my head. 'I think that's unlikely. She probably didn't tell Zeus that she was coming and too long an absence would have raised questions.'

'But what about Zeus?' persisted Sarah. 'Wouldn't he come here? He'd want to know what Hera had been up to.'

'Hephaestus has copies of health files for Simone and Marie,' said Helen. 'If Hera was looking for proof of Simone's claims, it would be in there.'

'Well, that gives us less than twenty-four hours,' I said. 'In the kangaroo court that I was at, I'm sure that the Archon was Zeus. If he is visiting the hospital, he'll be here tomorrow.'

'And we need to find out what's in those files before he gets to them,' said Sarah, 'or else that information could just disappear.'

'He could already have them electronically,' suggested Natalie. 'Or gained access to the reports sent to Hera.'

'I've no idea what is really in those files,' whispered Helen, 'but I do know that they're dangerous. Neither Hephaestus nor I can keep any of the notes we make. We have to hand over any hand written notes to the enforcers. Everything else is typed directly into the Company computer and the only part we have access to is regarding the current project. I only know that these files exist because I caught Hephaestus copying notes from the screen. He twisted my arm and threatened to break it if I ever mentioned them to anyone.'

'Why would he be copying notes?' asked Sarah. 'I know he's a dangerous guy, but that sounds risky, even for him.'

'My best guess would be that he was creating a little insurance policy for himself,' replied Helen. 'But that is only a guess.'

A thoughtful silence hung over us.

'You still have to get them,' said Natalie at last. 'You know how important they are and if we manage to break out of here, we'll need something to take to the police.'

'Assuming we can get out of here,' said Sarah, biting her thumbnail again.

I was scared too, but tried to be reassuring. 'We don't know who's looking for us, but I'm sure that my husband will be putting a plan into action. He was there when Ares came for Marie. He'll call the police and help in the search for me.'

'I'm not sure anyone knows I'm missing,' said Natalie. 'Ewan and I broke up before I came here. I hoped that one day we'd raise a family together. I never dreamt that I could be hidden away.'

'People are looking for us,' I insisted. 'In the meantime, we should do everything we can to prepare for escape.'

'It's only going to be another hour before we're called to the dining room. Why don't I take you to the examination room straight after?' suggested Helen, looking at me. 'I'll tell the enforcers that I want to retake your blood pressure, because it was too high. That's true, by the way. The central lab is almost opposite the exam room. If Hephaestus is hiding personal files, they'll be in there. The enforcers eat in shifts after we do; there'll be fewer around then.'

'But how can we get into the lab? You said your pass didn't allow you access,' I reminded her. 'You can't get in there alone.'

'That's true, but the enforcers aren't allowed in the corridor, only outside the main doors. There are two security cameras in the corridor, one at each end. We'd have to avoid the cameras and find a way to access the lab.'

'Well, even if we can't gain access, I think it's still worth a look,' I said. 'At least then we'd have a better idea of what we're up against.'

'Good idea,' said Natalie. 'I'll come with you.'
Soon enough, an alarm sounded and the door to the unit clicked.

'We have to move quickly,' said Sarah. 'The door unlocks when an enforcer touches the pad with a pass. That gives us thirty seconds to leave the room before it locks again.'

Outside the unit, a mean looking guy with a shaved head stood opposite the door. He was wearing a black sweater with pads at the shoulders and plain black trousers and shoes, as were all the other enforcers we saw on our way to the dining room.

'Doesn't look like they went overboard with the staff uniforms,' I remarked. 'How many are here?'

'I don't know how many there are in the building,' said Helen, 'but there are at least two men on each floor; one at either end of the corridor and always one outside our unit.'

I stared at one enforcer as we entered the dining room. 'Do they speak?'

'No,' replied Natalie. 'I don't think they're allowed to. They're here to make sure that we are where we're supposed to be, but they can't touch us. If you move to go down another corridor, they'll just step in front of you and block your way. I've tried.'

'They're here for protection,' said Helen. 'Apparently.'

The dining room was a large open space with tables and chairs in blond wood. A stack of plastic trays, smelling of disinfectant, sat at the end of a long counter. Behind the counter, shutters had been pulled down. Opposite the counter at the far end of the room was a large refrigerator with a glass door showing cartons of drinks and fruit.

'Welcome to the works canteen,' said Natalie, taking a tray.

A bleeping sound pulled our attention to the shutters, which slowly rose to reveal plates of food behind. Cupboard doors behind the plates obscured what may have been the kitchen.

'You can take one plate of hot food and one dessert,' instructed Helen, 'and you can help yourself to anything from the refrigerator.'

'I'd recommend taking an extra juice carton,' said Sarah, doing just that. 'You don't get cocoa at bedtime.'

Helen frowned at Sarah. 'Each meal has been calorie counted and prepared with care. All excess fat and calories have been excluded from the menu.'

'Wait till curry night,' Sarah continued. 'That's a real treat.'

I helped myself to a pasta dish with tomatoes and a single helping sized tub of frozen yoghurt. Glancing over my shoulder, I noticed the other women already sitting at a table. I reached out my hand and pushed against the doors at the back of the shuttered area.

'Locked.' I hadn't seen Helen move to my right. She took a plate for herself. 'You're not the first to try.'

At the dinner table, I sipped bottled water and tried to eat. I wasn't very hungry, but didn't know when I'd get to eat again. Helen seemed to read my thoughts.

'It's best that you try to eat what you can. What you leave is deducted from your daily calorie intake and noted in your health reports.' She moved only her eyes upwards. 'They are always watching you.'

I lifted my head as discreetly as I could and saw a round camera fixed to the ceiling. A glance around the dining room revealed a camera above each table.

'How are we going to get to the exam room?' I asked. Helen took a forkful of white fish and vegetables. 'Leave that to me. I know what to do.'

Natalie finished her meal quite quickly. She pressed a hand to her abdomen.

'Ooh, I shouldn't have eaten so fast. I think I'm getting a stomach ache.'

Helen finished her fish but didn't touch her yoghurt. She tugged my sleeve gently.

'Follow me and say nothing.'

We left the table and approached the enforcer at the door.

'I need to take Athena to the exam room,' said Helen. 'Her blood pressure needs to be retaken.'

The enforcer stared at Helen sternly, but remained silent. He pressed a finger to his ear and then nodded, stepping aside to let us pass.

'Ooh, ow!' yelled Natalie from the table. 'I need a dose of Andrews.' She puffed her cheeks as if expecting to vomit. 'Quickly!'

The enforcer nodded again and Natalie ran after us into the corridor.

'Are you all right?' I asked Natalie once I thought we were out of earshot. She winked at me.

'Never better.'

'You're always on camera,' Helen reminded us. 'Access to the stairwells is restricted. We need to get to the next floor in the elevator.'

Natalie held her hands against her stomach as we walked back the way we'd come, until we reached a dog-leg in the corridor. Behind this corner was a single elevator.

'Is there just the one lift?' I asked. 'That doesn't seem like much, the building looked pretty big from outside.'

'This site is really a collection of buildings,' said Helen. 'They only have the parts they need in operation. There is only this lift that I know of. It runs up the centre of the building like a chimney.' The lift whirred and clonked as it landed at our floor. Helen lifted her laminate pass. 'And you need one of these to access it.' She held the pass against a flashing red light next to the buttons and the doors hissed open.

I glanced at the display above the lift as we entered. 'We're not on the fifth floor, are we?'

'No,' said Helen, as the doors shut. 'That's S for subterranean. We're going to the ground floor.' She leant forward and pressed G.

I counted the buttons. There were four above. That meant that there were six floors in total; subterranean, ground and one through four.

'OK,' said Helen as the doors opened. 'Stay close. Don't forget, we're always watched.' She led the way across the corridor to a door with a small porthole window at the top. The window was of frosted glass with a snake and sword medical logo etched within. Helen held her pass against the flashing red light and once it had turned green, she pushed the door. Ushering us in ahead of her, she jerked her head back to the doors opposite.

'That set of double doors with the narrow windows, that's the central lab. See that plain door along the corridor? That's the surveillance room.'

Helen shut the door behind us and indicated that I should sit on the examination bed.

'I'll have to retake your blood pressure anyway,' she said. 'It'll be suspicious if I don't record another reading.'

Natalie leaned against the door with her arms folded while she waited. 'How do we get across the corridor to the lab?' she asked.

'There are two cameras on the ceiling in the corridor,' said Helen. 'Each has a range that covers an area from the end of the corridor almost to the middle. That means that there's about a yard of blind space across the middle of the corridor. We'll have to creep with our backs against the wall for a few paces, until we're opposite the door, then we can walk across.'

'How do you know this?' I asked. 'Have you been in the surveillance room?'

'Yes,' said Helen turning to look at Natalie. 'The surveillance room isn't the problem. Accessing the central lab will be the biggest headache.'

'We're going to a lot of trouble here,' commented Natalie. 'Do you think it'll be worth it?'

'I do,' I responded, stubbornly. 'Those files could be evidence of what Fireflight are doing and not just the drug trials, but kidnapping, coercion and murder.'

'All participants to return to the residential unit immediately!'

'Oh my God! It's him!' I recognised the voice, the only one to scare me more than Hephaestus. Zeus had arrived at the clinic earlier than expected.

'That's bad,' said Helen, her eyes wide with alarm. 'Recall only means one thing. Invasion.'

Chapter 6

'Who could that be?' I asked. 'Police?'

'Unlikely,' replied Helen.

'Shh!' Natalie put a finger to her lips. 'There's running in the corridor!' she whispered.

Helen gripped my wrist. 'If we don't get back to the unit, they'll come looking for us.'

'Wait,' I urged, twisting my arm free. 'If people are running about, there'll be confusion. We can use this moment to take a closer look at the other rooms.'

Natalie listened closely at the door. 'The running has stopped,' she said 'Let's go. Come on Helen, we need your pass.'

'I really don't think this is a good idea,' said Helen. 'We don't know who's outside.'

'You said that there are enforcers at either end of the corridor,' I said. 'There was no one outside the exam room when we came in.'

Helen didn't answer, but already Natalie had left her post and snatched the laminate from Helen's lab coat.

'Wait! You can't use that.' Helen looked startled.

'We haven't got time to debate it,' snapped Natalie. 'Get moving.'

Natalie bleeped the door open and peered outside before signalling for us to follow. She led the way with me close behind and Helen bringing up the rear. We tiptoed along the wall as Helen had instructed and walked in single file across the corridor to the door with the long narrow windows.

Natalie tried Helen's pass again, but this time the bleep was a lower tone, denying us access.

'They'll know my pass was used against this door,' said Helen.

'Oh, shut up,' complained Natalie. 'If we're going to find out what they're up to, testing your pass against forbidden doors is something you're going to have to get used to.'

I peered through one of the narrow windows into the gloom of the darkened room.

'I wish they'd left a light on,' I said. 'I can barely see anything.'

Helen came up close behind me. 'There's an automated light system,' she said. 'It turns the lights on when it detects movement and turns them off after thirty seconds of no movement.'

'I think I can make out a work bench and a panelled wall behind. Is that right?'

Helen nodded. 'Yes. The wall has wide glass sections and there's a door to the right. You have to press a button on a microphone to talk to anyone beyond the glass.'

'Why is that? What's the other side of the glass?'

'The mortuary.'

'Eww!' said Natalie. 'Enough of that. Let's check out the surveillance room.'

'We probably won't be able to get in there, either,' said Helen.

'Why not?' I asked. 'You said you'd been in there before and that the surveillance room wouldn't be the problem.'

Natalie bleeped the door open. 'Stop bickering. We need to see what's going on.'

Bright lights lit up the room as soon as we entered, and I was relieved to see we were alone.

'Take a look at this,' said Natalie, pointing to one of the desks. 'This screen has four images on it. I can see the dining room, the kitchen, and there are two views of our corridor.'

I ran to another desk. 'This one has what looks like a main entrance, a rear entrance and two car parks.' Natalie came over to look at the screen, while I sat at the desk.

'I recognise the rear entrance,' she said. 'I was brought in here through that way.'

'Me too, and look,' I said pointing. 'Our rescuers have the same idea.'

Helen leaned over my shoulder. 'Rescuers?'

'He's found me.' Relief flooded through me as I watched Nick striding across one of the car parks. A slender figure followed.

'Omorfia!' exclaimed Helen. 'That's my daughter!'

'I recognise her,' I said, my heart sinking. 'That's Aphrodite.'

A flicker of panic lit Helen's eyes. 'Aphrodite?'

'Who's that?' asked Natalie.

'She was one of the other women involved in a project at the time I was kidnapped.' I remembered Aphrodite. She had been brought to the house where I was held. She was in her early twenties and as beautiful as a summer's day, but vain and completely self-centred.

'No, not her,' said Natalie pointing. 'Who's that?' Another figure walked across the screen, disappearing from the first car park and reappearing in the next.

'That's Charles Little,' I said relieved. 'We're definitely getting rescued. He's a senior police officer.'

'The cavalry!' laughed Natalie. 'We should get back to the unit and tell Sarah. Then we have to find a way to attract attention.'

'No!' the word flew from Helen's mouth before she could stop it.

Both Natalie and I looked at each other before turning to look at Helen.

'I mean, what if they come for the girls?'

Natalie's eyes narrowed. 'Don't you mean, what if they come for you?'

I followed Natalie's thinking. 'You've been reluctant to help us from the beginning.'

'Hey,' responded Helen, pointing back at me. 'I've helped you as far as I can. If you upset this rocky boat now, that's on you. I'm only interested in getting to Omorfia.'

'What rocky boat would that be?' I tried to mentally put the pieces together. 'The deal you made to come to the UK to look for her? Did you offer yourself in exchange for her?'

'Wait a minute,' said Natalie, holding up a finger. 'What was all that about finding a phone to send a text to Marie? Where did you find it? And how did you destroy it?'

'I was taking a huge risk.' Helen touched her fingers to her chest. 'A risk I chose to take for you guys.'

'No,' I said. 'It was a risk you took for you. But why?'

Helen stubbornly kept her mouth shut.

Natalie suddenly reached out and grabbed a handful of Helen's hair. 'Spit it out,' she yelled. 'Where did you get the phone?'

Helen squealed as she grabbed Natalie's wrist. 'It belonged to Ares,' she said. 'She'd left her phone unattended. It was in the dining room last week.'

'We should get the hell out of here,' said Natalie, still holding on to Helen's hair.
'We should,' I agreed, 'But before I run to my husband, I want to know who might run after us. Well?' I asked Helen. 'How did you do it?'

'Ares got up from the table to fetch another bottle of water from the refrigerator. Hephaestus followed her and they were talking. Hermes left the table to get a dessert. Marie had told me her mobile number and I memorised it. It only took a moment to send the text. I told her that she was being watched and that she and Eric were in danger from a new project.'

'But how did you know that?' I asked.

'Hephaestus had told me that Gaia was going to be placed

in my care.'

Natalie released her grip. 'Clever. If news of that leak got out, they'd trace it to Ares' phone.'

'But what about the cameras?' I asked. 'There's one above each table.'

Helen ran her fingers through her hair and massaged her scalp. 'This is the only surveillance room, at least that I know of. It's not manned all the time and Fireflight don't record anything. They can't afford to be caught with anything.'

'And, of course, you would know that,' I said, 'seeing as how you've been working for Fireflight for almost a year.'

'No, I told you, I've only been here a few months.'

'But that can't be true,' I said, 'if Marie told you her mobile number and you memorised it.'

Helen didn't have the chance to respond as Natalie slapped her, throwing the weight of her arm behind the swing and making Helen squeal again.

'You bitch! You're a liar and a fraud. How can we believe anything you say?'

Helen faced another desk and stood with her hands resting on the surface and her head bowed while she caught her breath.

'There is nothing in my life more important than Omorfia. I don't care what you think of me, or how you think I used you. It was all for her.' She pointed to the screen in front of me. Omorfia and Charles were staring up at a security camera looking back at us.

I left my chair and sat at the third desk.

'There's got to be a way to open the exterior doors. What happens during a fire alarm test?'

'There's a big noise and we're instructed to stay where we are,' said Natalie.

'They must have a procedure for evacuation,' I insisted. 'What are they doing now?'

Helen stood up and rubbed her cheek with the back of her hand. 'If the enforcers have been unable to scare your friends away, they'll be packing boxes, deleting files and making a getaway.'

'We'll still need information to show your friend, the police officer,' said Natalie. 'I don't think we'll be able to find a server room now. We've got to break into the central lab. Those files on Marie and Simone are all we have.'

I looked at the images on the screen in front of me. 'This looks like the inside of our unit.'

In one square of the four, Sarah was nervously pacing back and forth.

'I didn't know they had a camera inside the unit,' said Helen, 'but I recognise the others.' She pointed to another square. 'That's the unit where Marie and Simone were kept.'

'And that one,' said Natalie, pointing to another, 'is where Sarah and I were before we were moved to the current unit.' She shook her head slowly. 'Like rats in a science lab; moved from one cage to another.'

'They appear to be empty,' commented Helen.

'Well that's something to be grateful for,' said Natalie. 'It's only us in here.'

'Where would everyone be meeting if they needed to evacuate?' I asked.

Helen turned her head towards the first desk. 'In the secondary car park behind the rear entrance.'

'Then that's where we have to go. We'll go back to the unit, collect Sarah and make our way to the rear car park.'

'No,' said Helen. 'Not you. I'll take Natalie there if you like, but you can't come. You'll put everyone else in danger.' She held her hand out to Natalie. 'I'm going to need my pass back.'

Natalie pulled her hand behind her back. 'You're joking! No way.'

'My husband is out there,' I said pointing towards the door. 'I'm as desperate to see him as you are to get to Omorfia.'

'You don't understand,' replied Helen, becoming agitated. 'It's dangerous. There will be enforcers left behind whose job it will be to restrain you. Now that they've recaptured you, they're not going to let you go again.'

A spike of panic poked me in the chest. 'What do you mean, recaptured?'

Helen sighed. 'That's what Ares' instruction was. The Company found out that you and Marie were meeting at the coffee shop. Ares wasn't meant to kill Gaia. She was sent to recapture Gaia and Athena for Fireflight.'

'Then why the hell would she kill her?'

Natalie was growing impatient, keen to get back to her friend. 'Ares is hot tempered and unstable. There's no way of knowing why she'd do anything.'

'I don't know why Ares would kill Gaia,' said Helen. 'But my best guess would be that Gaia knew something about Ares she shouldn't.'

Chapter 7

'I can't see any of the gods or enforcers on these monitors,' I said. 'That must mean that they've gathered in an area with a CCTV blind spot.'

Helen nodded. 'They could be on any of the disused floors or in any of the minor buildings on site. And even if the gods are planning escape, enforcers will still be left behind. You are too much of a prize to be lost again, Athena.' I shuddered inwardly at the name. I knew I couldn't trust anything Helen told me, but I was going to need to keep her close if we were to get out of here safely.

'OK,' I said, making a decision. 'Natalie, can you take Helen's pass and get back to Sarah? Tell her what's going on. We'll meet you back there as quickly as we can.' Natalie nodded. I grabbed Helen's arm. 'You are coming with me.' I marched Helen to the door and we watched as Natalie made her way back to the lift.

'We're going to the rear car park to let my husband in. Get walking.'

Helen turned left and led me to a fire door at the end of the corridor. 'There's no way to know if this is going to set off an alarm,' she said.

'I no longer care. Keep going.'

Helen pushed through the door and we walked out into a covered walkway which enclosed a square outside space.

'I recognise this area. I was brought in through that entrance.' I nodded towards another fire door on the far side. We walked past the silent fountain, my pulse quickening with every step.

Helen paused as she placed her hands on the last fire door. 'There's still another corridor to navigate to get to the last door.'

'Yes, I remember.'

'I don't know the number to exit the final door.'

'You're going to have to try and remember, if you want to get to Omorfia,' I said.

'You don't get it. I don't know the code. It's gonna be a six figure number.'

I was starting to feel suspicious. 'Helen, what is on the other side of that fire door?' Helen didn't answer. 'Every space, even the outside spaces, seem to have a corridor that takes you to somewhere else. You said that each corridor has two cameras. That has to apply to the internal corridors, but what about this one?'

Helen looked at me as she rested her hand on the bar to open the door. I momentarily let go of her arm to push against the bar. As I pushed the bar, Helen pushed me and we both stumbled through the door into the short corridor.

'I am Eileithyia,' said Helen. 'And this is Athena.'

'I know,' said the enforcer who had been outside the dining room. He looked at me. 'I have something to give you.'

I gasped as he reached inside a pocket, but he pulled out a security pass. 'This is a copy of Hephaestus's pass. Be careful how you use it. Anywhere you go, he can go too. The Network continues to do all we can.' The enforcer looked over his shoulder. 'I have to get out of here before the gods realise I'm missing.'

'My husband is out there. Do you know the code?'

'Of course,' he replied, frowning at Helen. 'We all do. It's three eighty-five, three twenty-three; Aristotle's birth and death.'

Helen no longer pretended to be shy about the code. She pushed past the two of us and entered the numbers to release the door. Outside, she stood on the cracked tarmac as if unsure of where to turn, but a voice came to me, filling me with renewed hope.

'We need to try around this corner.'

'Nick! Nick, I'm here!'

'Kim? Kim! Where are you?'

Nick came running around the corner of the building and swept me up in hug.

'I've only been gone for a day,' I laughed. 'I really don't need all these hugs.'

The enforcer hurried past us and mouthed to me, 'Good luck, Athena.'

'Oh, shut up,' Nick murmured. 'I need the hugs.' He glanced at his watch. 'OK, it's 7.30 and dusk already. We need to get out of the area before dark. We can be in Norfolk by 10pm.'

'We're not scheduled for a visit to your parents until next month.'

'Your schedule is going to need revising,' said Nick firmly.

'But they still have my phone,' I protested.

'Forget your phone. I'll take you to the shop and we'll get it cancelled and I'll buy you another.' He ran a hand through his hair. 'Look, I made several telephone calls while you were missing and Charles and I agree that we need to get you out of London.' He gripped my hand. 'We're in the other car park. Come on.'

'Where is my daughter?' Helen's voice disturbed our reunion. She zig-zagged a finger over the scene in front of her. 'This is all very cute, but I have priorities of my own.' She glared at Nick. 'Where is Omorfia?'

'Who?' Nick looked puzzled.

'The girl with you on the security cameras,' I said.

'Oh. She said her name was Aphrodite...' Nick's explanation was cut off as Charles and Omorfia walked around the side of the building and into view. Helen immediately threw open her arms.

'Morfi!'

'Mum? What are you doing here?'

'I came to find you, sweetheart.'

'You should have stayed in New York. It's not safe in the UK.'

'We should all leave,' said a stern voice. 'Mrs Anderson. A pleasure to see you again.'

'Good to see you too, DCI Little,' I said.

Charles Little had been the Senior Investigating Officer when I was kidnapped. He had shown not only a professional concern for my safety, but also a willingness to believe me when others didn't.

'But I'm not leaving without the other women.'
Nick's face fell. 'The other women?'

'There are two other women in the residential unit waiting for us. I'm going back in to get them out.'

'Are you crazy?!' Helen's voice suggested that she already thought I was. 'The police can come and rescue them. I'm outta here.' She gripped Omorfia's arm and started walking her away.

'Actually,' said Charles, 'This will be a matter for the local constabulary. I was persuaded to take early retirement after being told that Mrs Anderson's kidnap was the work of an isolated group of conspiracy theorists.'

'Fucking fabulous!' exclaimed Nick. 'You don't think you could have mentioned this a little earlier?'

I turned to look at Helen and Omorfia. 'I no longer care what you two do, but I'm not going to leave those women with Fireflight. Not when there's the risk of another project.'

'Another project?' Omorfia turned to look at me. 'How much do you think it's worth?'

I was shocked. 'There are other women trapped in there and you're asking about money?'

'Apparently,' said Charles, 'Ms Markham received an unofficial settlement to assist with the upkeep of her child.'

'So, you made a deal? What kind of deal?'

Omorfia remained silent. Losing patience, I turned and walked back through the short corridor and into the outside space with the fountain. I paused here to see who would follow. Nick and Charles were close behind. Omorfia followed Charles and Helen followed Omorfia, not wanting to leave her again.

'Who's looking after your baby?' I asked Omorfia, as we continued our journey.

'Laura. She's got Eric, too.'

'Herse was a participant in the last project, wasn't she?' I asked. 'The same one as you. How are you finding motherhood, Omorfia?'

'Tiring,' she responded shortly. 'It puts shadows under my eyes.'

Charles cleared his throat. 'When Nick called me, I called Ms Markham and Ms James. We formulated a plan of action. I admit, it didn't include re-entering the lion's den.'

'That's something I've had to learn about plans,' I said. 'There's always someone out there willing to spoil them.'

I led everyone down the concrete stairs to the unit and tried the security pass I'd been given against the flashing red light beside the door. It bleeped denial. I was surprised, but also relieved; if what I'd been given really was a copy of Hephaestus's pass, then he couldn't gain access to the women.

'Get the hell back!' yelled a voice from within. 'If you come in here, I'll kill you!'

'Natalie, it's Kim. Open the door.'

The door clicked and as I pushed it open, I saw Sarah crouching behind the table, and Natalie standing just to the side with a chair above her head. Sarah immediately smiled, but Natalie did not relinquish her chair until I'd introduced everyone.

'Let's get out of here,' said Nick. 'We should be able to leave the way we came in.'

'We might,' said Sarah, 'but Hephaestus has already been banging on the door. He said we would be moved. He was looking for you, Kim.'

'For me? Why?'

'He wouldn't say. We haven't heard anything from Hermes or Ares, though.'

I thought about that for a moment. 'If Ares is still to face the Archon tomorrow morning, it's possible that Hermes would have taken her somewhere else, someplace safe. You should be free from him for a while.'

'Great!' said Nick, clapping his hands together with a satisfied rub. 'Let's go!'

Sarah, Charles and Helen all moved towards the door, but Natalie and I stayed where we were.

'We don't know how many other women are out there,' said Natalie. 'Or even if there are other women on this site. But if she is to be believed,' she nodded her head at Helen, 'then The Company is already advancing its next project.'

'What's that?' asked Omorfia.

'Cryogenic Fertility Transplantation,' replied Helen. 'I

don't want you involved.'

Omorfia shrugged. 'They had me in a room like this. I had a little op and they took some eggs.'

'Egg harvesting is not a little op, Morfi.'

'Ares let me have whatever I wanted.'

'There's a different Ares now,' I warned, 'and if the payment you received was Fireflight's money, The Company is going to want some sort of payback.'

'All the more reason to leave,' said Nick.

'I agree,' said Sarah. 'I mean, what can we do? Let's just go!'

'We need to break into the central lab,' said Natalie. 'We've got to get those reports on Marie and Simone. We should split up before we're captured together.'

I held up the pass I'd been given. 'I can get you into the central lab.'

'Christ, Kim! Are you out of your mind?!' Everyone stopped to look at Nick. 'I didn't download a tracer app to find anyone else, just you. I didn't follow it to stop a project, or halt an illegal drugs trial. I came here for you.' He pointed towards the other women. 'I didn't come to rescue them, just you.' He took a moment before realising what he'd said. 'Sorry. No offence, but...'

'I can see the door!' shouted a voice from outside.

'That's Hephaestus!' yelled Natalie.

Charles and I pushed the door shut and stood with our hands pressed against it while Hephaestus repeatedly bleeped his pass at the red light.

Chapter 8

'Kim, I know you're in there. Open up!'

'Don't speak to him,' instructed Charles. 'You reinforce his status by engaging in conversation.'

'Don't worry,' I gasped. 'I have absolutely no desire to engage him in conversation.' No more sound came from outside the door, but there was no way for us to know if anyone was there. 'He might have left to find another pass for the door. There may still be an enforcer in the corridor.' I was breathing hard and could feel my heart pounding. I put my hand against my chest and closed my eyes, trying to think clearly. I sat at the table and Nick joined me and held my hand.

'Natalie and I can break in to the central lab, but we've got to arrange the safe escape of the others,' I said, thinking aloud. 'The two of you will have to scout out the corridors and one of you come back to lead us out to safety. You can do that between you, can't you?'

Charles didn't speak straight away. He stood facing me with his arms folded. He was wearing soft slacks, a plaid shirt and what looked like a golfing sweater over the top. I noticed he still wore a neatly knotted tie. He seemed to be wearing what somebody else thought retirement should look like. I'd never seen anyone look so out of place in casual clothes. He studied me with calm blue eyes for a moment and coughed gently, as if clearing his mind, not just his throat.

'We'll do it,' he confirmed, 'but not because you've asked us to. We'll do it because it's the right thing to do.'

I frowned at him. 'I don't expect you to do anything just because I asked you to. The women's safety is my only concern here.'

'You're taking charge and issuing orders,' he pointed out. 'That's what I'm used to doing. But if you're going to take on that responsibility you have to be prepared for the possible consequences and I'm not convinced that you are. Why did you even come here? Did you stop to think about what you were doing?'

'It wasn't as if I had much of a choice.' My voice was starting to crack again. 'A woman died in my arms today. She and I were dragged here, wherever the bloody hell here is!'

'Here is only thirty minutes' drive away from where you live. You should have called the police as soon as she called you,' persisted Little. 'That was a whole night and a morning of wasted time. If you had, they could have used an experienced decoy in your place and there's a chance she'd still be alive.'

'Now, hold on a minute,' said Nick, rising to his feet, 'that's not fair.'

'The police may not have sent anyone,' I pointed out. 'And if someone else had gone instead of me, Marie may not have even turned up!'

'No,' agreed Charles. 'And she'd still be alive.'

I could not believe Charles was speaking to me this way. I had allowed myself to be captured for a woman I barely knew, but with whom I felt an incredible affinity. I wanted answers, I wanted to know what had happened to her and, I believed, she had wanted me to find out.

'You have absolutely no idea what I've been though in the past months!' I yelled back, 'Or what this means to me. I do not deserve to be spoken to like that.'

Charles leaned in closer and I smelt carbolic soap and ironed lemon water. He spoke in calm and measured tones.

'Now you listen to me carefully, Kim. I'm not accustomed to having to give a lecture. If you had been a constable on my team, you'd already be on a disciplinary and you'd never work with me again.' He was deliberately keeping his voice under control, but I could see he was angrier than I was. 'You repeatedly make dangerous mistakes. You deliberately put yourself in danger and in so doing, you encourage the people who love you to follow you into danger.'

'Charles, that's my wife you're talking to.'

'You impose your own sense of right and wrong on to a situation and expect others to want it. And until you can understand the gravity of what you expect from others, then actually yes, you do deserve to be spoken to like that.'

'Thanks for the sermon, reverend,' interrupted Natalie, 'but has anybody thought about how we're actually going to get out of here?'

Nick reached for his phone. 'I can't get any kind of signal in here.'

'That's because you're in a subterranean area,' said Helen. 'You might have better luck on another floor.'

'Or sending a text,' said Natalie, narrowing her eyes at Helen.

'We need to find another safe space,' said Charles. 'Who controls this door?'

'I do,' said Natalie, holding up Helen's pass.

'And is this lab you were talking about a secure area?'

'No,' I said, 'Hephaestus has access to it, too.'

'But what you want is in there?' I nodded. 'Who should accompany you?'

'Helen and Natalie.'

'Then you three should stay together. That leaves the two other ladies, Nick and me. I propose that while you look for the information you need, the four of us search for an escape route. I'll then come back for you three.'

Sarah nodded agreement while Natalie and I looked at each other.

'That's not going to happen,' said Natalie. 'We want to stay close.'

Sarah sighed. 'I'm not the bravest of people,' she said, 'but I'm good with computers. If Fireflight are accessing their systems remotely, they could be deleting any number of files. If we are to stop them, we need to rescue as much data as we can.'

'And we still can't be completely sure there aren't other

women here,' said Natalie. 'I'm going to check for myself.'

'This is unnecessarily risky,' said Charles, clearly irritated.

'Sorry,' said Natalie, unapologetically. 'You're overruled. We're staying together.'

Natalie led the way to the lift, but there seemed little point in trying to avoid the cameras. I kept Helen in front of me so that I could keep an eye on her. From the lift, we tiptoed in silence to the lab, conscious of low voices at the end of the corridor. I bleeped us in and Natalie stood guard just inside the door. Lights flickered on as we entered, bouncing bright shafts off the surface of a central table.

Sarah made her way to the only computer in the room, on a high bench to the right of the door. An ancient looking printer sat on the other end of the bench. Beyond the lab table, the glass windows of the mortuary looked dark and menacing.

'I think I can isolate this PC.' Sarah's fingers danced over the keyboard. 'They don't seem to have very robust security on their systems, but I guess they weren't expecting anyone else to use them.'

'They're using Greek characters as protective instructions,' said Nick looking over her shoulder. 'Some of what's here must have been typed using a Greek keyboard.'

'Luckily it seems to be responding to instructions in English,' said Sarah. 'If I can get their central server to ignore this PC, we should be able to see what's been saved here.'

'That won't be much,' said Helen. 'All my reports and results were saved directly.'

Sarah ignored her as she continued to type. I gripped Helen's arm.

'Come on,' I said. 'We have our own job to do.' I pushed Helen towards the door to the mortuary and indicated for her to open it. Overhead lights responded to our movement and Omorfia and Charles followed us in.

'They've moved her,' said Helen.

Charles frowned. 'Moved who?'

'Gaia. The woman who was shot.' Helen pointed to the stainless steel mortuary table. 'There isn't provision for safe storage of a body here. They must have moved her soon after I identified her.'

Omorfia shivered. 'It's creepy in here. Can't we just leave?'

'Where are her notes?' I asked. 'There are always notes.'

Helen moved to the bench under the windows and shuffled a few folders. 'I think these are what you're looking for. The latest report is always on the top.' I opened the file.

'This is an unwritten autopsy report.'

Helen shrugged. 'Perhaps they were planning to do that here.'

'By whom?' I asked incredulous. 'Hephaestus? Is he even qualified?'

'Does he seem qualified to you?'

'Where will it happen now?'

'How should I know? They'll probably bring in a professional, though, to make the paperwork look legitimate.'

'You know what Helen? You should take off that white

coat. You really haven't earned it.'

'Think what you like about me, but I've had a career long enough to know that when you have a subject like Gaia, anything is possible.'

I could feel my cheeks getting hot. 'Marie is not your lab rat anymore. None of us are.' Charles placed a calming hand on my arm. I handed him the file.

'Those reports will show you that she was unlike any other participant,' continued Helen. 'No participant ever responds exactly the way they should to any drug or treatment, but Gaia did.' Helen looked back at me unable to hide the excitement shining in her eyes. 'Perfectly. Every time.'

I wrapped my arms around me and tried to ignore the numbers counting in my head. 'So why did Ares kill her?'

'This project isn't about the women. It's about the children.'

'What do you mean?'

'Most immuno-protective responses are passed from the mother to the child, but there are many things that a child can inherit from the father; height, jaw structure, even dental condition. What if the best of both could be combined to produce a child that had advanced capabilities? Those children would rule the world.'

My thoughts strayed to Eric and what his mother had told me in the coffee shop. 'What the hell did you do?'

Helen's eyes were still shining. 'We tested that theory.'

I stepped forward and grabbed Helen's shoulders. 'What did you do?'

'Kim, stop.' Charles' calm demeanour could not stop the counting in my head. 'We have the file. Let's just get out of here.'

'What did you do, Helen?'

'We injected a test serum from Hephaestus into Gaia. We measured how much she absorbed to calculate what she might pass on to the child.'

I wasn't sure I wanted to know the answer to my next question, but still, I asked. 'How much could that be?'

A cloud of puzzlement passed over Helen's face. 'Well, I don't know. I haven't been able to test him yet.'

Chapter 9

One, two, three...

I pressed my head between my hands to pause the counting. 'Your plan wasn't just to reclaim Gaia, but to reclaim her son.'

Helen said nothing, but her eyes went to Omorfia and her fingers went to her locket. I guessed that whatever tests had been planned for Eric, weren't ones she wanted for her daughter.

'What is this serum, Helen, that you injected into Gaia?'

'Come on, Morfi. We're leaving.' Helen reached for Omorfia's hand.

'We should all go,' said Charles. He looked at his watch. 'It's just after eight. We don't know what it's going to be like here at night.'

I turned to the files on the bench that Helen had flicked through. 'I want to know what this is. I want an answer before I leave.'

'Knowing this isn't going to help you,' said Helen. 'The construction recipe and the ingredients aren't kept in the same place.'

Flicking through the papers I found a sheet with what looked like diagrams of hexagonal shapes. 'What is this?'

'That is a chemical structure for a basic glucose. It says so on the file cover.'

'It says it's a syrup, but it doesn't say what it's for.'

'Syrup is used as a carrier for oral drugs. Wait a minute, that's not glucose. That's a drug,' Helen said, peering at the file.

'How can you tell?'

'The letters and numbers beside the diagram say what it is.'

'Do you recognise it?'

'No. Why would it be in the autopsy reports folder?'

'Probably to make sure you didn't recognise it.' I tore at the paperwork, separating the diagram from the rest of the page.

'Hey! What are you doing? Leave it.'

'In just a few hours, most of what's here will be going through a shredder,' I said. 'The Company will still have this information somewhere else. I'm making sure we have it, too.' I folded the slip of paper several times and tucked it into my bra strap. 'You're not going to get to examine me again, Helen.'

A sharp rap on the glass made us all turn towards Nick, who was mouthing words to us from the other side of the window. I opened the door.

'You better come out,' he said. 'We've found something.' I walked back into the main area first, closely followed by Helen.

'I found the participant files for Marie and Simone pretty

quickly,' said Sarah, 'but there's no email or outside access from this computer. We're having to print them out. They make for very interesting reading.'

'They were on different drug programmes,' said Nick. 'Gaia's programme was called Golden Apple, that seems to be the current project.' He glanced at Omorfia, still standing in the doorway to the mortuary. 'Simone's programme was called Adelfi.'

Helen gasped. 'But it can't be! That was abandoned.'

Nick shook his head as he pulled pages from the printer.

'It doesn't look like they've abandoned anything. Some of the details in the reports refer to studies dating back twenty-five years.'

Helen's hand covered her mouth, but she didn't speak.

'What is Golden Apple, Helen?' I asked. 'What did you do to Marie?'

Helen took a deep breath before answering. 'Golden Apple involves subjecting a female participant to a series of three compounds. The result is to engineer a stronger and more intellectually evolved child.'

'And Adelfi? What was this other project trying to do?' I asked.

'We're not entirely sure.' Sarah leant back in her chair and massaged her neck. 'Nick and I have had to try to translate what we've found between us, but it looks like they were trying to combine the chromosomes of two women to produce a child without male genetic abnormalities.'

'I know it's all evil and that they really do need to be

stopped,' said Natalie, 'but why is a eugenics programme such a bad idea? I'm not trying to make excuses for their violence but, if they really can eradicate hereditary disease...'

Sarah looked shocked, but Nick answered her question as he gathered the papers from the printer.

'This is uncontrolled research; once you've succeeded in pushing the boundaries, the temptation will always be there to push them again. It's like the thrill of a gambler's lucky streak. What are the boundaries and how would you enforce them?'

Charles turned to look at Helen. 'You seem to know what the Adelfi project is,' he said. 'Perhaps you should share.' Helen stood silently, her eyes wide. She glanced around the room, and seeing everyone looking at her, reluctantly started to speak.

'Some gods were born independently,' said Helen. 'Without both parents. The theory suggests that all that is necessary to reproduce is two female chromosomes which can be activated in a host without sperm. It's basically pregnancy without sex.'

Omorfia really didn't believe the possibility. 'Ooh, kinky,' she grinned raising an eyebrow. 'I like it.'

'But this is serious,' persisted Charles. 'Could it really happen?'

'Trust me, sweetie,' smiled Omorfia. 'Outside of this clinic, that would never happen. Sex is far too much fun for this to be realistic. It has to be for the continuation of the species; ask any rabbit.'

'But is it viable?'

I shook my head. 'The Company's aims aren't altruistic, they're financial. It could be linked to the project they were working on last year.'

Charles frowned, not understanding. 'But why would they want an enhanced population? How would they make money out of that?'

'Maybe not an enhanced population, just a controlled one,' I suggested. They could charge whatever they like for a drug like this.'

'And inside the clinic?' asked Charles. 'What are the options for an enhanced population in here?'

'Too restrictive,' said Helen. 'The resulting child will always be a girl. They'd need another way to expand the gene pool.'

'Like recruiting donors independently,' I said, remembering last year's events.

Charles handed the file he was holding to Nick. 'Then the projects probably are linked. One project could be used to support another.'

'Well, that's the general idea,' said Hermes.

We turned to see Natalie held with a hand over her mouth and a knife at her throat.

Omorfia stepped forward to greet her ex-lover.

'Hello again,' she said.

Chapter 10

'Hello Aphrodite. Nice to see you.'

Nick's face froze at the sight of this intruder. 'Who the fuck are you?'

I thought it was up to me to make the introductions. 'Nick, this is Hermes. When we first met, he was Ares.'

Nick's hands balled into fists. 'So, you're the one who kidnapped and assaulted my wife.'

'Where's the other Ares?' asked Sarah.

'Not here,' replied Hermes, shortly.

'There's no need for this,' said Charles, stepping forward. 'Please. Put the knife down.'

Hermes smiled at the crazy old man.

'I'm used to getting what I want. The knife ensures that I do.' He lifted his fingers slightly to expose the casing. 'Recognise it, Athena?' I didn't, but wasn't sure how wise it would be to say so. 'A little present from my predecessor.' I looked into Natalie's terrified eyes and silently begged her to stay calm. 'She is not the one you're here for. Who do you really want? Me?'

'Both you and Aphrodite. You'll be taken to a new location.' Hermes looked at Nick. 'Sorry, but you're not invited.'

Nick immediately stepped in front of me. 'There's no way you are ever getting near my wife again.' Nick spoke threateningly. I touched his arm, not wanting him to do anything rash.

'There's no need for anyone to get hurt,' said Charles. 'Why don't we just talk about this calmly?'

'Good idea,' agreed Hermes. He threw Natalie away from him and she fell into Sarah's arms. He pointed the knife like a spear at Omorfia's face. 'In there,' he instructed.

Omorfia stared back at Hermes, but appeared unafraid. She looked at him as if she took what he was saying as a challenge.

Hermes looked at me and jerked his head in the direction of the mortuary. Omorfia and I walked slowly to the open door.

'No!' yelled Nick. 'Not again!' He ran in front of Hermes and pushed me away, both of us falling against the mortuary windows.

Hermes reached out for the front of Omorfia's shirt. 'I swear I'll slash her pretty face to ribbons!'

'No, stop!' Charles crashed into Hermes, pushing all three of them through the door and into the mortuary.

Hermes turned his attention to Charles, grabbing the front of his sweater and pointing the knife at his neck. Omorfia regained her balance and quickly pushed the door shut and locked it before Helen or I could barge in.

'Why the hell did she do that?' asked Nick.

'Omorfia loves me and she loves her daughter, but she

also loves money,' explained Helen. 'If Hermes is here to reclaim her, she'll want to know how much she's worth.'

'Wow,' said Natalie, rubbing her neck. 'That chick's a real piece of work.'

Nick examined the mortuary door. 'There's no lock on this side, just a door knob. How can we get in?'

'We can't,' sighed Helen. 'There's a smaller knob that locks the door. It sits inside the larger door knob. It has to be turned from inside.'

I pressed my hands against the windows. 'I can't hear anything they're saying.'

'It's a soundproof room,' said Helen. 'Fireflight can't afford for anyone to know what they say to each other while the tests are being performed.' She pressed a button on a small rectangular panel at the bottom of the windows. 'Morfi! Can you hear me?'

It was Hermes' voice that came through the speaker. Charles was leaning against the bench on the other side of the glass with his hands behind his back. I could see a microphone on a small stand on the bench. He had his thumb pressed against the button.

'Do you know what brought mommy dearest to the UK?' Hermes sneered at Omorfia, seemingly enjoying the moment, his attention and the knife focused on her. 'You did. When Helen found out that that you were involved with Fireflight, she begged Troy to send her here so that she could look for you.'

'How come you know so much about it?' asked Charles.

'I don't think it's likely that Fireflight would have shared this much with you.'

'There is a certain amount of trust that comes with the job,' said Hermes, stretching an inch taller. 'I am the messenger of the gods, after all.'

'That means that if information is leaked, they know who to blame.'

Hermes nodded. 'That's true, but accessing useful information is a privilege, and one that I'm happy to exploit, especially now that I know both Fireflight and Troy want Eileithyia.'

Omorfia looked pale. 'Fireflight can't have her.'

'Fireflight already have her. Do you honestly think you have any say in the matter?' Hermes almost laughed. 'Fireflight take who they want. You, me and Helen.'

Omorfia softened her expression and reached out to touch Hermes' jacket.

'Do you remember that day in that grotty little cottage, when I told you I was pregnant? It was true; you have a daughter.' Omorfia ran her fingers over Hermes' collar. Hermes put the knife down on the bench, keeping his eyes on Omorfia. 'Her name is Harmony. A friend is looking after her at the moment, but I know that you'd like to see her. Helen has a granddaughter she's never met. Let me take her home. Let me take her to Harmony.'

'Zeus already knows about Harmony,' said Hermes. 'I heard him talking about her to Hephaestus about a week ago. He's already making plans for her education.'

Omorfia's hand flew to her mouth and Charles turned his head to stare at us through the glass panels.

'No, no. That can't be true.' Helen pressed her hands against the glass. 'Get out of there!' she yelled. 'Just run.'

I gripped Helen's arm. 'What's going on?'

'Fireflight's plan for the new procedure meant reclaiming the freed participants. All the women that Tony had released were to be returned to Fireflight for Golden Apple. Zeus doesn't want Harmony. He wants Aphrodite.'

'I can help you,' said Hermes. 'I have friends on the outside. Together we can stop Zeus getting to Harmony. But I'm going to need some sort of commitment from you.'

'Don't listen to him,' instructed Charles. 'This is a pack of lies. There's no way anyone can get to your daughter.'

'Shut up, old man,' spat Hermes. 'This has nothing to do with you.'

'You're not going to intimidate any woman again, and you're not getting to any child!' Pushing Omorfia aside, Charles lunged at Hermes and managed to land a respectable punch, but he was no match for the younger man. Hermes lashed out with a powerful hook and sent Charles into a spin, crashing against the bench and crumpling on to the floor. He landed heavily and rolled over, clutching his left wrist.

Omorfia and Hermes glared at each other while Charles scrambled to his feet and stood back, just a couple of paces behind Omorfia. He was clearly in a lot of pain.

Now that Charles' thumb was off the microphone, Helen

and I yelled through the speaker on our side, urging Omorfia to run for it, but Hermes had already threatened her daughter; Omorfia was standing her ground with Hermes and refusing to run.

Hermes took another step towards Omorfia, expecting a response. Helen and I banged our hands against the glass and tried to shout down the microphone again, but Charles' thumb was back on the button.

'Stop!' screamed Omorfia. 'OK, enough! I'll do it! I'll come back.'

'No!' yelled Charles. 'Don't believe him.'

Helen gasped, bringing her hands to her cheeks. 'Oh, dear God! No, not my baby.'

'You will?' persisted Hermes. 'For Harmony?'

'Yes,' whispered Omorfia. 'I'll do it. I'll be Aphrodite. For Harmony.'

Suddenly Charles stepped forward and reached out a hand. It looked like he had tried to pat Omorfia's behind; an action that astonished me. I had always thought that he was the kind of guy who frowned on that kind of behaviour. Omorfia barely seemed to notice. Then Charles stepped back. Now it was my turn to gasp and Helen saw it too.

'Oh, my God!'

Omorfia's hand went to the back of her jeans. She lifted out the knife and engaged the blade. As Hermes took another step forward, he walked directly into the knife.

Chapter 11

Omorfia unlocked the door and went straight to her mother. 'I want to leave now.'

I grabbed Helen's arm. 'You're going to have to stay a little longer.' I pulled her into the mortuary with Charles, who was kneeling beside Hermes, pressing his good hand by the side of the knife.

'Why are you even bothering to help him?' Helen wrinkled her nose at the bully on the floor.

'That's an interesting question, coming from someone who swore to do no harm,' said Charles. 'A dead man can't be questioned.'

Helen reached for a box of latex gloves. 'I took a modern oath which didn't mention doing no harm. Unfortunately, I can't refuse to help when asked, either.'

In the main room, Sarah and Nick had turned their attention back to the computer. I peeked out of the lab door and seeing that the corridor was clear, hurried over to the examination room. The room was empty.

'It seems that we have this floor,' I said re-entering the mortuary, 'at least for the time being.'

'I don't think he should be moved,' said Helen. 'It may be even too risky to get him up on the mortuary table.'

'Soon it'll be used for you,' groaned Hermes.

'If I were you,' advised Charles, 'I wouldn't say anything else without a solicitor.'

Helen nodded at Charles' wrist. 'You should let me strap that for you.'

'Ok, but quickly.' He turned to look at me. 'How do we know where the enforcers are?'

'We can't be sure,' I said, 'but the surveillance room is next door.'

'I'll take a look.'

I'm coming with you,' said Natalie, shivering slightly. 'I don't want to spend another minute anywhere near that psycho.'

'Kim, take a look at this!' Nick beckoned me over to the computer.

'What have you been looking for?' I asked.

'I've been looking for you,' said Sarah. 'I wanted to find out who Athena was. But then, Nick told me that Athena's mother was Metis. And we found this.' She clicked a key and a page opened up on the screen.

'It looks like your mother buried a report in Fireflight's systems,' said Nick. 'We know that Fireflight has a dangerous anaesthetic; Thanatos. Your dad told us that your mother was secretly working on a stabilising compound. I think we might have found it.'

'What's Thanatos?' asked Sarah.

'It's a killer,' said Nick. 'An assassination compound.'

'This is wonderful! This could be what we've been looking

for. This is proof that Fireflight are using dangerous and illegal drugs, and not just for fertility tests.'

'It's interesting, but until we know what supplies of Thanatos Fireflight have, we can't use this information.'

I knew that Nick was just trying to be sensible, but I was disappointed by his lack of enthusiasm. 'Anything we can take with us could be useful. We'll need as much as we can to pass on.'

'Pass on to who, exactly?' Nick was becoming annoyed again. 'You heard what Charles said earlier. No one is coming to our rescue. I came to rescue you.'

'Look, we have, at least, some data. Let's take it and go.'

'First sensible thing I've heard you say.'

I left the lab and turned right to the surveillance room. Helen and I eyed each other warily as we passed.

Charles lifted his head as I entered. 'I need a word with you.' The ridge between Charles' eyebrows deepened as I walked into the room. He pointed his right arm back towards the door.

'Who, exactly, is that in the mortuary?'

'What do you mean? That's Peters; he was Ares when he kidnapped me. I told you about him, I gave you an exact description.'

'You gave me the description of a man who had experienced a TKO at the hands of Anthony Brownlow, and who did not receive immediate medical treatment.' Charles' head-masterly tone suggested that he no longer believed what had happened to Peters.

'Well, I'm sorry if you think I was being neglectful, but I didn't have a phone handy to call 999.'

Natalie turned away and pretended not to hear.

Charles glanced at the door, before returning his gaze to me. 'Do you know what TKO stands for?'

'Total Knock Out, I believe.'

'Correct. When the forensic team examined that house, they expected to find a dead body. Nobody who gets knocked out can just wake up and be as they were before. My guess is that his unconsciousness must have been acted out for your benefit.'

'But I saw it. Tony was there. Peters was punching me. He saved me.'

'Perhaps only because you still had something he needed.' Charles expression had softened slightly, but I didn't want him to pity me.

'Don't you dare say it! Don't even suggest it!'

'Kim, I'm only hypothesising, but if that man is who you say, and beating you wasn't getting the information he wanted, they would have had to try another way.'

I held my hands against my burning cheeks. During my kidnap, Peters' demanded that I reveal an account code that would release thousands of pounds to finance an illegal drugs trial. My stubborn refusal unleashed a dark storm of fury. I flinched as I remembered the pain he inflicted.

'I wasn't just used; I was manipulated.'

Charles smiled sympathetically. 'Is everyone ready to go?' He held his bandaged wrist against his chest and rubbed it gently.

'Are you OK?' I asked, diverting the conversation.

'I'm fine, just badly bruised. Look, I think we have a route of escape.'

'There are only two corridors and an outside space for us to navigate,' I said. 'We're already on ground level.'

'We might have to take the pretty way,' said Natalie. 'We can see the quadrangle with the water fountain, but the last corridor to the outside isn't on the monitors. I've tried several times, but I can't find a camera, so we'll have to assume that enforcers will be waiting there. We know that they are at either end of the internal corridors.'

'So how are we going to get out?'

'I searched around for a fire escape route and found hard copies of drawings for each of the floors,' said Charles.

'I couldn't find anything on the monitors,' said Natalie. 'Sometimes it's worth going old school.'

Charles ran a finger over a large sheet on one of the desks.

'The enforcers think they have us contained on this floor. That's giving them time to block off the nearest exits. I propose that we move to the third floor and turn east. There is another lift at the end of that floor which doesn't stop at this one. We'd have to get off on the first floor and try the far stairwell to get back to ground level.'

'That really is the long way round. Why the third floor?' Charles used his good hand to spin the drawing around so I could see for myself.

'My God! Really? Another lab and a control room.'

Natalie nodded. 'Helen didn't say anything about them, did she?'

I looked at Charles. 'You should take the others to safety without Helen, Omorfia and me. We are goddesses and The Company want us back. We're a danger to you.'

'I don't care about Helen and Omorfia,' said Natalie, 'but none of us thought we had any hope of escape until you came here.' She shook her head. 'We decided we'd stay together as a group. You're a part of that group, too. We're not leaving you behind.'

Charles shrugged. 'Over-ruled again.'

I stood in the doorway to the lab, with Charles and Natalie just behind. 'Charles has found a way out, but we'll have to stick close together.'

'What about him in there?' asked Sarah, jerking a thumb over her shoulder.

'Leave him,' instructed Charles. 'I'll make a call as soon as I can get a signal. An ambulance will come.'

As each person turned to look at us, I realised someone was missing. 'Where's Omorfia?'

'She just went across to the exam room to the john,' said Helen.

I turned and pushed the door to the exam room and the other door at the far end. 'She's not here.'

Helen pressed a hand to her chest. 'Maybe she ran for it.'

'We'll find her,' said Charles, with more confidence than I felt, 'but we haven't got time to hang around. We should go.'

Nick and Sarah bundled up their printed sheets and followed our anxious little band to the lift.

Exiting on the third floor, we followed a near identical row of rooms along the corridor.

'OK, this is Lab One,' said Charles, stopping outside a heavy looking door with a single, narrow strip of glass on one side. 'The control room is two doors down.'

'We should go and check that out first,' said Nick. 'There might be a way to shut off the alarms and automatically open the outer doors.'

'I think we should see what's in the lab, first,' said Natalie. 'I want to know what else has been going on around here.'

'Before we start another argument,' interrupted Charles, 'maybe we should agree to split up, just for a few minutes.'

I kept hold of Helen's arm while Natalie used Hephaestus' pass to open the lab door, then handed it to Nick.

We blinked as bright lights flickered on. Two shapes relaxed as now they could finally move. Natalie screamed as Zeus and Hephaestus both took a step forward.

Zeus fixed me with a hard stare from within his black balaclava.

'We need to talk.'

Chapter 12

'Run!' yelled Nick, grabbing my arm from behind. 'Head for the lift.'

Already Charles was pushing Sarah ahead of him, but Zeus had grabbed Helen's wrist and Hephaestus had grabbed mine.

'Let go of her,' shouted Nick, as I was pulled in a violent tug-of-war.

Charles reached out to Natalie. 'Run. Quickly!'

'I have questions,' said Zeus, ignoring Nick. 'Where are Simone and the child?'

'Hera already took care of her,' I shouted back. 'Was that on your orders?'

Zeus' head tilted as if asking an unspoken question.

Helen struggled against the grip of his glove. 'You already know she's been assassinated,' she sobbed. 'Is that what you have planned for us, too?'

'Not if you do as you're told,' said Hephaestus.

Nick swung a kick at Hephaestus' left leg, knocking his cane away. Hephaestus screamed and bent over with the pain. I twisted my arm free and Nick pulled me through the door. I glanced over my shoulder and saw Zeus let go of Helen like he was dropping a hot stone.

Helen ran past me and caught up with Natalie as they chased Sarah to the lift. Charles clutched his wrist to his chest as he stumbled behind.

I could see the lift at the far end of the floor.

Helen and Natalie dashed into it as Nick and I ran through the corridor. I noticed Nick had dropped the pass. 'Leave it,' he yelled.

Helen was already pressing the lift buttons, but Natalie had one hand against the closing steel and was beckoning to us with the other.

'Come on, run!'

Nick was ahead by two strides and pushed Charles into the lift first, then reached back for me. Hephaestus was behind me, catching up with a long legged lope. He swung out his cane. The rounded top caught in my hair and I squealed as strands were pulled from my head.

'Quick, Kim!' yelled Natalie, just as Charles pulled her back and the doors closed within arm's reach.

Nick's hands smacked against the doors and Hephaestus' hand grabbed the back of my neck, pushing my head forward and ramming my face against the unforgiving metal.

'No!' Stars burst in my eyes as I was roughly dragged backwards.

'Get your hands off her!' Nick charged at Hephaestus, but this time grabbed at his cane, twisting it from his grasp.

Hephaestus swore as he stumbled backwards towards the fire door beside the lift. Nick stabbed at him with the cane, pushing him through the heavy door and into the stairwell.

Hephaestus made a dive for Nick and reached for his cane, but Nick was already holding it high like a baseball bat.

As Hephaestus moved in, Nick took a swing and the smooth head connected with his jaw. Hephaestus twirled like a dancer before pitching sideways down the stairs to drop, unmoving, on the halfway landing.

Nick reached out his hand to me.

'We can get past him, Kim. Come on!'

But I had decided that I was not going to let Zeus slip by me again. I ran back the way we had come, scooping up the dropped pass along the way. I slammed the laminate against the flashing red light and pushed open the door into Lab One. He had gone.

'Shit! God dammit!'

Nick ran, puffing, through the door. 'For fuck's sake, Kim! What the hell are you doing?!'

'He's gone. We almost had him.' I wasn't sure if my fast heartbeat was because I'd been running, or because I might have encountered Zeus.

'Christ, Kim! He almost had you. Again.'

'He wanted Simone back, too. I think he assumed that she'd been freed. I don't think he knew she'd been assassinated.'

'Forget about Simone.' Nick grabbed my arm. 'We have to go.'

'You looked at Omorfia.'

'What?'

'When you were talking about the Adelfi project, you

looked at Omorfia.'

Nick frowned and rubbed his chin. 'When Sarah and I were reading about it, the pages we found said that Aphrodite was to be the face of the project. I didn't think that was something I wanted to say in front of her mother.'

'Wait!' I knelt down to pick up something winking at me from the floor.

'What's that?'

'It's Helen's locket.' The chain was long enough for me to slip it straight over my head.

'She must have lost it in the struggle with Zeus.'

'I don't think she'll be coming back for it. I think she'll chase after Aphrodite again. It looks like both of them have given us the slip.'

'We can't hang around here,' said Nick heading for the door. There are probably enforcers on the other floors. Let's check out the control room.'

I turned away from Nick slightly as I lifted the slip of paper from my bra strap. I folded the paper again and tucked it inside the locket. Looking around the room, I let my eyes drift over the benches, computers and whiteboards. I wished I knew what they were up to. I wished I knew how to stop them.

The lights in the control room flickered and buzzed as we entered. The rooms on this floor seemed older and faded, as if the deeper we went into the hospital, the darker and more sinister it became.

'There has to be some sort of override switch,' said Nick,

sitting at a bench. He agitated a computer mouse and the screen in front of him came alive. 'Look, I can see the quadrangle. There's Charles and Sarah.'

The display of buttons on the desk next to him looked like the main control panel on the bridge of the Starship Enterprise.

'They need to go through the covered corridor and enter a six figure code on the panel to open the last door.'

Charles was already following the women into the corridor, when we noticed a figure in black jogging his way on to the quadrangle. Within moments, he would be in the same outer corridor as the group.

'We need to find the override,' yelled Nick. 'Quickly!'
I scanned the display in front of me and saw the switch just as the enforcer reached the corridor. Emergency override. I pressed the button.

Enter code:

'Fuck! How do we find that?' Panic was seeping into Nick's voice.

'It's Aristotle's dates of birth and death.'

Nick typed 385-323 at the same time as the enforcer entered the corridor.

Chapter 13

'We can't see in the corridor! Did they get out?'

Nick clicked the mouse and pressed buttons on his keyboard. 'I don't know. I can't bring up an image.'

'I'm going down there. We have to leave.'

'Kim, wait. I'm checking for enforcers.'

'I don't care about the bloody enforcers. I'm going.'

Nick rose from his chair. 'Kim.' He held my face in his hands and made me look at him. 'Take a breath. Take several. We'll go together.'

Holding hands, we reached the lift and made our way back the way we came in. We exited into the ground floor stairwell and entered the quadrangle opposite the covered corridor.

'We should try and be quiet,' hissed Nick. 'There's no way to know who else is out there.'

'I'm scared.'

'I am too.'

We stood in front of the door to the outside corridor.

'Ready?' asked Nick.

I shook my head. 'Yes.'

We pushed the door together. There was no one inside.

'Everyone got out,' I said. 'I'm not sure if that's a good

thing or a bad thing.' Nick and I clasped hands as we ran to the other end of the corridor.

'There's only one way to find out,' he said.

Nick tapped in the numbers and the door clicked open.

'Stand back and identify yourself,' shouted Charles.

'Kim! You're OK.' Natalie ran forward. 'We were so worried when you missed the lift. What happened to Hephaestus?'

'I think he might have a broken jaw,' I said. 'Where's the enforcer we saw on the monitors?'

'He ran for the exit,' said Sarah, pointing. 'The rats are deserting the sinking ship.'

'We should leave, too.' Charles looked at his watch. 'I've already called for the police.' He looked at Nick and me. 'I'd suggest discretion is the better part of valour.'

'We're going to Norfolk,' said Nick without thinking.

'I'm not going to your parents straight away,' I said. 'There's something else I want to do first.' I looked around our little group of anxious faces. 'I know you've been recruited once. But I'd like to recruit you again. To the resistance. We call ourselves The Network.'

'I've heard about The Network,' said Charles. 'You are political antagonists.'

'Actually, we work in much smaller ways, but do what we can to derail Fireflight's plans. We try to discover their latest project, identify the main players and disrupt their money routes.'

'And how successful are you?' scoffed Natalie. 'They are

major players. They have the backing of Big Pharma. Who are we? A bunch of nobodies.'

'This is an ongoing war, not a single battle. If you say yes to me now, you've got to accept, we're in it for the long haul. I want you to reach out to the other women.'

'What other women?' asked Natalie.

'Well how many are there? Weren't there others with you?' Natalie answered my question. 'We three are the only ones left in this programme. At least, that we know of. Laura is out there somewhere...'

'She's looking after the children,' interjected Charles. 'Omorfia called her.'

'...Marie and Simone are dead. We could be too.'

'Only Laura?' I looked over at Charles and Nick. 'Five women.'

'What were you expecting, Athena? An army?' retorted Natalie. 'Each of us was born with about two million eggs in our ovaries. A woman of childbearing potential has about 400,000. That's Fireflight's army right there.'

I paused to think for a moment. 'This is dangerous. I'm asking too much.'

Natalie sighed. 'Look, I'm sorry I snapped at you. It's just... Well, we've heard all this before, you know? Women have been recruited and talked about stopping Fireflight, but nothing's worked. Then, when you told us about Marie, it seemed pretty hopeless.'

'I know you're scared,' I said. 'I am too. But when Marie made contact, she asked for my help.' I didn't know if I could make this work, but if I was going to raise an army, I'd have to inject some morale into the remaining troops. 'You all have skills that make you valuable to Fireflight. Those same skills are valuable now. We may not know everything, but we know that Fireflight is working on a programme designed to give eugenics an acceptable face. We can't halt that programme unless we can disrupt their systems at the source. That's what I intend to do. And I need your help.'

Sarah raised her head. 'Are you serious?'

'Absolutely.'

Natalie stepped forward and held out her hand for me to shake. 'All right. I'm in.'

'Welcome to The Network,' I said.

A wail of police sirens brought our attention back to the moment. Charles looked anxious.

'Kim listen to me. This is your last chance to leave and I strongly recommend that you take it, because if you don't, what will follow will be an endless stream of police interviews and incrimination. This is not the first time something like this has happened to you, and the police will definitely focus on that.'

I nodded. 'I know, but I have to face them sooner or later.'

'No, you don't.' Nick pointed to the car park behind him.

'I'll drive all night if I have to. Let's get the hell out of here.'

'Drive me home, Nick. I'll talk to the police in the morning.'

'Kim...'

'I'd rather face them and their suspicion, than run away and wait for retaliation.'

'Do you remember the sergeant I introduced you to?' asked Charles. 'She's DI Kelly now and still works in Major Crimes. If her team will agree to take your statements in the morning, we can meet up with Herse, I mean Laura, and the children in the afternoon.'

'I'll stay,' said Sarah, hugging the paperwork to her chest. 'I've got plenty to tell the police.' Natalie nodded her agreement.

'Wait a minute,' said Nick, distracted by a sheet in Sarah's arms. 'I'd like to keep that page on me, if you don't mind.' He lifted the top sheet from the bundle.

Back at home, I couldn't wait to jump in the shower. I needed to wash away the day's events. Robed and with a towel around my head, I sat at the dining table with a notepad and pen and wrote down as much as I could about what had happened that day.

Nick pulled a sheet from his pocket.

'What's that?'

'I think it's a copy of a pamphlet. I took it from Sarah's collection of papers.' He folded it into thirds. 'It talks of the Adelfi project. There's something about it that's troubling me. Perhaps we should give this to DI Kelly, too.'

I turned my attention back to my notes.

'It's just before eleven,' said Nick looking at his watch. 'Are you hungry? Do you want anything? Cuppa tea? Hot chocolate?'

'No thanks. I want to get this done. I just think it's a good idea to write down as much as I can.'

'You were a witness to crime; you're not actually under any pressure to talk to the police.'

'But I want to. If I don't, there'll still be unanswered questions.'

'I have some unanswered questions.'

I sighed and put down my pen. 'What is it Nick? You don't seem very happy to have me back home.'

'I'm utterly delighted to have you back home. But I don't think you realise how much danger we're in.'

'I'm home now. Here with you. You once said that you never wanted anything more.'

Nick sat at the table and ran his fingers through his hair. He scratched at his temple with his little finger and left a smear of ink at his hairline.

'I should never have bought you that fountain pen for your birthday,' I said. 'You always make a mess with it.'

'You didn't even ask me how I found you.'

'You downloaded a tracer app.'

'I told you that; you didn't ask.'

'I didn't have to question it. I knew you'd come.'

'You couldn't have known. You weren't to know if I'd been captured, too. I've been thinking about how incredibly easy it was to locate the hospital. It's almost as if Fireflight wanted me to know where you were. I don't think they expected me to bring friends. Less than ten hours ago,' said Nick, suddenly looking extremely tired, 'we witnessed the murder of a woman in a public place and I watched helplessly as you were bundled into the back of a car.'

'You saw that? I'm sorry. You need some cleansing lotion and cotton wool.'

'All I could do is hold that poor little boy and beg him not to cry and reveal our hiding place.' Nick followed me to the stairs and watched me walk up. 'You haven't even asked about him!'

In the bathroom, I spread my hands across the sink and took several deep breaths, trying to shrink the shouting numbers in my head. Don't think too hard, I told myself. Think logically, not emotionally. Emotional thinking is overwhelming. I walked back down the stairs slowly and squirted make-up remover on to a fluffy ball. Nick was still waiting at the foot of the stairs.

'Tell me about Eric,' I said. I started to clean away the ink.

'He seems a curious little guy,' smiled Nick. 'He didn't really cry that much. Too young to understand what was going on. He seemed to recognise Laura.'

I applied more lotion. 'Laura? The girl Charles was talking about?'

'She's a friend of Gaia – I mean, Marie. Apparently, she was a project participant, too. Charles found her after you were released last year.'

'Oh yes, she was Herse. There. You're all done.'

'Aphrodite called Laura and she offered to look after the children. I'll drive you to the police station in the morning, but I don't think I want to go inside. I've already told DI

Kelly everything I can.'

'You've already spoken to DI Kelly?'

'Yes, of course. I had to report the murder and your kidnapping. The police were already swarming over the coffee shop, by the time I left, but Kelly seemed more interested in the murder than the fact that you were taken.' Nick swallowed and dropped his head. 'I was so scared of losing you again,' he whispered.

I hugged him and he held me tight.

'Sometimes I envy you, Kim,' he sniffed. 'Emotions don't affect you the same way.'

'My emotions are giant sized monsters waiting to engulf me,' I said. 'There's nothing enviable about that.'

I felt him smile against my neck.

'Don't leave me, Nick,' I whispered. 'I can't face this without you.'

'Don't worry,' he said. 'I'm not going anywhere.'

Chapter 14

I complained to my father about the monster that lived under my bed.

'OK, Kimmie. How big is this monster, then?' asked Dad. I paused to consider. 'Two feet, six by six feet, three.'

'That's the size of your mattress, Kimmie. Did you see that on a sticker?'

I probably did, but didn't want to lie to Dad. 'But the monster takes up all the space, Daddy. If that's how big my bed is, that's how big the monster is.'

'And how big do you think that space is?' he asked. I held my arms out to my sides as far as I could make them stretch.

'I see. Well, what do you think would make a monster as big as that go away?'

'Light, Daddy. Lots and lots of light.'

'Kimmie, we've talked about this before. Children need darkness to sleep. Too much light will keep you awake.'

'Well, just a bit of light, then.'

Dad rubbed his chin. 'Hmm. How about torches? I could put one torch under your bed and you could hold on to the other one.'

I eagerly agreed.

'You're pandering.' The sing-song tone of Mother's voice

hinted at her impatience, but she kept her eyes on her paperwork.

I jerked awake. I have no idea how often Dad had crept into my room to close my book and turn off the torches, but when I woke in the morning, the smaller one would be beside my book on my night table and the larger one would be standing on the floor within easy reach of my pillow.

The thought of having to talk to the police made me feel small again. I'd rather face the monsters.

'Mrs Anderson, thank you for coming. This is Detective Constable Kent, and thank you for the notes'.

DI Kelly's wardrobe seemed to have become significantly more expensive since the last time I saw her, incongruous in the sparse interview room. Kent, a young, thick-set, bulldog of a man with no neck, lifted his eyes from his notes to jerk his head in acknowledgment of my presence, but remained silent.

'We're here to capture a picture of what happened yesterday at the coffee shop. The casework regarding the murder of Marie King and your kidnapping will be handled by DCI Gardner, but I will be conducting this interview. I understand that this may be difficult, but please, walk me through the events as you remember them.'

DC Kent wrote fast and only lifted his eyes from time to time when I stopped speaking. He didn't refer to my notes at all. Kelly was business-like and polite, but there was none of the friendly sympathy I had experienced when we first met.

'I'm interested to know why you would agree to meet a

stranger, knowing that such a meeting could potentially be dangerous.'

'It's because of the danger that I went. Marie was terrified.'

'I meant dangerous for you.'

'My husband insisted on coming with me.'

'And consequently, you were both witnesses to a horrific crime.'

'Yes.' I felt as if I was sitting in front of my secondary school headmistress again.

DC Kent's pen hovered over his notepad while Kelly spoke.

'It seems quite strange to me, Mrs Anderson, that this group, whoever they are, should be so interested in you. Why would they go to all the trouble of kidnapping you a second time?'

'I'd like to know that, too,' I said.

'Clearly you have something they want.'

'Clearly. But Fireflight have not yet been kind enough to tell me what it is. And you know this group is Fireflight; Sarah's paperwork would have given you this information.'

DI Kelly shuffled some papers on the desk. 'Ah, yes. Ms Millwood. What paperwork would that be?'

'Sarah found paperwork that explained what Fireflight were up to.'

'And did she have permission to acquire this paperwork?' I couldn't answer, so DI Kelly tried another question. 'Do you know where she is?'

'What? No, why? What's happened?'

'I'm afraid I'm not at liberty to discuss the specifics, but if you see her, perhaps you could let us know.'

'So, she's missing?'

'The CCTV imaging we have recovered so far show you were escorted to a car and driven along Conner Street. What can you tell me about the car?'

'It was a dark blue Mercedes and smelt like it had been recently cleaned.'

'And from the coffee shop, where did you go next?'

'We were taken to the abandoned hospital.'

'We?'

'Gaia, I mean, Marie and I.'

'How many people were there at the abandoned hospital?'

'Well, I'm not sure.' I did a quick mental calculation. 'Eleven of us, but I don't know how many enforcers there were.'

DI Kelly referred to her own paperwork and listed them for me 'The people you have named as Hermes, Hephaestus, Ares and Zeus; the participants, Natalie Scott and Sarah Millwood; Dr Helen Markham, her daughter, Omorfia Markham, former DCI Charles Little, and of course, your husband, Nick, and you. Eleven people. A workforce, perhaps.'

'We weren't all working together!'

'Weren't you? Two accused are in hospital with serious and potentially life altering injuries and five witnesses are missing.' DI Kelly stared at me as if their disappearance was my fault. I couldn't help wondering if it was.

'Five?'

'Dr Markham and her daughter, Sarah Millwood and the mysterious Ares and Zeus. You saw an enforcer running for the gate as you and former DCI Little debated when to come and see me.'

'We didn't debate when to see you…'

'The enforcer,' interrupted DI Kelly. 'Could that have been Ares or Zeus?'

I thought about that. 'I don't know; it could have been either one. I couldn't tell if they were a man or a woman.'

'And then there's the question of the car.'

'The car?'

'The Mercedes in which you were taken.' DI Kelly took a sheet of paper from DC Kent which she carefully placed in front of me. She lifted her eyes to see if I had any comment to make. When I didn't respond she continued.

'That is the forensics report for the car, which was found abandoned in an industrial estate twenty miles away, burnt to a crisp. Forensic evidence is therefore scant, but shows that the driver was, at least at one time, David Peters, also known as Hermes, and that the deceased female you saw placed in the boot was Marie King, confirmed as the mother of the infant, Eric King.'

I pushed the report back across the table to DI Kelly, 'I don't know what else I can tell you.'

'You could tell me where the remains of Marie King are now.'

'I've already told you. She was taken to the same abandoned hospital as I was.'

'Was she?'

'Isn't she there?' DI Kelly did not reply. I suddenly felt very tired. 'Then I have no idea where she is. How the hell would I know that?'

'David Peters remains in hospital, seriously wounded by Omorfia Markham and assisted by your friend, former DCI Charles Little.'

'That's hardly fair. They were defending themselves.'

'Philip Moore, known as Hephaestus, is also in hospital, seriously wounded by your husband, Nick Anderson.'

'He was defending me!'

'But the whereabouts of the assassin you named as Ares remains unknown.'

'I have no idea where she is either.'

'Why would she assassinate Ms King, but leave you unharmed?'

'She didn't take the time to tell me.'

DI Kelly dropped her head to her hand and scratched her brow, a small smile lifting the corners of her mouth. 'Puzzling, isn't it, that so many who come into contact with you suffer death or serious injury, and yet you seem fine.'

DI Kelly and I seemed to have very different definitions of the word 'fine'. I stared back at her as the numbers shouted in my brain.

Later, Nick and I met with Charles and Natalie at the multi-storey car park in the town centre.

'That was a really weird interview, Charles. I felt like I was being told off.'

'I felt the same yesterday,' said Nick. 'It's as if Kelly knows there's something going on, but is annoyed that she's not in on it.'

'I never doubted her ambition,' said Charles, 'but a little bird told me that the new DCI appointed to Major Crimes, Gardner, is a good egg. He'll have his work cut out, though. I don't think the police can deny Fireflight's existence anymore, not now that they dared to capture you a second time. That was a huge risk on their part.'

I pulled my coat closer around me against the sharp afternoon wind. 'What did Kelly mean when she asked me where Sarah was? Is she missing?'

'Nobody's seen her since the carpark yesterday,' replied Natalie. 'Charles gave me a lift to the police station and Sarah rode in the back of a police car.'

Charles led the way towards the courtyard, where a row of boutique shops lined the entrance. 'From what I can gather, Sarah didn't speak to the police, or hand over any paperwork. She must have changed her mind at the police station.'

'But she'd have to speak to the police,' I protested. 'Wouldn't she?'

'She's a witness,' replied Charles, 'they can't make her speak to them, but they'd certainly have questions for her.'

'There's the café,' said Natalie, pointing. 'I told Laura we'd meet here.'

'It's a shame you couldn't arrest everyone straight away,' I smiled.

'It's really not so bad,' said Charles as we reached the door. 'Unfortunately, Ares has disappeared, but Hephaestus has been arrested, so has Hermes and there were at least half a dozen witnesses to Gaia's murder.'

'Marie,' said Natalie. 'Her name was Marie.'

'Marie,' repeated Charles, nodding apologetically. 'And you are also free,' he added.

'Yes, but so are Zeus and Ares.' Natalie glanced around her and shivered involuntarily. 'God only knows where they are now and what they're up to. I can promise you one thing; we've not heard the last of them.' Natalie suddenly squealed and pointed to the upper parking levels. 'What the fuck is she doing?!' She gripped Charles's arm. 'Stop her, Charles, say something!'

Herse sat on top of the safety wall, three storeys up, with her feet dangling casually, almost as if she was facing the sea and admiring the view.

Nick and Charles, with reason in their voices and panic in their eyes, started taking cautious steps across the courtyard to the paved area under the multi-storey balcony.

'Herse, just don't,' instructed Charles. 'Whatever it is, we can sort it out. I can have people here in less than four minutes to talk to you.' I noticed his fingers go to the supporting strap around his wrist, the memory of danger and pain.

'You can't call her Herse,' said Nick. 'She's not that

person anymore. It's Laura.'

Nick was trying to be practical, but I could hear a definite note of fear in his voice.

I put my hand to my chest and took a deep breath as those spiteful little numbers started in my head. One, two, three…

'Laura,' I heard Natalie call, 'Laura, just stay where you are. Don't move.'

I glanced across to the entrance and saw a car go in.

'Please don't go to the top,' I silently begged. 'Don't scare her.'

Next to the entrance was a pedestrian doorway. I didn't stop to think, I just ran towards it. I barged through the rough grey door and wasted five seconds in front of the lift. It was already on the top level. I headed for the stairs and bounced up two at a time.

'Kim, wait,' I heard Nick shout. 'I'm coming with you.'

I didn't wait, but could hear his footsteps close behind me. 'Don't do anything until I get there,' I whispered. 'Leave the children in the car. Please leave the children alone.'

In a dozen paces, I was on the first level, past the lift entrance and starting up the stairs again, all the steps, two at a time. 'Two, four, six, eight, who do I appreciate?' the familiar children's rhyme was racing through my head. 'I appreciate Nick and my friends, those who know of the anxiety monster who lives inside me, and love me anyway.'

I passed the lift and started on the last flight. I was getting tired. 'Don't think too much. Press on, press on.'

At last, I pushed through the doors and ran out on to the

upper parking level. There were only a few cars parked here and there. I was momentarily lost until I heard chilling screams coming from below. I ducked my head and covered my ears with my hands. I don't know what I thought I would do when I got here, but I was too late. Laura was gone.

Nick charged through the doors and almost knocked me over. 'Don't go over there, Kim,' he said as he gripped my arm. 'Come away.'

I looked to my left and saw a Ford Mondeo neatly parked at the far end, with one rear door open.

I released myself from Nick's grip and ran over. I saw the sleeping baby, cosy in her car seat within. She was a beautiful little girl, pretty in pink, with long pale eyelashes. She had her head turned slightly towards me and contentedly sucked her thumb as she slept.

'Hello Harmony,' I whispered.

I walked over to the boundary wall where Laura had been sitting and noticed the scuff marks where she had climbed up. The wall was at chest height and managed to hide what I didn't want to see. For a selfish moment, I was glad I'd run in to the car park when I did.

Propped up against the wall, out of the way of other cars, was another baby's car seat. The baby in this one didn't seem quite so content. I knelt before the grizzling infant and instructed him to hush and to my surprise, he did.

I suddenly felt immensely sorry for Laura. She presumably took her own life believing that she'd never be a parent, but who other than a parent would take a fretful baby from a car so that he didn't disturb a sleeping one? Now here were two young children whose future was horribly uncertain.

I unclipped Eric's straps and held him up in front of me. We took a good look at each other, observing, noting, questioning. Nick crouched beside me, his eyes already red rimmed.

'Poor little bugger.'

'Hello Eric. We haven't been properly introduced. I'm Kim. Your mother asked me to look after you.' I looked at him and he looked at me. 'Yes, I know that sounds ridiculous, but it wasn't my idea.'

I heard footsteps rushing towards us and the wail of sirens approaching.

'This is only the start of a very crazy life for you,' I said. I knew that was true. 'But I promise. If ever you need me, whenever you need me, I'll be there for you.'

'Perhaps we should arrange for you to have your own locker, Mrs Anderson,' said DI Kelly. 'You're spending almost enough time here to make that a possibility.' DC Kent smiled politely, but didn't speak.

'I wouldn't mind my own locker,' I said responding to her joke, 'as long as I don't have to stay in one of your hotels.'

DI Kelly lifted her head, but didn't smile. 'How well did you know Laura James?'

'I didn't know her at all. We'd never met.'

'And yet she chose to take her own life in front of witnesses, including you. A very specific group of witnesses. Friends, one might say.'

'What a shame you can't ask her.'

DI Kelly's eyes grew cold at my flippancy. 'You've said that you think she took her life because she couldn't conceive.'

'I don't know, but I presume so.'

'...Because she waited to see you and others arrive, knowing that the children would be cared for, and then her job would be done.'

'I don't know; I guess...'

'Where is Omorfia Markham? And please don't guess.'

'I have no idea.'

'Even though you'd met her before, talked to her, befriended her?'

'She wasn't my friend...'

'But she left her daughter behind, to be found by you.'

I dropped my head and sighed. I doubted that Omorfia would still be in the UK, but couldn't explain why I thought so. My best guess would be that if she was agreeable to another project, she'd be in Greece. It would be too risky to The Company for her to still be in the UK.

'What will happen to the children now?' I asked.

'Social Services have already been informed and foster care will be arranged. Would you like to put yourself forward?'

I looked up, surprised. 'Me?'

'Apparently, it was Ms King's dying wish that you look after her son.'

I was probably the least qualified person I knew. And staying with me could only put Eric in danger. 'Oh, yes. Well, actually I...'

'Yes,' interrupted Kelly. 'As we thought.'

'What about Dion?'

'Dion?'

'The child who was born at the hospital. His mother was Simone.'

'We have no information about anyone called Simone or Dion. There is nothing to suggest that there was a child at the hospital.'

I took that to mean that any paperwork left behind had

already been destroyed. Unless Sarah resurfaced with the paperwork she had, no one would know where to start looking for Dion.

'Go home, Mrs Anderson.' DI Kelly rubbed her eyes. 'I'm sure we'll be talking to each other again soon.'

Back at home, I was restless and anxious.

'I can't find the correct furniture polish,' I complained. 'Not the multi-purpose one that does glass as well, I want the one with beeswax.'

'The house is already clean Kim. Stop fussing. Why don't we get a takeaway tonight?'

'Not from the Chutney Pot,' I said, referring to the local Indian takeaway. 'There were grubby fingerprints on the new menus they put in with the food on our last order.' I reached for the little basket containing the dusters and found the beeswax polish behind. Nick must have hidden it there.

'Then how about I cook tonight?' Nick was trying to sound cheerful. 'I'll make your favourite chilli.'

I wiped a dry dust cloth along the top of our wedding picture and then sprayed polish on to a separate cloth. Many people spray polish directly on to surfaces and never think to dry wipe first. Both spraying and wet polishing can send dust particles in the air. If you want to be sure to capture all the dust, you should always use two cloths.

Nick touched my shoulder and made me jump. 'What's the matter, Kim?'

'Nothing's the matter.'

'Kim...'

I closed my eyes. 'Nobody is looking for Dion.'

'But there's no evidence that there was a child at the abandoned hospital.'

'I believe Natalie and Sarah. He was there and Tony hid him from Hera. Why would he do that? This little boy is special, Nick. And he could be in danger.'

'Nobody knows where to look. And I know what you're thinking. There's no way for you to know where to look either.'

'I've got an idea.'

'No. I'm not letting you.'

'Not letting me what?'

'I'm not letting you have another idea. Your ideas are dangerous. They always lead to trouble. Leave it to the police. They'll get a lead and we...' he bent forward to kiss my nose, 'should keep our noses out of it.'

I tried to distract myself with television until Nick told me that dinner was ready.

'Kim, I've cleaned the kitchen.' I answered Nick's call to help carry our dinner to the dining room.

'Oh, no! there's a chilli stain.' I immediately set down the flatbreads and reached for the baking soda and granite cleaner.

'The kitchen is clean, Kim. Everything is in the dishwasher, the ingredients have been put away and the surfaces have been wiped.'

'But there's a stain,' I said, pointing to a pink smear next to the hob. I pulled a clean cloth from the basket under the sink and dabbed the chilli with the soda before applying the cleaning spray.

Nick took our plates to the dining table and had already started eating before I sat down.

'For God's sake, Kim! I forgot to clean a chilli stain. You're behaving like I deliberately sullied your personal space.'

I couldn't have put it more succinctly myself. 'Well, you kinda did.'

Nick took a deep breath and tried to sound reassuring. 'I know that when I spill something, I have to clean it so there's no trace. But spilling is a natural occurrence during cooking. You're going to have to be more tolerant if you want me to make your favourite chilli.'

He was deliberately missing the point. 'Failing to clean spills straight away could stain our granite worktops.'

'I know. That's why, whenever I forget, I wonder if I should fess up and face you, or move to another country and start a new life. You have no idea how annoying this is. Thank God, I don't get so wound up about things.'

'Oh, Nick. You do. All I have to do is move the pepper mill three inches to the right and you can't find it. You behave like someone broke into our house to steal just that.'

Nick looked up with a mean glint in his eye. 'To get my own back, all I have to do is turn one of the sofa cushions upside down.'

I slammed my fork back on to my plate and the flatbread jumped half an inch.

'They have an easily identifiable geometric pattern.'

'Which looks exactly the same both ways up!'

'It does not! The closed edge of the pattern should be in the bottom right corner and the open edge should be in the top left. That's the logical image for a puzzle.'

'The only puzzle around here is why it's so bloody important.'

With clenched fists, I stood up and walked from the room. Nick half turned in his chair.

'Where are you going now?'

'To move your pepper mill.'

Nick followed me back into the kitchen.

The anxiety monster in my head was counting again. 'What did I do to you, Nick?'

'What do you mean?'

'You've been pushing my buttons since yesterday. The stain, the cushions, even the magnets on the fridge.'

'I just don't get why they have to be exactly two inches apart in straight lines.'

I didn't mean to raise my voice again, but I couldn't help it.

'What the hell did I do to hurt you?'

'You hurt yourself!'

The silence that followed Nick's shout, echoed in the kitchen like a clash of cymbals. Nick closed his eyes and tried to speak more kindly. 'I worry about you constantly.' He gripped my shoulders gently. 'I know it's difficult for you to share things with me but when you agreed to meet Marie, I knew you would be launching yourself into a dangerous situation again. And I knew that the monster in your head wouldn't go back to sleep until you'd found the answers you were looking for.'

I nodded. My anxiety monster was the third person in our marriage.

'The best I can do most times is turn her volume down,' I said. 'Sometimes she'll go into hibernation, sometimes for weeks, and then something will happen and she wakes up again.'

'Well if your monster is going to take us on another journey, to find, um...'

'Dion.'

'...Dion, then we need to come up with an idea of where to begin the search. Come into work with me tomorrow; the boss is out of the office and there's something I'd like to show you. If I can skive off for a couple of hours, I'll buy you some new clothes for the trip.'

'I don't need new clothes,' I protested. 'I have loads of new clothes.'

'No, you have old clothes that you've only worn a few times. You keep hold of your very old clothes and won't throw them out. You only buy yourself new clothes every few years.'

'But Nick...'

'Stop arguing. I'm taking you shopping.'

Chapter 16

'This is Patrick,' said Nick. The man he was introducing me to looked to be just a little younger than himself, but significantly less tidy. Patrick's tie was wonky, his sweater was bobbly and there was a pale stain on his shirt collar.

'Is that mayonnaise?'

Patrick sniffed at the stain. 'No; salad cream.' I couldn't bring myself to shake his hand.

'Er, Patrick,' said Nick, keen to avoid awkward explanations, 'why don't you show us the work your team have been developing?'

Patrick's face lit up and he reached to the table behind him to show me a small black box and what looked like a pair of blacked out binoculars.

'VR headsets have been around for a while,' he explained, 'but it's only in recent years that the CGI has become uniquely realistic. This technology has developed really fast, leaving previously expensive technology redundant. But now, with this little box of tricks,' he held up the black box for me to see, 'we can bridge the gap between real life data and CGI. So, previously, if you had wanted to go on an archaeological dig with Howard Carter, you would have had to choose between being a character at a dig site, or watching Carter at a real one.' Patrick handed the funny looking binoculars to me. 'But now you don't have to choose. You can really be there.'

'Try the headset,' said Nick. 'I think you're going to like this.'

'Who's worn this before me?' asked my monster.

'Actually, no one,' replied Patrick. 'We've only just got licence approval for this experience. You're our test volunteer.'

With an encouraging smile from Nick, I slipped the straps over my head and adjusted the binoculars.

'I'm on a pathway,' I looked down. 'There are flowers beneath my feet.'

'You're on the path that leads up to the Parthenon,' said Nick. 'The flowers are thrown for the Midsummer Parthenaic celebration; a festival to honour Athena.'

'It feels like a long walk.'

'It might be bigger than you expect. Don't forget, the Parthenon was a religious complex. There would have been several buildings and statues.'

Following the path and turning right, I found myself at the foot of some huge, wide steps leading up to the Parthenon, with open fire pits on low stands on either side of the entrance. Doric columns framed the entrance with banners draped from the outer two.

I walked through a set of tall, narrow doors into a large room with internal columns creating a walkway through the middle. Behind the columns on either side, I saw decorated pots and bowls, as fresh and beautiful as those in a shop window.

An open doorway at the other end of the room led to a large rectangular outside space with more buildings to my left. Fifteen feet ahead of me, there were more wide steps leading to a low platform on which stood Athena, with a fire pit at her feet.

'I can see her! She's made of bronze.' Athena stood several metres tall with a shield in her left hand, balanced against the ground and a spear in her right. She wore a tall headdress which added another half metre to her height.

'That's the Warrior Athena,' said Nick. 'Keep following the path.'

I walked around Athena to the right and saw more buildings on the plateau. Following the pathway, I reached the front of the temple. The pediment across the top showed images representing the founding myth; the contest between Poseidon and Athena. The statues of two warriors guarded the entrance. Behind them were eight Doric columns, each decorated with a blue banner with an owl embroidered in silver thread.

I held my breath as I walked through the tall, narrow doors and into the temple. On both my left and right, life sized statues stood on lower columns, resplendent in colourful clothes. On the floor, more flowers had been scattered, leading the way to a shallow pool, shimmering with golden reflections.

Just beyond, the giant goddess stood majestically. Forty

feet tall and dressed in gold, she gazed over the top of my head to the rest of Athens. In her left hand she held the top of her shield. Her right arm was extended and in the palm of her hand stood the winged goddess, Nike. Her ivory skin shone with an ethereal glow. I could almost imagine her lowering her head to look at the unworthy mortal standing at her feet and my heart beat a little faster at the thought.

I snatched off the headset. I felt breathless with excitement and finally felt that I had a purpose. 'We need to go to Athens.'

Nick walked over to take the headset from me. 'This was just to give you an idea about Athena,' he said, 'what she might do. We don't know if Athens is where we need to go.'

'We don't know where Dion might be,' I agreed. 'But the Olympians are most likely to be in Athens. They were in Crete last year because they were chasing Daedalus, but I think they'll be in Athens, now.'

'You can't possibly be sure.'

'I'm not. But it's a place to start.'

I turned to see a look of complete bewilderment on Patrick's face as he watched this confusing exchange, his eyes moving from Nick, to me and back again.

Nick held up the headset. 'Any chance I can borrow this overnight?'

A little while later, Nick left me at the door of a women's clothes shop.

'Here, take this,' he said handing me our shared credit card. 'There's another shop I need to go to. I'll come back for you in about half an hour.'

I chose a skirt and blouse, a summer dress and some comfortable looking shoes. Not knowing what our trip was likely to have in store, I wanted to have all bases covered.

'Four items?' asked the shop assistant. 'This way.' I followed the young girl to the changing rooms and watched as she opened a concertinaed door to a cubicle. 'Just come to the front counter when you're ready.'

I pushed the door closed and removed the blouse from its hanger. I turned to hang the other clothes on the hook above the seat. As I did so, I noticed a grubby smear on the right hand side of the mirror. Pink dust had been dragged along the top corner. Immediately an argument started in the back of my head.

'It's only make-up,' said my logical brain. 'Someone's already tried to wipe it away.'

'It's disgusting,' said my monster. 'There's no way of knowing where that's come from.'

I rummaged in my handbag, looking for tissues. The pocket where I kept my usual supply was empty. I rummaged again. The pocket where I kept my emergency supply was also empty. I could feel my heart speed up and I started breathing heavily.

Leaving the clothes where they were, I grabbed my bag and ran for the ladies' room. The paper towel dispenser was empty. I dashed into a cubicle and locked the door. The toilet roll holder was empty. I placed both my hands against the cubicle door and tried to take some deep breaths. It was then that I noticed, I was still holding on to the blouse.'

'Hello? Hello? Are you in there?' called the assistant.

'Um, yes. I just needed the loo.'

'You can't bring clothes into the toilets,' she insisted. 'Didn't you see the sign?'

'No, I didn't,' I responded truthfully. 'And I don't see any toilet paper. Could you get me some?'

The assistant ignored my question. 'We have a zero tolerance approach to shoplifting. I could call the police.'

'Would they have toilet paper with them?'

The assistant banged on the cubicle door. 'Could you unlock this door, please.'

'Could you get me some toilet paper?' I fanned a hand against my burning cheeks. I couldn't let the assistant see me like this. I'd look as guilty as hell.

'Open this door!'

'Do you really want to see me sitting on the loo?'

'Open this door or I'm calling the police!'

'And tell them what? That there's a strange woman sitting on a toilet in your ladies' room?'

'Right.' I heard the clip-clop of the assistant's shoes as walked towards the door. As she opened it, another voice drifted through.

'What the hell's going on in there?'

And as if by magic, my monster fell silent. Nick paid for my clothes while the assistant sent me killer looks from the other side of the counter.

Nick stared sternly at the road ahead as he drove me back

home.

'I wasn't trying to steal anything.' Nick didn't answer. 'I'd forgotten I was holding the blouse. I just went looking for tissues. Oh, for God's sake, Nick! It was a minor panic attack!'

'Nothing about your panic attacks are minor,' said Nick quietly. 'And they're becoming more frequent.'

'Well, can you blame me? It's not as if we've lived a nice uneventful life lately. It's probably in response to the stress of the last couple of days.'

'Stress? I think we can describe it as a little more than stress, Kim. I think you should go and see Dr Bridges again.'

'No,' I said. 'Absolutely not. No more doctors. And definitely not Bridges. He practically accused me of attention seeking. He said that Dad's absence in my life had created a sense of parental abandonment.'

Nick gave me a sideways glance. 'Don't you think he might have a point?'

I clenched my fists and tried to stay calm. 'No, Nick. I don't. People don't believe in Fireflight; they think I'm a conspiracy theorist in need of therapy.'

'Nobody has said they think you're crazy.'

'No. Nobody's that honest.'

'Maybe we should delay any trip until you're a little calmer,' suggested Nick trying to sound reasonable.

'Come off it, Nick.' I unclipped my seatbelt as we pulled into our driveway. 'What do you think is going to make me calmer? Those tablets that Bridges prescribed; the ones that made me feel drunk? You know my mind doesn't work that way. What I want is another meeting with the Olympians. I want to talk to Zeus.'

Nick swallowed and I saw his lips tremble when he spoke. 'I wasn't sure I'd see you again after your last meeting.'

Nick walked into the living room ahead of me. When I entered, I saw that he'd emptied his own shopping bag on the coffee table. There were half a dozen disposable mobile phones scattered across the surface.

'Well, if we are going, we'll need to be prepared,' he said. 'We should take two each; hang on to one and have the other in our hand luggage. If we make a call or contact someone in Athens, we should get rid of that phone then use the other. Four should be enough for the trip. I'll programme the numbers in before we leave.

I looked up from the collection before me. 'You really think we should go?'

'No, I really think we shouldn't. But your anxiety is only going to get worse if we don't and I won't get any sleep until we do. So let's just go there and see what we can find out. But this time, we stay together, OK? No wandering off to meet strangers without me.'

I flung my arms around Nick's neck. 'Oh, Nick. Thank you.'

'We should call Charles and let him know what we're planning. I think it would be smart to keep our friends here informed.'

I nodded my agreement. 'Maybe he and Natalie can look

out for each other while we're away.' I hugged Nick again. 'I don't always have the words to say this, but I do love you, Nick. I'll never be able to express how grateful I am to have you in my life.'

I felt Nick smile against my shoulder. 'There's one thing I can think of,' he said.

I pretended to be shocked. 'Nick! It's not even dark outside.'

'I know. How about we be really naughty and not bother to put a towel down first?'

'You were the one who said it was unromantic to change the bed linen afterwards.'

'When you said you wanted to change the linens the first time,' he said, 'I thought you meant in the morning, not immediately.'

'When can we go?' I asked.

Nick smiled his sweet, crooked smile. 'Straight away.'

'No, Nick. I mean the flights.'

'Oh. I'll book them online tomorrow.'

PART 2

Chapter 17

'Are you sure you don't want me to pack your case for you?' I asked Nick when he pulled the suitcases from the loft.

'I'm sure,' he said. 'I know your system of folding is efficient, but I'm quite capable of packing for myself.'

I was wiping my case with an antibacterial wet wipe when I felt a bulge in one of the outside pockets. 'What's this?' I pulled out a carved wooden plaque with a picture of a loaded donkey being led by a small boy. 'We didn't pick up souvenirs when we were in Crete, did we? You always said they were a waste of money.'

Nick reached into the outside pocket of his case. 'I've got one, too.' Nick's plaque was an image of a saint. 'It's Saint Andrew,' he said. 'The patron saint of Greece.'

I was worried. 'Where the hell did they come from? Did someone tamper with our luggage?' But Nick smiled.

'They must have come from Perry and his mother. They're icons, little tokens that are supposed to keep travellers safe on their journey.'

'Speaking of little tokens, I'll leave Helen's locket here. I have a feeling it's going to be dangerous taking it to Athens.'

'I have a feeling it's going to be dangerous taking you to Athens.'

'That's sweet, but...'

'But what?'

'Can we really afford this trip?' I was starting to have second thoughts. 'I know you've got projects on at the university, but I'm not bringing much money in right now. I can barely cover the food shopping.'

Nick looked up and raised his eyebrows slightly. 'We're not that badly off. Your earning is useful, but we're managing.'

I pouted. 'I hate having to rely on you.'

'I don't mind.'

'I know. And I'm not being ungrateful, but I'm used to having my own money. I'm not getting enough freelance work.' This was true, but not the real reason I was questioning the wisdom of the trip.

'You've had a few assignments. I quite like the idea of you working from home. I know where you are.'

'I'd have better earning potential if I was employed. Every company I approach is scared of me.'

Nick suppressed a snort of laughter. 'They are not scared of you.'

'They are! Every Finance Manager's job I apply for has suddenly been filled as soon as I give my name.'

'There'll be other opportunities.'

'I can almost hear the wheels going around in their heads. "There's that crazy conspiracy chick who gave away her company's account codes".' My phone buzzed.

'Who's that?'

'I've just had a text from Natalie.'

'Oh, yes?'

'She says she's going to look after Harmony until Omorfia can be located. She suspects she's in Athens.'

'Well, it seems you're both thinking along the same lines.'

'She says she doesn't know anything about Dion, but she has a friend in Athens who might help us.'

'Really? Who?'

'Someone called Elena. She's sent a phone number.'

'How can Elena help?'

'She doesn't say. But I guess it's a place to start.'

'Well, we'll make contact when we get there and see what Elena knows.' Nick waggled a fatherly finger at me. 'But we go together, remember? No wandering off without me, or I'm bringing you straight back home.'

I licked my finger and crossed my heart. 'I promise.'

We took an early morning flight.

'I don't feel that I know enough about Athens,' I complained as we took our seats on the plane. Nick had the seat by the window. 'I've brought some leaflets with me, but they feel inadequate. Athens has so much history, I don't know where to start.'

'Don't worry,' said Nick. 'I can fill you in on most things. You'll like the hotel I've booked. It's bright and modern and has excellent reviews.'

'I checked it out myself. One reviewer commented that they didn't change the glasses in the bathrooms the whole time he was there.' Nick shot me a worried look. 'But never mind,' I added quickly. 'We can buy some plastic cups when we land.'

Once we were all seated, the stewardess walked down the aisle checking that everyone was belted in.

'Excuse me, what aircraft is this?' I asked.

'It's an Airbus A380, ma'am.'

'How many seats are on this plane?'

'About 853.'

'And how many toilets are there?'

'Kim, don't.' Nick had that warning tone in his voice.

'There are eighteen toilets.'

'So if everyone on this flight went to the toilet, each one would be used more than forty-seven times.'

'Kim, stop it. You're being irrational.'

I smiled politely at our stewardess. 'How often are they cleaned?'

'After every landing, ma'am.'

'I'm going to need a large packet of tissues, please.'

Nick dropped his head into his hands and avoided eye contact with the cabin crew until after take-off.

'Kim, I've been thinking,' he said eventually.

'That's dangerous. It can bring on headaches.'

Nick ignored me and continued. 'As Natalie is caring for Harmony and Marie wanted us to look after Eric, then maybe,' I turned from the in-flight magazine to look at Nick. '...we should, you know, think about it.'

I was shocked. 'Are you mad!'

'It was her dying wish, Kim.'

The numbers started counting and my hands felt clammy. 'If there was a course for parenting at the university, I'd fail it miserably.'

'There is a course for parenting at the university.'

'Don't joke, Nick. It's a terrifying idea.'

'I'm not joking. It's called parentcraft classes. They're designed to show expectant parents the basics of childcare. They're run after hours and open to the public. As I work there, we could get a discount...'

'Stop it! Don't. It's still a terrifying idea.'

'I know. I'm scared too. But Marie did ask us and we don't know what is going to happen to Eric now.'

'He'll be placed with experienced foster carers who can adequately respond to his needs.' I reached out to touch Nick's arm and stroked the back of his wrist with my thumb in what I hoped was a placating gesture. 'I honestly don't think my anxiety could cope with that,' I said reasonably, 'and I certainly wouldn't want to impose my anxieties on to a child. I'm currently living a dangerous life and we can't be sure that Eric would be safe with us.' I squeezed his wrist gently. 'You would make a wonderful dad, Nick. But I'm not a mother.'

I turned back to the in-flight magazine and slowly breathed out, feeling like I'd dodged a bullet. Nick turned his face to the windows and stared at the clouds.

'No, but you could be.'

Nick was right about the hotel. I liked it very much. The plastered exterior had a lemon tint, elegant against the dark grey framed windows. Our whitewashed room was in a contemporary style, with white bedlinen and towels, all neatly folded.

'Do you like it?'

'I haven't inspected the bathroom, yet. But yes, I like it.' The relief on Nick's face made me laugh. The room was one less thing for him to worry about.

'We're less than ten minutes' walk from the local cafes,' said Nick picking up a brochure, 'and less than 20 minutes from the Acropolis. Check out the views. There's a little courtyard just below. Do you fancy a drink?'

'Maybe later.' I said, dropping my hand luggage on the bench under the wall-mounted TV. 'I'm thinking of calling Natalie's friend.'

'We don't have to worry about that right now.' Nick squeezed my shoulders. 'We've just spent nearly four hours in the air. Let's relax for a while; we can take a stroll to one of the cafes for lunch.' I didn't answer, but Nick read my expression. 'OK,' he said dropping his arms. 'Go make your call. I'm taking a nap.' He flopped on the bed and rolled on to his side away from me.

I sat on the chair by the window and looked out on to the courtyard. Why was I here? Had I really come all the way to Athens to chase shadows?

I pulled the phone that Nick had given me from my bag and made the call.

'Ne?'

'Elena, please.' This is only a phone call, Kim. There is

no reason to be anxious. I had to pull the phone away from my ear.

'Mama! Tilefono!'

'Ya sas.'

'Elena? This is Kim Anderson. I don't suppose you know who I am...'

'Yes, you are a friend of Natalie.' The warm, softly spoken voice was calm and welcoming. 'I am a friend of Natalie, too. She comes on holiday often, but this year she says she has been in trouble. And you have been in trouble, too?'

'You could say that. I think I have been in more trouble than most. Natalie said she thought you could help me.'

'When Natalie called, she told me what had happened to her. I have a friend who thinks the same thing has happened to his wife. He thinks he knows where to look. Maybe you can help each other?'

'Can we talk to your friend?'

'Of course. His name is Khaled. He is eating at our place tonight. You will come too?'

'Oh, we really wouldn't want to put you to any trouble.'

Elena laughed. 'Oh, you English are funny. You always say eating is trouble. In Greece we eat to live and live to eat.'

I could feel myself blush. 'It's just that my husband and I haven't made any plans for this evening.'

'Come anyway. At eight o'clock and have tea.' She gave me the address.

I sat on the edge of the bed and watched Nick's back as it moved gently with his breathing.

'That's first contact,' I said, relieved that the phone call hadn't been as stressful as I feared. 'We're visiting a new friend at eight. Nick?'

I reached out to touch his back and he snored in response. Maybe taking a nap wasn't a bad idea.

Chapter 18

A couple of hours later, Nick and I strolled into the square and were surrounded by cafés.

'Which one would you like to try?' he asked.

I pointed to a nearby place with wide open windows. 'That one. I read about it in one of the brochures.'

We seated ourselves at the coffee bar at the back of the café and Nick ordered semi sweet coffee, while I asked for a frappe.

'I'm starving,' said Nick.

'It's only 12 o'clock, our time.'

'Yeah, but it's 2pm in Athens, and I skipped breakfast. What time did you agree to meet this friend of a friend?'

'Elena. At eight.'

'Well, then I suggest we have something more substantial now and a snack later. It might be too late to eat by the time we get back to the hotel. You should destroy the phone you used, too.'

Nick ordered a gyros wrap, which looked like a whole meal in a pitta. I stuck with a Greek salad.

'You're so boring,' he said with his mouth full. 'This is amazing. Want a bite?'

'No thanks,' I said with half admiration, half disgust. 'I'll stick with this. Besides, you know I don't like tzatziki.'

'It's only a yoghurt dressing. You like yoghurt.'

'I don't like cucumber.' A creamy blob of dressing landed on Nick's trousers. 'And now you're getting it all over you.' I reached for a handful of napkins and noticed a young woman sitting in the far corner of the café, watching us.

She was wearing a caramel coloured coat that draped over the sides of the chair, beneath which I could see a mustard coloured top. Her head was loosely draped with a deep blue scarf, which highlighted the depth of her dark eyes. She smiled shyly before returning to her coffee.

'Do you want anything else?' asked Nick while ordering a second cup of coffee.

'No thanks.' I looked up, and again the young woman was watching us. She dropped her head, embarrassed.

'Nick, do we know her?' I whispered, nodding my head towards the woman.

Nick risked a glance. 'No. Why?'

'She's watching us.'

'You're paranoid.'

'She is.'

The woman must have guessed that we were talking about her, as she hurriedly picked up her bag and dashed out into the square, keeping her head down and her eyes averted.

'No, wait!' I dropped from my chair and rushed after her. I couldn't see very much against the harsh glare of the sun, but thought I could spot the blue of her headscarf amongst the crowds. She was already several metres ahead of me and then suddenly turned right.

'Wait!' I ran after her and took the same right turn, only to find myself in another square of smaller buildings. The woman had disappeared.

I had promised Nick that I wouldn't go anywhere without him, and within a matter of hours, had broken that promise. When I got back to the pavement outside the café, the disappointment in his eyes hurt more than the noise of his shouting.

'Would you mind telling me what the hell that was all about?'

'I think she knows who I am. Or maybe who I was. I think she wanted to tell me something.'

'Well let me tell you what I think. I think you saw someone who was only looking at you. I think you scared her, and when she tried to leave, you chased her.'

'She knows something, Nick!'

'What could she possibly know that you need to know right now? How to make friends and influence people the Athenian way?' Nick started marching me back to the hotel.

'We're staying in one place until we have to go out this evening, and when we do we're taking a taxi.'

The car took us via the Vouliagmenis highway to a small but smart and modern apartment building in Glyfada. Elena's apartment was surprisingly spacious, with white walls and buttercream furnishings.

Khaled was already at the apartment when we arrived. He was younger than I expected and was softly spoken. He looked unshaven and in need of sleep, his shoulders stooped with tiredness. Elena introduced us and Khaled dropped his head shyly as he shook our hands. Hot, sweet tea and hard aniseed biscuits were waiting on the small table by the window.

'Please, sit,' insisted Elena, indicating a comfortable sofa. Elena was a little shorter than me, perhaps five feet, five, with a pretty oval face. Tiny lines around her eyes were still very faint. She had long dark hair that she had swept over one shoulder.

'When Natalie told me of the trouble she had experienced at the hands of Fireflight, I knew that this was serious. I visit with the food sellers near the coast and at the end of the day, they share the food with the visitors. Sometimes they go to the camps, there are many all around the city. Sometimes they go to the farms.' Elena's soft voice had a rolling accent that whispered her S's, making them sound like a lisp. 'I have heard the visitors talk of Fireflight. They ask for workers who do not return. Khaled here works at a tomato nursery not far away.'

'When was the last time you saw your wife?' I asked.

'Three weeks ago. We were staying in an empty building with my brother. Adamus and I walked to the farms to ask for work. We returned in the evening, but Gamila was gone. Now we live at the farm.'

'The authorities have been very strict with the visitors,' explained Elena. 'The buildings were abandoned at the beginning of our financial difficulties and the visitors moved in, but they are unsafe for people. Many visitors have been moved to Elaionas, there are over fifteen hundred people there now.'

'Gamila is not in Elaionas. I am sure. I have been there to ask. My wife would not have left me unless she was taken.'

'But what makes you think Fireflight have anything to do with this?' asked Nick.

'We know their name,' replied Khaled. 'They come to the camps looking for workers who don't come back. I am terrified they have taken Gamila.'

'Khaled says he knows the way to the hotel the Olympians are using. Janna!' Elena called towards the kitchen, 'bring more cups.'

'How did you discover this?' asked Nick. 'Do the Olympians own the nurseries, too?'

'As far as I know, not this one,' whispered Khaled. 'But one day, I was asked to help load some crates on to the back of a truck that was delivering to the Hotel Fortune. Sometimes we go to Central Athens, but not often. I overheard the driver talking about the use of the Fates in a new project.' Khaled lowered his eyes. 'My Greek, it's still not very good. But I am sure I was right.'

'Then what did you do?' I asked.

'I saw the truck again another day, by the Hotel Fortune.'

'That could have been just a regular delivery,' said Nick. 'What makes you think the Olympians are there?'

'It was the same driver and passenger as before.'

'Even so...,'

'But they are there!' Khaled suddenly lent forward to grip Nick's wrist, his eyes desperate. 'Why would they let strangers deliver to the hotel? Please! You must help bring my wife back to me.'

A clatter of china interrupted us as a girl with a long blonde ponytail walked towards us. We immediately stopped talking, but Elena smiled and introduced her.

'This is Janna, my daughter. We can speak in front of her, she knows of the work I do.' Janna left the cups on the table and dropped herself on the sofa at the back of the living room, apparently uninterested in our conversation. 'Janna studies fashion and design at the university,' boasted Elena. I couldn't help wondering if Janna had good hearing.

'Khaled will need to return to the nursery before morning and I am working this evening. Janna can take you to this hotel Khaled has told you about, but I do not want her to wait for you.'

I nodded my understanding.

'You must be careful,' she said to Janna, 'and make sure you stay away from migrant streets. I have heard there is a new sickness there.'

'I don't want to go through those streets, anyway,' replied Janna. 'You can smell them before you get there.' She wrinkled her nose as she spoke.

'Not in my backyard,' I mumbled. Nick widened his eyes at me with a look that told me to shut up.

'It's awful,' continued Janna. 'Those allodapous, they're so grubby. Even the children.'

'Do you have a bathroom in this apartment?' asked Khaled, almost casually.

'Of course,' said Janna, 'it was refitted only last year.' Elena looked at the floor and bit her lip, but it was too late to stop her spiteful daughter from speaking.

'I had a bathroom in Syria.' Khaled nodded slowly, as if recalling a fond memory. 'My father-in-law and I fitted it ourselves. On the day our street was destroyed, I couldn't help thinking, "I'll never be able to fix that".' He sighed and took a sip of tea. 'Now my brother and I use a bucket of hot sea water between us. That is all we are allowed, one bucket for two people each morning. That's not so bad,' he shrugged. 'At least we can boil it.' Khaled's eyes dropped to the floor. 'It is still better than living on the island beaches like our friends,' he said quietly. 'They have nothing and nothing is coming. This is true in Greece and in life; when you lose your money, your friends forget you. Only those who love you will remember to ask how you are.'

'I don't think it would be very smart to visit the hotel this evening,' said Nick. 'We are strangers asking awkward questions, after all. Perhaps we would be better off searching for ourselves in the morning.'

Before I could answer, Khaled agreed. 'If I can leave the farm before sunrise, I can meet you here. That would be better than allowing a girl to walk in the dark.'

'I can take care of myself,' pouted Janna.

'Yes,' I said, cutting Janna off. 'Tomorrow.'

Nick arranged a hire car at the hotel and the next day we

met Khaled outside Elena's apartment building at 8.30.

'I read that it shouldn't take us more than 25 minutes to get to the city centre,' said Nick, 'but the roads are already busy.'

'If you park behind the War Museum,' suggested Khaled, 'we can walk there.' Nick was happy to comply rather than fight the workday morning traffic in Athens.

As we strolled through Likiou, Nick marched ahead, tourist guide in hand, following his map even though Khaled had told him he wouldn't need it.

'The hotel is the biggest and most famous in all of Greece,' he said.

Khaled and I slowed our pace to talk while my husband took charge of our journey.

'Coming to Greece must have been something of a culture shock,' I said. I was keen to hear more of Khaled's story, but didn't want to ask questions that he would be reluctant to answer.

'It was, but even though we have an uncertain future, I am pleased just to be here. There is life in Athens that you won't experience anywhere else.'

'But that is true of any of the Greek islands,' I replied, remembering Crete with a certain fondness I hadn't felt before. 'Each seems to have their own take on what Greek life is and each is unique.'

'True, but there is an extraordinary resilience in Athens. Not just in the people, but everywhere. Their strength is all around us; in the robust flavours of their food and wine, in their love and generosity, in their spirit and the courage they instil in their children.'

'You speak as if you have already made Athens your home. Don't you feel that you might want to go back to Syria one day?'

'It is too soon to know. What kind of life would I be taking my wife back to? The one we had in Idleb doesn't exist anymore. I stood and watched while the street where I was born was burned. My time here may be temporary, but life is temporary. Athenians don't think too far into the future. They have their troubles, the same as any other people, but they have been here for thousands of years. They will still be here tomorrow.'

Khaled speeded up his pace a little to join Nick on the corner of Irodou Attikou. We'd come to a stop as a procession of noisy demonstrators passed across the front of us, blocking the street. Most of the demonstrators appeared young, and filled the road like a swarm.

I turned to look back the way we'd come, to see if perhaps we could take another route, but did not get the chance to suggest this to Nick. I was about to call to him when I became aware of a shadow on my left.

One hand pressed over my mouth and nose, restricting my breathing while something cold and sharp pressed against my neck. A hoarse voice hissed in my ear.

'Scream and I swear to God, I'll slit your throat.'

Chapter 19

I could see Nick and Khaled walking ahead of me. Unable to yell, I felt helpless as I was dragged backwards and into a narrow passageway, away from the busy street. My summer sandals skidded over ancient cobbles for a couple of metres, and then I was turned around and pushed up against the cold stone wall of a building.

The young woman before me had fearsome blue eyes, striking against her coffee coloured skin. The anger within them shot poisoned beams straight through me. Her light brown hair was twisted into dreadlocks that sat on her shoulders and bounced and swayed with every movement. She twisted the knife as she pointed it at my neck and I saw the light of the bright sunny morning glint on the blade.

'Who the hell are you?' I didn't dare take my eyes off her, but calling for help would have been useless anyway. The noisy parade was making too many screams and shouts of its own to hear any of mine. The woman pushed her free hand against my chest and the cold from the stone building behind me pressed chilling fingers into my body.

'You really don't know? Well, I suppose I shouldn't be surprised. You only care about yourself, don't you? My name is Medana. Does that mean anything to you?'

'I've, I've never heard that name,' I stammered. 'We've never met.'

'No, we haven't. When I heard that Athena was coming to Athens, I thought it was time to correct that oversight. My friend, Leander, told me that you were in Crete last year. He showed me a picture of you from the security desk at the Labyrinth. But you are not Greek.'

'I'm British.'

Medana shrugged. 'Fireflight is international. They take who they want from wherever they want.'

'You know about Fireflight? What do you want from me?' I wondered if Medana had been sent to assassinate me. Medana looked me up and down.

'Don't you know it was your meddling that put me in danger?'

I held Medana's wrist and tried to pull the knife away. 'Look, I'm sorry if anything happened to you, but...'

'If anything happened to me?!' Medana twisted her arm away from my touch and redirected the blade to the underside of my chin. 'You don't know, do you?'

I shook my head, uncomprehending. Medana's expression softened slightly. The pressure against my chest eased and she took a step back, but continued to point the knife at me.

'Do you know the nightclubs? At least tell me you know Athens.'

I shook my head. 'I've never been here before.'

'Ahead of us is the National Garden,' she pointed back

towards the street, 'And beyond it is Athena's Temple Nightclub. That is where I was raped.'

'Oh, my God!'

'Because of you. It's your fault that I spent a week in hospital and six months in therapy. It's your fault that I had to drop out of university. I thought you should know what happened.'

'Because of me? What do you mean?'

'The guy who attacked me called himself Poseidon. I didn't know his real name. He approached me on campus. He said Fireflight could get me a high level job. Athena had been dropped from one of their projects, so they had to find someone else. He said I was destined for great things, a heroine. But I said no.'

'So he raped you? Why didn't you leave Athens? I would have.'

'I tried.' Medana dropped her head, but not the knife. 'I rented an apartment with my sisters in Gibraltar for a while, but that didn't work out.'

'Can't you go anywhere else? Where are you from?'

'Pick any place you like. My parents were travellers. They named me after a village in Slovenia. My sisters said, "Ana, stay with us, go back to Uni," but that was impossible. I came back to Athens to find Poseidon. And kill him.'

'How are you going to do that if you don't know his real name?'

Medana's cold eyes met mine again. 'You're going to tell me.'

'But, I swear, I don't know.'

'Then swear that you'll find out.'

'But the police, your family...'

'No-one can help me. Except you. There is CCTV everywhere in the city, but the police cannot find him. I know they are lying; I have clever friends, I found you.'

Medana reached into a pocket in her ill-fitting jeans. She pressed an image on her phone and held it up for me to see.

'The day after I was admitted to hospital, a friend found this on the internet. Look at it,' she demanded. 'I want you to see.'

The images were jerky, but quickly, Medana's terrified face could be seen as the person holding the phone pushed against her again and again. Medana was crying as she screamed and begged her attacker to stop.

'No Medana. Enough.' I held my hands up and turned my face away.

Medana continued to move the phone in front of me with one hand while brandishing the knife with the other. 'Look at it, Athena. You did this.'

'Medana, stop. I promise, I didn't know.'

'I don't care that you didn't know,' she persisted. 'You're still to blame.'

'OK, OK,' I said, finally relenting. 'I'll find out who he is.'

Medana lowered the phone and the knife. 'The student network has eyes everywhere. I will find you again, Athena,' she said. And then she was gone.

I held my hand against my chest for several seconds as I tried to regulate my breathing. I stumbled back out on to the pavement and scanned the crowds, but Medana had disappeared into the throng of students weaving through the streets.

Looking to my left, all I could see were banners bouncing above young heads, but then I heard my name called from behind me.

'Kim! Kim! There you are. Did you get lost in the crowd?' Nick turned to call to Khaled. 'It's OK. I've found her.' Then he saw my face. 'What the hell happened?'

It took me a moment or two to gather my thoughts.

'There was a girl. Dangerous and angry.'

Nick dropped his head. 'Oh, dear God. Not someone else. Who was it this time?'

'She said her name was Medana. She wants me to find Poseidon. She dragged me back there.' I pointed to the passageway behind me.

'OK, that's it,' said Nick. 'We're going back to the hotel. I've had enough of this game. We should call the airport and try to get a flight back home. It's too dangerous for you to be here.'

'But Nick, I promised her. I said I'd find out who attacked her.'

'Someone attacked her? That means someone could attack you, too. You can't save every lame duck, Kim. And if this girl knows who you are, then Fireflight will know that you're in Athens...'

'They probably knew the moment we landed.'

'... and that makes this whole business far too risky. I know you had a plan, and I'm sorry, but I think we should leave.'

Nick stood with his hands in his pockets, looking up and down the street. The movement of students reminded me of a murmuration of starlings I had seen in the UK. We would have to break their mass to reach the other side of the street and walk back the way we had come to find our hire car.

'Perhaps a cup of sweet tea would calm your nerves,' suggested Khaled.

We found a café just a little further down the street. I sipped my rich, dark tea and smiled gratefully at Khaled while the cacophony of protest swarmed past the steamy windows.

The ridge between Nick's eyebrows deepened as he watched my shaking hands.

'What the hell happened?'

'She grabbed me from the street. It all happened so quickly.'

'Couldn't you yell for me?'

'No, she had a knife.'

Nick reached for his phone and started thumbing through the screen. 'I'm changing our flights.'

'Nick, no. Please wait.'

'This is the trouble with disposables; there's a limit on what you can do.'

'Nick, listen. I have no intention of going back home until I've found out what's going on here in Athens. We knew it could be dangerous and we chose to come anyway. This is an ongoing war and I'm in it for the long haul.'

Nick placed his phone face down on the table. His shoulders drooped as he spoke. 'Who is this girl? What can you tell me about her, where has she come from?'

I breathed slowly through my nose as I pictured Medana.

'At first, I thought she was one of the students from the demonstration. She was dressed like one. She said she had come back to Athens from Gibraltar.'

'There are student groups all over the city,' said Khaled. 'The students are peaceful at the university, but gather in groups when they wish to protest.' He looked up at me with solemn brown eyes. 'They will be walking towards Syntagma Square.'

'But why is she here?' asked Nick.

'She wants to find Poseidon, the guy who attacked her.' I shivered involuntarily as I recalled the images on her phone. 'Her rape was captured and uploaded on to the internet.'

'But why would the attack be on the internet? Did the guy want to get caught?'

I cradled my hands around my glass cup. 'He probably wanted to prove himself to Fireflight. Anything can get uploaded to the internet these days. Most of us wouldn't go digging, but I'm sure Fireflight would know where to look.'

'How did Medana find it?'

'She said a friend found it.'

'Do you believe her?'

I paused to think about my answer before I spoke. 'No, I

don't think I do. I think it's more likely that she was sent the video to scare her into compliance. She'd already refused an offer from Fireflight. What I don't understand is what Fireflight want with her in the first place. And how would she know who I was unless someone had told her?'

Nick closed his eyes and dropped his head into his hands.

'What is it?' I asked.

'Poseidon raped Medusa. It's about you.'

'What about me? Medusa was an ugly monster killed by Perseus, right?'

'Athena turned Medusa into the monster as a punishment for defiling her temple. The rape of Medusa was blamed on her beauty and Poseidon couldn't help himself.'

I was shocked. 'That's disgusting! How could she possibly be blamed?'

'Kim, we're talking about a period in history where women had no voice and men had all the power. Even under these horrific circumstances, Medusa would still have been labelled a seductress. Stories told about women have always focused on women's sexuality as a dangerous and potentially evil force.'

'Why is that? Why should we be burdened with such an unfair image?'

'I think it's another portrayal of the curse of Eve.'

'Surely this can't have anything to do with menstruation?' Khaled squirmed in his seat. 'There are some stories not told outside the home,' he said, clearly uncomfortable with the frankness with which Nick and I talked. 'But their privacy doesn't make them easier to hear.'

Nick smiled apologetically at Khaled and lowered his voice.

'That's a later religious interpretation, true,' he continued, 'but the curse is a punishment. What was Eve being punished for?'

'For eating the forbidden fruit of the tree of knowledge,' I answered.

'In part, yes, but...'

'She seduced Adam into eating the forbidden fruit, too.'

'Right. So the punishment suggests that if Eve was seduced by the snake, maybe you can't help yourselves; you're all bad girls. And religion, from the oldest to the modern day, has been treating you the same ever since.'

I couldn't speak for a few seconds. 'Well, fortunately we're better educated. We've moved on since then,' I said.

Khaled looked up. He raised only one eyebrow. 'Oh, you think so?'

'You can't trust this girl,' continued Nick. 'Fireflight will always be trying to get to you.'

'If Fireflight know that Medana has found me, they will use her to get to me.' I drained my cup. 'Come on. We've got work to do.'

Nick and Khaled rose to their feet.

'Where are we going now?' asked Nick.

'We're going to find Poseidon.'

Chapter 20

'We're going to talk to the police,' said Nick.

'What about the hotel?' asked Khaled.

Nick shook his head. 'I'm sorry for dragging you out here, Khaled, but I think it's too risky. Even if I can't persuade Kim to go home, one dangerous adventure is enough for today.'

'You won't be able to persuade me to go home. And the day is still young. We'd still have time to check out the hotel. Whoever is there might know of Poseidon.'

'No, Kim.' Nick spoke sternly, reminding me of my father. 'Not today. And you still have to report this to the police.'

I opened my arms in a frustrated gesture. 'What do I tell them? That another woman was attacked while I was in the UK and blames me?'

'You tell them that you were ambushed in the street and threatened with a knife.'

'She's a desperate woman, Nick. She just wants some answers.'

Khaled quietly interrupted us before our conversation could descend into rowing. 'Perhaps you speaking to the police will remind them of what happened to her. But the central Athens police station is a long walk from here.'

Nick nodded. 'Let's see if the crowds have thinned out.'

Out on the street, only a few stragglers from the demonstration were loitering on the pavements. Nick gripped my hand as we crossed the street and headed west towards Rizari Park.

Khaled held out his hand. 'I must leave you here,' he said. 'I will lose tonight's bed if I am not back at the farm by this afternoon.'

'Will you be able to find your way back?' I asked.

Khaled smiled. 'I have friends who deliver to other hotels. I can get a lift back. Thank you,' he said, a serious look coming into his eyes. 'Thank you for believing me.'

Nick gripped Khaled's arm. 'Take care, Khaled. We'll catch up with you before we fly home.' I watched him walk away before Nick and I turned towards the car park.

I followed the map while Nick drove up Alexandras Avenue and we saw the Hellenic police building just ahead. It was an impressive looking place. About twelve storeys high, the complex towered over the street. Thick square columns supported the front of the lower level, while a pair of palm trees stood like sentries either side of the main door. Above, a wide bank of windows bounced sunlight back on to the street. Nick was able to park nearby and we walked back on ourselves.

'I think this is the main east to west thoroughfare,' said Nick reaching for my hand. We dodged the busy traffic to reach the main entrance. Nick approached the officer sitting behind the main desk and although Nick spoke in Greek, the officer rose from his chair to point his pen towards the street and eastwards. His welcoming smile quickly faded as Nick tried to argue.

'No,' insisted Nick, starting to lose his temper, and slipping back into English. 'We are not driving back. My wife needs to speak to someone now.'

'What's going on?'

'He says we're in the wrong place. We need to go to the Tourist Police Office.'

'Where the hell is that?'

'Somewhere around Dragastsaniou. Apparently it's hard to find, but because we're tourists, that's where we need to go.'

'Let's just get out of here,' I said. 'I'm already starting to feel edgy.'

'They need to be told, Kim. We're doing the right thing, making a report.'

'Surely there are other police buildings in the city. Let's go.'

Nick pulled away from me and stood in the centre of the foyer and yelled in Greek. All the hustle and bustle around us stopped and all eyes turned to Nick. I could feel myself shrink with embarrassment.

'What the hell did you say?'

'I demanded that someone come and talk to us,' said Nick. A couple of uniformed officers were walking briskly towards the entrance. 'Look, it's working. Either you get to make a statement, or I'm about to get arrested.'

Five minutes later, I was sitting across from a uniformed female officer with a telephone in the middle of the table between us. The officer completed a form, while the voice from the telephone explained what was happening. This was a very dispassionate experience. The officer relayed her questions to the translator, not to me, and both the officer and the translator seemed bored at having to go to the effort of taking the details about what had happened to me.

'Tourists are advised to be careful of the students,' said the translator. 'You were clearly caught up in the student demonstration marching towards the Parliament buildings.'

'I have no way to know Medana is a student. And they weren't marching.'

'We believe she is,' responded the translator. 'Many of the young people travel to the university from camps outside the city. Their demonstrations often descend into riots. We advise tourists to stay away from the demonstrations.'

I felt my cheeks get hot. 'I didn't go looking for trouble. She attacked me. And she knew who I was. How could she know?'

'We will look into that for you. Please leave your contact details with the officer.'

Nick was waiting for me back at the foyer. 'How did it go?'

'Tediously. I feel like the form that was completed will go to the bottom of a very deep pile and may never see the light of day again. What about you? Are you OK?'

'While the Hellenic Police recognise my right to express myself, I've been warned not to make a habit of calling the officers stupid donkeys.'

I giggled in spite of myself. 'You called them stupid donkeys?'

'I couldn't think of a suitable translation for brainless asses.'

We walked out on to the bright street. It was not yet spring in Greece, but already the day's temperature was high.

'I'm sure the police, as well as other Greeks, must be pretty fed up of tourists complaining about their time in the city,' I commented as we walked back to the car. 'I know that it's a part of their culture to be friendly and accommodating, but it must be trying at times.'

'The Greek relationship with tourism makes me think of a temperamental and distrustful marriage,' said Nick. 'Greece genuinely needs the sunny tourist traps but the holiday companies are like a young and flighty wife; always looking for somewhere better.'

I laughed. 'Well, that's a unique take on things.'

Nick smiled down on me. 'How are you feeling now?'

'Calmer. But we've still got to get back to our hotel.'

'That shouldn't take too long. We can stop off and I'll buy you an ice cream along the way.' Nick started the car.

'Khaled said he was sure he heard the truck drivers talking about The Fates. Who are they?'

Nick sighed. 'You're not going to let go that this is a working trip for you, are you?' I couldn't answer. It was true.

'He could have been mistaken. Even he said his Greek wasn't very good.'

'He's worried about his wife, Nick. I think we should take this seriously, even if he's wrong.'

'Well, I hope he is wrong, because if he's not, whatever he comes across isn't going to be good.' I looked at Nick as he drove and waited for him to continue. 'The Fates were three goddesses who determined how long a person's life would last. Clotho spun the thread of life, Lachesis measured it and Atropos cut it at life's end.'

'They're already starting to sound like drugs, or more likely, compounds. Fireflight aren't starting up again; they haven't stopped working.'

'It seems that whatever they do, their projects support each other,' agreed Nick.

'Right, but we don't know how. Instead of buying me an ice cream, how about buying me a coffee at an internet café? I'd be interested to see what we can find.'

The internet café, just a few streets from our hotel, had little lunchtime trade.

'I know it's quiet, but let's just get some coffee and do what we need to,' suggested Nick. 'I don't think we should hang around.'

I nodded and offered to queue while Nick logged in to his email. I watched his hands fly over the keyboard and smiled as I saw him type my name.

'You are not going to believe this,' he said when I returned. 'I've had an email from someone calling herself Princess Pixel.'

'Lucky you. Is she looking for a date?'

'No, not that kind of email. She's found out that Dion, that kid you were worried about, was smuggled here by Tony Brownlow.'

'Tony?' I felt goose bumps rise on my arms, despite the sun's warmth from the windows. 'Is he still alive?'

'She doesn't say.'

'Don't respond,' I warned, suddenly worried. I sat beside him. 'We have no way to know if this person is a friend.'

'True, but I think I know who it is. How many princesses do we know who are good with computers?'

'We don't know any princesses. This could be a trap.'

'Whose name means princess?'

'Sarah? Oh my God! Is she OK?'

'Yeah, seems to be, but she's not revealing much, so she's being cautious.'

'I'm not surprised. If she's doing some digging for The Network, she needs to be doubly careful.'

Nick blew in his coffee. 'I think she knows. She seems pretty tech savvy. And talking of being careful, you better get rid of that disposable phone.'

'Does she say anything about The Fates?'

'No. I'd guess that she doesn't know of them. But she does say that Dion was adopted by a winemaking family who are already part of The Network.'

'Where is he?'

'The tone of her email suggests that he's here in Athens.'

'Well, Sarah won't have been able to send us any proof of that. How can we verify her findings?'

Nick brought up a search engine. 'Let's see what we can find.' He entered Winemaking Families. 'Apparently Troy is the biggest producer and seller of wine around here.'

'Troy? As in the ancient city?'

'They're a major American owned multinational. They're a global investment company and have interests in all sorts of different businesses; wine, foodstuffs, heath supplements, fitness and healthcare.' Nick brought up their US webpage and clicked on "all about us". 'Here, listen to this. "100 years ago, our founder, Lucas Troy, arrived in Manhattan with a pocket full of loose change and heart full of dreams. He persuaded a delivery driver to give him a job and at only 17 years of age, was delivering some of the most expensive wines in the world to some of the most exclusive restaurants in the US. After studying under the best vintners in Greece and Turkey, Lucas made his fortune selling wine all over the world, before deciding to share his expertise and diversify into investment".'

'Wait a minute! Helen said she was working for Troy. What building do they have in New York?'

Nick put down his cup and tapped on the keyboard. 'That's their head office, but they have offices all over the world; Geneva, Canakkale, London.'

'Can you send them a message through their webpage?'

'Kim, you've got that look in your eye again. I really don't think this is a good idea.'

'I'm not going to chase after Helen, I promise.' Nick gave a look that said he didn't believe me. 'But I don't think it's a coincidence if Dion was adopted by a family in Greece. What if this winemaker is connected to the same Troy that Helen worked for? We have no idea where this boy is and there's no way to know if he's safe until we can check them out.'

Nick tapped at the keyboard again. 'They have a building here in Athens.' He let out a low whistle. 'It looks like a palace.'

I leaned across to take a look. 'They have a link for events,' I said. 'What's coming up?'

'A party to celebrate a new partnership. Tomorrow night.'

'A partnership with whom? Fireflight?'

'Well, they wouldn't put that on their internet pages, would they? But there is no way we can go.'

'They did mention it on their page.'

'No, Kim. Absolutely not.' Nick set his mouth in a grim line and clicked back to the image of the building. 'Look. You see that?'

'No. See what?'

'That light at the entrance. That could mean that the building is being used as a registered brothel. There's no way to know who could be there.'

'And how the hell would you know?' I asked.

'Prostitution is legal in Athens in a registered building. Some of the guys at work... Well, let's just say, they've had some interesting holidays.'

'It's just a light, Nick. Buildings like that have lights everywhere.'

'But why that kind of light, exactly there?'

'It's not even red.'

'It doesn't have to be. Look at the rest of the website. This Troy look like they're a big deal. If they have major offices around the world, they could also own any number of buildings in the city. Who knows what they could be used for?'

'I'd expect a big company to own several buildings, Nick. They could be perfectly legitimate.'

'But what if you're right? What if Fireflight are there? Where there is Fireflight, there will be enforcers.'

'Where there is Fireflight and sex, there will be Aphrodite. She might not know anything about Dion, but she'll be able to answer other questions for us.'

'You're guessing again. We can't know if Aphrodite will be there.'

'Yes, I am guessing. But if I'm right, I'd love to have the opportunity to get my hands around that pretty little neck of hers.'

Nick sighed and dropped his head. He took another gulp of coffee. 'It looks like I'm buying you an evening dress, then,' he said.

Chapter 21

Back at the hotel, Nick headed straight for the bathroom.

'I need a shower; I've got to wash the day away. The menu in the hotel restaurant is pretty good. Do you fancy eating in tonight?'

I stood still in the middle of the room feeling uneasy. I could hear Nick talking in the bathroom and the hiss of the shower. Everything seemed perfectly normal, but it wasn't somehow.

'Kim?' Nick poked his head from the bathroom door. 'What is it?'

'Something is different. This room is not how we left it.'

'Well the cleaners have probably been in.'

'No, that's not it.' We had not put anything in the bins and they were still in the same place. The flyers we had picked up were still on the bench under the TV. Nick's jacket was still flung over the back of the chair; he had decided not to take it when we went out. 'It's your jacket. It's facing the wrong way.'

'What do you mean, facing the wrong way?' Nick walked into the room with a towel around his waist.

I pointed to the jacket. 'When you fling a jacket on to a chair, you hold it by the collar and lay it down.'

'I do.' Nick indicated his jacket. 'Just like that. You're always telling me off about it.'

'But when we left this morning, the open edge of your jacket was facing the window, now it's facing the bed.'

'Are you sure?'

I narrowed my eyes at my husband. 'I can tell when one of the fridge magnets is less than half an inch out of alignment. Yes, I'm sure.'

Nick couldn't argue with that. 'Would housekeeping need to move my jacket?'

'No, I think this room has been searched.'

'Searched? What the hell could they have been looking for? We had the phones on us.'

'I want a different room, Nick. Talk to reception.'

'I will. But what were they after?'

'Well, what did you have in your jacket?'

'Nothing. Only...'

'Only what?'

Nick walked back into the bathroom and turned off the shower. He came back holding his trousers and fished in the pockets. He pulled out a crumpled piece of paper.

'What is that?'

Nick unfurled the paper. 'This is the copy of the pamphlet of the Adelfi project. I took it from Sarah.'

'I remember. You said there was something about it that troubled you.'

'Yes, but I still can't put my finger on it. Look.'

I sat on the edge of the bed while I studied the picture

and the wording. 'It's all in English.'

'Yes, so?'

'You said that some text on the computer at the hospital was in Greek.'

'That's right. This is obviously an English translation.'

'But that suggests to me that the original text was written here, in Greece. You and Sarah thought that perhaps a Greek keyboard had been used, but I don't remember seeing any at the hospital, do you?'

Nick sat beside me. 'No.'

'When you discovered that Aphrodite was to be the face of the Adelfi project, was there a picture with the Greek text?'

Nick frowned as he thought back. 'No, I don't think so. Only on that.'

I held up the pamphlet. 'So who's this?'

'Well, it's Aphrodite, obviously.' Nick laughed. 'A bit of an odd choice for a reproduction programme.'

'Exactly!' I stood up suddenly, nearly dropping the pamphlet. 'I've been trying to figure who she is. Now we know.'

'It's Omorfia.'

'No, it's not. Look again.' I handed the pamphlet to Nick. 'Do you remember Helen's reaction when she found out that the Adelfi project was still running? No wonder she's so protective of Omorfia. She's already a child of Fireflight.'

'I agree, it's not an exact likeness...'

'But close enough. That explains why Omorfia went back to Fireflight.'

'It does?'

I tapped my finger on the picture. 'That's not Omorfia's face. That's Helen.'

'Are you sure?'

'Well, no. But if I'm right, it explains a lot of things.'

'Perhaps you could explain this to me.'

'Helen might have been Aphrodite, once. Which means that she was probably still working for Fireflight while she worked for Troy. Helen was trying to trace Omorfia, who might have been conceived through the Adelfi project. Somehow Helen found out that she'd been freed from Fireflight and came to the UK, maybe to see if it was true.'

'Well, that's a happy ending. They found each other.'

'They found each other all right, but they are still very far from a happy ending. Omorfia became Aphrodite again and has re-joined Fireflight.'

'That was only a threat from Hermes. He told her that Zeus had plans for her daughter, but Helen said that was wrong. He can't get to Harmony.'

'I don't think it's her daughter she's protecting. It's her mother. Think about it. Hermes told Omorfia that Fireflight and Troy are fighting over Eileithyia. That's Helen.'

'I don't know why. She's not an Olympian.'

'No, but she is important to the Golden Apple project.'

'But this pamphlet is talking about the Adelfi project, not the Golden Apple project.'

'It doesn't matter. Whatever project they're working on helps support the others. What happened in the legends regarding the Golden Apple?'

'The goddesses Hera, Athena and Aphrodite all wanted the golden apple and each had to convince Paris that she should have it.'

'And who won?'

'Aphrodite. She promised Paris the most beautiful woman in the world.'

'Right. The golden apple wasn't the prize, Helen was.' I started to pace as I ordered my thoughts. 'Aphrodite won the golden apple, which means that Fireflight definitely want to use her. It's possible that wherever Omorfia was sent, Helen would follow and they could both be here in Greece.'

Nick nodded. 'I'm sure she would want to follow her, unless of course, she was sent somewhere else. But the original Aphrodite and Helen didn't come from Athens. Helen came from Sparta and was taken to Troy.'

'So if Helen of Sparta went to Troy, where would Helen of Fireflight go?'

Nick paused to think about that. 'Probably Canakkale, the most likely place in Turkey. It's right next to the original site of Troy, at Hissarlik. But how could we find out?'

I smiled. 'Well, luckily for us, I happen to be a goddess. Perhaps a call to Perdika is in order.'

'That's in Crete,' said Nick, remembering the restaurant. 'I don't have the number.'

'I can remember it.'

Nick rolled his eyes. 'Of course you can.'

I pulled another phone from my bag and brought it to

life.

Perry and his mother Sofika, were the owners of Perdika, a charming little restaurant in Crete. Nick and I had travelled there looking for clues after I was released from my kidnapping last year. Perry's bravery and knowledge of Greek culture had convinced me to recruit him to The Network.

Perry seemed pleased to get my call. I was relieved he was willing to speak to me after the danger we had been in ten months ago. The kindness we had been shown by Perry and Sofika, had enhanced my admiration of the generosity of the Greek people and confirmed my belief in the necessity for The Network.

'It is good to hear from you Athena.'

'It's nice to speak to you too, Perry. I'm sorry to have to bother you, but I need a favour.'

'It is never a bother to help Athena. What do you need?'

'I am in Athens looking for Eilytheia. Her name is Dr Helen Markham. I need to know if she has been to Turkey; perhaps to Canakkale. Can you check with Kiki and find out if any money was spent on travel to Turkey in the last three months?'

I remembered Kiki as a grumpy teenager who was helping her grandpa record Fireflight's accounts. The two of them had taken an enormous risk when they shared details of hidden money Fireflight was using.

'Of course. May Kiki contact you? On this number?'

'Yes, I'm afraid I don't have a number for her myself, and this request may be a little less obvious or suspicious coming from you.'

'I understand. I will tell her to use a disposable phone to text you.'

'Thank you, Perry. I'm grateful.'

'You can thank us better in person. If you are in Athens, you are only a brief flight away from Crete.'

'I'd love to see you, Perry. But I don't know how long we'll be here. I'll be in touch.'

'Take care, Athena. Be safe.'

Later that evening, we wandered down to the hotel restaurant and asked for somewhere quiet to eat. The young man showed no surprise at our request and led the way through a side door. I was expecting to be shown to the courtyard, but we stepped into a separate outside eating area.

The outside dining space looked like it had once been an external alleyway running along the side of the hotel. Now painted and with a tiled floor, it felt cool, welcoming a breeze from the courtyard beyond. Black painted lanterns hung from the ceiling every six or seven feet, and each was enveloped by the embracing starlight of a hundred LEDs.

Nick ordered soutzoukakia for both of us and it was while I was finishing my meal, that the text came from Kiki. The belligerent teenager I remembered seemed to have mellowed slightly.

'Kiki has found some interesting figures,' I commented. 'She says she's seen additional columns of figures in the spreadsheets, but can't copy them. I suppose it would be too risky to try and send them.'

'That was how her grandpa discovered Fireflight's hidden money last time,' remembered Nick. 'How is old Plutus?'

'She doesn't say, but it looks like she's following his methods. The hidden columns show huge deposits made by Troy.'

Nick paused in his chewing to absorb this news. 'Deposited by someone called Troy, or the company, Troy?'

'Judging by the figures Kiki is quoting, I'd say it would have to be a company. They're several thousands of Euros paid over several months. Starting from the second week of May last year.'

'I recognise that date. That's when you were released.'

'It's also when Omorfia and others were released. Kiki says that last week's and this week's payments didn't arrive, they've mysteriously stopped.'

'Does Kiki know why, or who stopped them?'

I turned my phone around so that Nick could see for himself. 'I don't think so, and I don't think that Kiki would have done that, even if she could intervene. It's too dangerous.'

'But no one else other than the higher up members would have had access to those accounts.'

'Which means the halt on those payments must have come from outside and Troy suspended the payment themselves.'

Nick pushed his plate away and took a slow sip of water.

'Maybe Sarah managed to send paperwork to Troy and they got cold feet.'

I shook my head. 'Unlikely. Any company willing to become involved with Fireflight isn't going to be scared off that easily. Somebody talked to them and I think it was Omorfia.'

Nick almost laughed. 'Omorfia loves money and wasn't scared by Fireflight's procedures. Why would she want to damage their deal?'

'She seems to love her mother,' I pointed out. 'She was probably trying to complete the deal without the goddesses or Helen involved. For her, this could have been an all-round win. Fireflight regain Aphrodite, she makes a deal and gets a payment; Helen isn't a part of it; I'm out of the picture and Hera, the interfering witch, is none the wiser.'

The waiter put a fresh carafe of water on the table.

Nick turned his attention back to the phone. 'But something's gone wrong. Whoever is paying Aphrodite, Fireflight or Troy, must be getting something for their money and that money must be coming from somewhere. And,' he continued, looking up, 'This isn't evidence that Helen went to Turkey.'

'All the more reason to go to that party. We can ask Omorfia tomorrow.'

It was already 9 am when we left our new hotel room. It was just as lovely as the previous one, but didn't have a bath; it had a double width shower unit instead.

'Ooh,' said Nick approvingly. 'We could make good use of that.'

We took the 9.30 tram to the Attica district.

'I don't want anything cream, grey or silver,' I said as we walked into the boutique. It was another bright day and the sunlight streaming in through the large windows bounced light off every sequin, illuminating the shop like a nightclub on Valentine's night.

'What's wrong with cream or silver?'

'I become invisible,' I complained. 'I'm so pale, I disappear.'

Nick stroked my arm. 'Oh, I don't know. I think I can see a little colour coming through. It'll be nice to see you in a proper dress.'

I cast an uncertain eye over the mannequins and then over the life sized portraits that adorned the walls. Every picture was of a glamorous model with forever legs and pudding bowl breasts.

'I couldn't possibly wear a dress like that,' I said, pointing.

'Even with a Wonderbra, I'd never have the chest for it.'

'I like yours the way they are,' whispered Nick, reassuringly. 'Bite-sized.'

An assistant, who looked like she had just retired from modelling the dresses she sold, approached and Nick spoke to her, indicating me. The assistant gave me a critical once-over and turned to another rail.

'If she comes back with thigh split, cleavage bursting, transparent nothingness,' I hissed, 'I'll divorce you.'

Happily, I was presented with a collection of five dresses, all of which covered me adequately and fitted well.

'I like this pale blue one,' I said, twisting in front of the mirror. The halter neck design showed off my shoulders and fell gracefully to my ankles. 'How much is it?' I looked at the label and almost fainted.

'They're all likely to have similar prices,' said Nick. 'Relax. I'm paying.'

'How? With a quick loan?'

'Kim, I'm buying you a dress because I want you to have something nice. You need the dress, because if you don't have it you'll look out of place at the villa.'

He was right, of course, but it felt ridiculously extravagant for something that I was unlikely to wear again. Nick handed over his credit card.

The assistant looked towards the shop windows. 'Poso atychos. I think it will thunder this afternoon.'

Nick and I both turned in the direction of her gaze to see a dark band of cloud moving in from the east.

'Bad weather looks like it's coming in from the sea,' said Nick. 'The tourist brochure said that storms here are brief, but can be pretty dramatic. We should get back to the hotel, or we might risk getting caught in it. No time for sightseeing today.' He turned to smile at me. 'Never mind, I'll take you for a walk on the beach tomorrow.'

I didn't mind taking a tram back to the hotel. It turned out that I quite liked tram riding.

'I could get used to this,' I said when we got back to the room. 'I should let you buy me things more often.'

Nick kissed my cheek as I dropped the heavy paper bag on the bed. 'Yes, you should.'

I pulled the dress-box from the bag to hang the dress up straight away. 'What's this?'

'Hmm?'

'Is this your receipt?' I held up a slip of paper that had fallen from the box.

'No, I have that in my wallet.' Nick took the paper from me and then looked at me with his eyes wide. 'What is the weather doing now?'

I looked at the window. 'I think the sky has cleared. We were lucky not to get caught in bad weather.'

'Yeah, lucky,' repeated Nick. 'We were tricked with a classic diversion. Look.'

I took the slip of paper from him, but what was written on it was in neat Greek handwriting and meant nothing to me. 'What does it say?'

'It says that Eileithyia took a day trip to Canakkale before coming to Athens, and we should take care.'

'Someone knows of our conversation with Perry.'

'Someone knows we were looking for Helen.'

I thought about that. 'Do you think this room is bugged?'

'That sounds a bit old fashioned.'

'But possible. And you spoke to our waiter at dinner last night in Greek.'

'Of course. I think it's good manners to speak the language of the country you're visiting.'

'But what if it's unnecessary? What if he could speak English?'

'It's still good manners,' said Nick.

'I can't help feeling that even though we're surrounded by danger, we have friends protecting us, even if we don't know who they are.'

'How are we supposed to tell one from the other?'
I turned the slip of paper over in my fingers. 'We might not be able to, but I'd like to think that we have more friends than enemies. We'll have a clearer idea of who they are when we visit the villa.'

'Maybe we should take a walk in the National Gardens at lunch time,' suggested Nick, 'have a breather before we take the plunge tonight.'

We strolled from our hotel to Vasillisis Sophias Avenue and into the beautiful public park. As soon as we passed the first of its famous palm trees, the noise and bustle of the city was almost silent.

'This garden is home to 7000 trees,' said Nick. 'Queen

Amalia is said to have planted the palm trees herself.'

I pointed to a structure on the left. 'What's that?'

'The remains of a Roman Villa, apparently.'

We held hands and followed a long narrow path, not caring where it led.

'I heard a guy at the hotel say that any path you take here will lead you to a lake.'

I doubted that was possible. 'Is that really true?'

'It could be. There are six of them.'

I paused to pull a shoe off and wriggled my toes. 'Are we allowed on the grass? My feet are hot.'

Nick smiled. 'Yes, I think so.'

I held my shoes in one hand and took Nick's with the other and we explored the park together until it was time to leave.

When we got back to the room, I headed straight for the bathroom. 'I'm going to take a quick shower and wash my feet.'

'Leave some hot water for me,' called Nick. 'I might want a shower, too.'

I slid open the double doors to the shower and felt relaxed by the massage of the warm water. I had just finished washing my hair when Nick entered naked, with a towel around his waist.

'I just wanted to make sure you weren't using all the hot water,' he said.

'Not much chance of that,' I replied. 'We're only using water that's just warm; the weather's too hot for anything else.'

Nick dropped his towel and joined me in the shower. 'As long as it's warm enough to get a lather,' he said. 'You know I'm always willing to share my shower gel.'

'That's kind of you. I'm not clean yet.'

Nick smiled as he wrapped his arms around my waist. 'Good. Then we can both be dirty.'

I laughed as Nick kissed me in the space below my ear. He continued, tracing a line down my neck, towards my collarbone and to the hollow at the base of my throat. I held his head in my hands as I kissed the top of his head and ran my fingers through his thick hair, allowing the water that splashed from my shoulders access to his scalp. His hair curled almost immediately at the touch of the water.

Nick's journey of kisses carried on down my body, towards my navel. Ignoring the water, he knelt before me and I gasped with surprise as his mouth travelled on to my belly and even further south.

'What are you doing?'

'Worshipping my goddess.'

I reached out either side and pressed my hands flat against the giant marble tiles; cold beneath my palms and contrasting sharply with the hot, wet steaminess of the shower. I dropped my head back and felt the shower water tumble over my hair and down my back, as soft as summer rain.

I left the bathroom after Nick. He had gone to find his suit. I pinned my hair up, and decided against a necklace. I wore long drop earrings instead.

'Wow,' said Nick when he saw me in the dress. 'Did I remember to buy you new lingerie to go with that?'

'No,' I smiled.

'Shame.' He reached out his hand and our fingers entwined. 'Never mind, there'll be more shopping to look forward to when we get back to the UK.'

I lifted his hand and turned his wrist slightly to glance at his watch. 'Well, I'm afraid round two will have to wait. There's a party to go to.'

Nick's face fell. 'You're such a spoilsport.'

We took a taxi to the address on Troy's website and arrived just before eight. This was the hour when Athens came alive, the time when friends and families came together to eat and drink after the sun went down.

The half-moon driveway was busy with cars coming and going and light shone from every window of the house. Music and laughter spilled from the open doors. The villa was magnificent and I guessed that the original winemaking family must have been extraordinarily rich to have built a house in the Kifisia hills.

As soon as we walked through the palatial entrance, I realised we were at a different kind of party.

Two young women greeted us, one to take our coats and my bag, the other to offer us champagne. They were both beautiful and flirtatious. The offers their eyes hinted at were not lost on either of us.

In the centre of the entrance hall was a large, circular table with an enormous bowl of flowers in the middle. Every available inch in the bowl was stuffed with blooms, toppling over each other and flowing down towards the table top. The shine on the surface mirrored the flowers, doubling the impact. What should have been a display of beauty was now an ostentatious display of wealth.

I pressed my hand against my chest. 'I have a bad feeling about this place.'

Beyond the table, a sumptuous chaise longue was pushed up against the wall. The woman reclining on it was wearing an evening gown and a pair of Jackie Onassis sunglasses. She lowered the glasses as we approached to give Nick a tired end-of-shift stare.

'We're looking for someone,' I said. The woman stared blankly back at me and I elbowed Nick who translated the message and received one back.

'She says she doesn't do couples.'

'Tell her we're looking for Omorfia.'

Nick did so, but the woman only shrugged and shook her head.

'What about Aphrodite?'

That name needed no translation and the woman's eyes immediately widened on hearing it. She said something and then replaced the sunglasses to indicate that our conversation was over.

'She says that Aphrodite is either in the garden to the right or by the pool at the back of the house.'

I walked through the doorway to the right, and saw at the other end of the room, a set of double doors leading to a pretty patio with a gigantic looking garden beyond. I noticed a woman, in her early thirties, sitting on a wicker chair in front of the doors, reading a magazine, before I realised that Nick was not behind me.

'Excuse me, I'm looking for Omorfia?'

'Beauty is everywhere,' she replied. She crossed her legs and her long, shimmering dress slipped across her knees.

'No, I mean I'm looking for someone called Omorfia.'

'I don't know who that is, but I am beautiful, am I not?'

'I'm not looking for a date.'

The woman shrugged, her dark hair gliding on her shoulders, and turned her attention back to the magazine.

'You look familiar to me.'

The woman tilted her head towards me and smiled. 'I'm sure that if we had met before, I would have remembered.'

'Why are you here? In this place?'

'Why do you think? We all have to work.'

'But you shouldn't be pressured into doing anything you don't want to do.'

'I'm not. Apart from the need for money. The financial crisis has been going on for many years.'

'But you still have to stay here, to earn money for The Company?'

'Are you a reporter?'

'No.'

'You ask questions like one. Foreign reporters are always looking for the dark side of business. Look, I'll tell you what I tell them. I can work what hours I like. We get a health check every year and we are licenced. It's the women on the beach who are not, the Syrians. I feel sorry for them, but we are legal, they are not.'

'But you work for Fireflight.'

'They are a big company. They make medicines. What does it matter who runs the house? The work is the same.'

I walked through the doors and into the garden. I strolled across the patio towards a large square of grass, which led the way to the beautiful flower garden. The rich turf felt spongy beneath my shoes.

A voice from behind surprised me.

'How are you, Kim?'

Chapter 23

'Helen! I was wondering if I'd see you in Athens.'

'I followed Omorfia to Greece. I have property in Laconia.' Helen linked an arm through mine and led me across the grass towards the flower beds. 'Isn't this incredible?' She waved her free arm over the flowers. 'Everything you see in this garden was imported and paid for by wine. Everything that's here owes its place to the determination of the winemakers.'

'Did you find Omorfia?' I asked.

Helen smiled. 'I did. She's here with other freed women.'

A chill tickled the back of my neck. Omorfia returned to Greece as Aphrodite. Who were these other freed women?

'They are completely safe here,' she continued, 'and knowing you're in Athens has created a real buzz. I'm already monitoring three pregnancies. Isn't that wonderful?'

'I'll be going back to the UK in a few days,' I said.

Helen stepped towards a green painted bench and indicated for me to sit beside her under the honeysuckle. 'I'd like to persuade you to stay longer. Your presence would be wonderful for morale. These women have been through so much. To have you here would mean a lot to them.'

I looked down at my feet and wriggled my toes inside my

shoes. 'You know what I've wanted to do? More than anything else?'

Helen shook her head.

'I wanted to walk barefoot in the grass in my garden.'

She laughed, then. 'You can walk how you like in this garden. You can go wherever you want.'

'But this isn't my garden. Home is in the UK.'

Helen nodded sadly. 'Well, I can't say I'm not disappointed. I honestly thought you'd be willing to help the others.'

I looked up at her. 'I will help them. But I won't help you.'

'What do you mean?'

'The American project. Was that the Golden Apple? The advancement of the next programme?' Helen didn't reply. 'I found out you went to Turkey. Just as Helen went to Troy.'

Helen's face clouded and her eyes grew cold. 'Do you think the original Helen wanted to go to Troy? Do you think she had a choice? Of course not. She was forced to go.'

'Even mythologists can't agree on that,' I said. 'Some say she was seduced; some say she was kidnapped. No one knows.'

'You know nothing of her and you know nothing of me!'

'I know that it's your face on the Adelfi campaign,' I spat back. 'The face to launch a thousand shipments.'

'That's Aphrodite.'

'That was Aphrodite. That was you. Before you were replaced with your daughter.'

Helen swallowed slowly. 'I was relocated.'

'You were sent to the UK. But before coming back to Athens, you went to Canakkale. There's only one reason why that I can think of. You needed to go to Troy to fix the deal that Aphrodite damaged.' I stared at Helen, but she stubbornly kept her mouth shut. 'Who are Troy, Helen?'

'They are a powerful global investment and development company.'

'Developing what?' I asked. 'Drugs?'

'They invest in healthcare, yes.'

'And they've been investing in the Golden Apple programme?'

'They'll invest in any programme that benefits them.'

'But they know of Omorfia. Who else knows that she is your daughter?'

Helen sat up a little straighter, feigning a confidence I doubted she felt. 'The Olympians are not related.'

'You are not an Olympian, but Aphrodite is. What's the average lifespan of an Olympian in Fireflight? What could they do to her if they found out about your meddling?'

Helen stared back, unspeaking, so I tried another question. 'What is Fireflight doing to the other women, Helen?'

'What do you mean?' Helen's false innocence was becoming annoying and I finally lost my temper. I reached out and gripped her wrist, twisting it harshly. Helen squealed and tried to wriggle away from me.

'I mean, I want to know what The Fates are and how they're being used. And if I think you're lying, I'll call for an enforcer of my own.'

'OK, OK, I'll tell you.'

I loosened my grip, but still kept hold of her wrist. 'And don't lie to me.'

Helen glanced nervously around the garden. 'The Fates are separate compounds that can be easily mixed with a simple carrier. They're safe enough to be administered as a syrup to a pregnant woman. That's the formula you found at the hospital.'

'I remember.'

'But the effects on the mother and foetus are dramatic.' Suddenly, the refreshing breeze took on a more unpleasant chill.

'How dramatic?'

'Very. Most times, if an expectant mother has an unexpected issue, like food poisoning, say, then she could be really sick, but the baby is usually protected. However, if the food poisoning comes from something that could cross to the baby, that could be really dangerous.'

'What was Fireflight's interest in this?'

'They wanted to see if the compounds they'd created could neutralise the threat of a dangerous situation.'

Mentally, I found myself back in the coffee shop with Gaia. It was only last week, but felt like a lifetime ago. 'Tell me about Marie.'

'Kim, listen...'

I retightened my grip on Helen's wrist and willed myself not to tear her hair from her head. 'Tell me about Marie.'

'Ow! OK. Marie was working in a separate lab, on the Golden Apple project, but we didn't tell her that. She was given one dose of one compound each day and then two days of an antagonist.'

'Antagonist? What's that?'

'I don't know, Hephaestus created it.' I squeezed Helen's wrist again. 'I swear, I don't know!'

'OK. What happened?'

'It was incredible. Something we'd never seen before.'

'What?'

'Marie had a month of this procedure, but started reacting after the first week.'

'Reacting? How?'

'The first dose was Clotho. Her hair looked thicker, shinier. Her skin looked smoother. The second was Lachesis and she started filling out, looking stronger.'

'And the third? That was Atropos, I presume?' Helen looked surprised, but answered my question. 'Yes, Atropos.'

'What did that do?' I momentarily held my breath, concerned about the answer.

'Nothing. There was no effect. Until...'

'Yes?'

'Until we delivered the antagonist. The follow up blood-work I did, showed that Atropos had no effect on Marie. It only activated when she received the antagonist. I still don't know how, but the antagonist was neutralised. Isn't that amazing?'

Helen's voice was full of wonder, but I remembered the fear in Marie's eyes and how she had guessed what was to come; that she would be sacrificed and parts of her body redeployed like bits of a broken up car.

'Helen, how could you know how The Fates worked?'

'What do you mean? I administered them.'

'Yes, but you know how they worked, not just what they are. Unless...' I was starting to feel a little sick. 'Unless you helped create them. Was that what you were doing when you were with Troy in New York?'

Helen's eyes were still shining. 'This is incredible research. We've barely scratched the surface of what these compounds can do.'

I let go of Helen's wrist and stood up. 'You need to get out of Athens.'

'But I have responsibilities here.'

I took a deep breath and tried to speak calmly. 'I know that you only came here to protect Omorfia. But she's a big girl, now. Do you still have possession of your passport? Get out of Athens, Helen. Retire – from both Troy and Fireflight. While you still can.'

I left her in the garden and didn't look back.

Chapter 24

I walked around the perimeter of the house, looking for Nick. I'd had enough. It was time to leave. I wandered towards the rear of the property and saw the swimming pool.

Omorfia was standing in the bright spotlights by the water's edge, dressed only in a tiny pair of bikini pants and a loose fitting white blouse. Nick was standing just a few feet behind her. His anxious eyes darted towards the side of the house where two enforcers stood like a pair of bouncers outside a nightclub.

'Athena, there you are. You're late to the party.' She pointed to a small garden table on which stood a tray with a filled jug and glasses. A small knife sat next to a bowl of oranges and lemons. 'Have a drink.' Omorfia looked like she might have had one or two already.

'I've spoken to Helen,' I said. 'I told her to leave Athens. You should do the same.'

'I live and work here now.' She threw a hand back towards the house. 'This is my business, or it soon will be.'

'I can get you out of here, Omorfia. Come with me back to the UK.'

'Why? There's nothing for me there.'

'Apart from Harmony.' I held out my hand towards her.

'Please. Come with me.'

Aphrodite laughed. 'What is the point of following you, Athena? What have you done with your life? Nothing. Fireflight have promised me my own premises and I will be very rich.'

'I hardly think operating a brothel can be called having your own business. But it seems that the only things you've ever loved are sex and money.'

Aphrodite's face hardened. 'It's perfectly legal here. My clients will be some of the richest and most powerful men in the world.'

'You're playing a dangerous game, Omorfia. Did you contact Troy before making a deal with Fireflight? Did you want to find out if you'd be worth more to them and offer yourself to the highest bidder?'

Aphrodite didn't answer. She spread out her arms to take in the pool and view of the hills beyond. 'Look at what you turned down.'

'I know you were trying to protect Helen,' I continued, 'but Fireflight probably already know your true relationship. They could be using you to keep Helen in line.'

'You could have been something great, Athena.'

'I won't be a puppet for the company's schemes.'

Aphrodite turned to Nick. 'Do I look like a puppet to you?' She pointed at me, almost dismissively. 'You turned your back on the chance to be a heroine.' She crossed her arms to lift off her blouse 'You've even started to let yourself go, whereas I,' Aphrodite dropped the slender slip of fabric at her feet and stepped over it to approach Nick, 'embrace everything.'

She strode towards him confidently, draping her arms around his shoulders, as sleek and unfaithful as a hungry cat.

She turned her head to look back at me.

I took a deep breath. Now would not be the time to give in to emotion, however much I wanted to scratch her eyes out.

'Well, let's take a look at what you've achieved. None of the women want anything to do with you, Harmony is being fostered in the UK and Troy don't want you. You have no back up and no means of continuing. So I'll thank you to take your cheating, silicone stiffened, botoxed fakery off my husband!'

Aphrodite turned from Nick, to give me the full force of her spiteful glare.

'Look at yourself,' she cried, almost laughing. 'There's nothing feminine about you. Who are you, anyway? Just some nobody from nowhere.'

'Well, what were you expecting?' I spat back. 'I've spent these past months discovering who I am. I may be ungainly and unenhanced, but I have absolutely no desire to be like you – or anybody else, for that matter. I am me. I am Kim.'

A sternly spoken statement came from the back entrance to the house. 'You're an ordinary mortal who has no authority, here or in the UK.' Helen stood there, holding a mobile phone. 'I've just spoken to the Olympians. You are no longer a goddess.'

I picked up Aphrodite's shirt and chucked it back at her. 'Well I guess that means we have nothing more to talk about.'

I looked at Nick. 'Let's go.'

'Hold her still,' yelled Helen.

The enforcers ran towards me and one grabbed hold of my arm as Helen pulled the plastic safety cap from the top of a syringe.

'No!' Nick ran in front of me and into Helen, pushing her over. The needle fell from her hand and rolled towards the pool. Nick stamped on it with the heel of his shoe before it reached the water. The other enforcer ran to Helen, but she pushed him away.

'Hold her,' she demanded, scrambling to her feet. She pulled herself up with the help of the poolside table.

Nick turned his attention to the second man and managed to land a punch. The enforcer staggered backwards and spat out a gob of blood. Finding his footing, he stepped forward just as Nick moved in front of me.

'Oh no!' Helen looked shocked as she stepped backwards and the bloody paring knife bounced on the wet poolside.

'Nick! Are you OK?' I reached out to my husband, but Nick couldn't answer as his hands went to his left side. He slowly started to fall backwards and the three of us, the enforcer gripping my arm, Nick and me fell into the pool.

I bobbed to the surface quickly and saw Helen grab Aphrodite's arm and pull her back into the house. The enforcer with the fat lip looked over to the three of us in the pool and abandoned his colleague to his fate.

'Nick, tell me you're OK.' I paddled over to him as he floated on his back while ribbons of blood oozed through his fingers.

I pointed at the soaked enforcer. 'Help me get him out of the water.'

Between the two of us we pulled Nick out and on to the side of the pool. Already women from the house were stepping out to see what was going on.

'Nick. Nick!'

He blinked up at the bright stars, the dark sky as deep as a blanket. 'Look at that sky! It's so blue. It's beautiful. So are you...'

'A phone!' I yelled at the women. 'Somebody call an ambulance!'

'...and brave. Beautiful and brave Kim.'

Chapter 25

Flashing blue lights threw eerie shadows along the lawn by the side of the house. As the paramedics jogged towards us, the enforcer backed away, but I gripped his wrist.

'You're working for me, now.' I looked him directly in the eye. 'I am still Athena. Do you understand?'

He nodded, water dripping from his black curls. His scared expression turned to one of sad resignation. Helen had abandoned him. She and Aphrodite were likely to flee Athens, but I think he also knew that I could not promise him safety.

The paramedics pushed my hands away as they took charge and tried to stem the bleeding. They applied dressings and strapped Nick to a trolley. As he was pushed across the lawn to the ambulance, I turned my attention to the enforcer once more.

'I want to know who ordered this. Who did Helen speak to? Find out, then meet me at the hospital with a car.' Think logically, I reminded myself, not emotionally. But the numbers came into my head anyway. One, two, three, four... 'Kyria?'

I was interrupted on an even number. That was good; even numbers represent symmetry and equality. A paramedic was holding the ambulance door for me. He lifted a couple of heavy blankets from a cupboard and draped one around my shoulders before laying one over Nick. I didn't realise how cold I was until I felt the warmth of the blanket. He then strapped me into a small hard chair with my back against the tinted windows before strapping himself into a similar chair nearest Nick.

'Are, are you OK?' shivered Nick.

I looked down at my hands, which were shaking. I could feel myself shivering as badly as Nick. 'I'm fine. Are you cold?'

'A bit. Maybe it's shock.'

'Are you in pain?'

'Not too much. I'll get a painkiller in a minute.'

The paramedic interrupted with a few questions, which Nick was able to answer.

'What do they want to know?' I asked, worried.

'It's just routine, Kim. He's going to insert a fine tube in the back of my hand. It's easier to administer medicine that way.'

'Don't forget to tell them you're allergic to seafood.'

'I don't think that will matter in the hospital.'

'It's reassuring that you can speak Greek. You know what's going on.'

'It's not that bad. I'll be OK.'

I couldn't tell if Nick was lying. He'd said the same thing when he fell off the ladder fixing the garage roof. He was in hospital for two days with concussion.

As the bright yellow vehicle zigzagged its way through the

busy streets, I made a mental list of all the things I had to do. I should speak to the Athens police, I should call Elena and let her know what had happened, perhaps I should call Charles Little, too. And I should call Nick's parents.

'I don't have a phone,' I said. 'We left our coats and my bag at the villa.'

'The hospital will probably call the police. You'll have to tell them that.' He said something to the paramedic, who responded and reached inside his uniform. He handed me a small card.

'What's this?'

'It's a phone card,' said Nick. 'There's a payphone in the entrance to the hospital and the hospital shop sells them.'

'Did you use your fountain pen again,' I asked. 'You've got a smudge on your temple.'

Nick managed a smile. 'You'll have to wipe it off for me when we get to the hospital.'

The inside of the ambulance became momentarily darker and then the back doors opened. We'd been driven into an underground parking area where a large set of double doors stood open and an unshaven doctor in green scrubs, perhaps a little older than Nick, waited to take charge of the patient.

'I am Doctor Christoph,' he said as the trolley was pushed up a ramp and through the doors. 'I will be responsible for your husband. Please wait in the family room and I will come and find you.'

We'd entered through the rear of the hospital and people were bustling around me as Nick was wheeled away.

'But I want to stay with my husband. Please...'

The friendly paramedic pointed me towards an area with old and stained chairs and a TV showing a cop drama.

'I want to stay with Nick.' My protestations fell on deaf ears as my husband and the doctor disappeared behind automatic doors. A tight ball knotted itself inside my chest. I pressed my hand against it and the fear that it was composed of, flew from my mouth as a frustrated squeal. I silently commanded my heart to slow down, as I realised that there was nothing I could do now but wait.

I stood next to the payphone, facing the doors through which Nick had disappeared. I had to call Nick's parents; they should have been my first priority, but the thought of having to explain to Patricia what had happened was more than I could bear. I stared at the phone for a moment before calling a different number.

'This is Charles Little. I'm unable to come to the phone at the moment, so please leave a detailed message after the tone.'

'Detailed?' I asked. 'That could take some time.' I could hear a tremor in my voice and other visitors were starting to look at me. I lowered my head, embarrassed. 'I'm currently in a waiting area at Athens General Hospital, wearing an evening dress and a blanket. I'm shivering, but I don't know if that's because I'm cold and wet or because I'm anxious. Nick has been stabbed.' Those word sounded terrible coming from my mouth; cold and unfeeling, but already I was becoming angry. 'It was Dr Helen Markham. She's an

American specialist in prenatal and infant health. I thought you should know.' My cheeks felt hot. I lifted a hand to my face and found that it was wet again. 'I, I think I might need a friend.' I ended the call before I started crying.

'The Kyria Anderson?' Dr Christoph was standing beside me. 'Your husband has a small wound but dangerous. We have cleaned it and he has a tube inside to drain. I want to operate tonight.'

'Operate?'

'To find more damage. With your husband, there is one wound but two chances for damage.' Dr Christoph demonstrated by pushing two fingers from his left hand into his right fist. 'Go in and come out.'

'I see. Will he be all right?'

Dr Christoph's eyes slid from my face momentarily. 'We hope. We take his blood pressure 20 minutes, then 20 minutes again.'

'I understand. Can I see him?'

Dr Christoph nodded. 'He has been sent for X-rays and scan. He will come back to the Trauma Room. In fifteen minutes?'

'Trauma Room?'

'The room where we examine.'

'Oh, OK. Thank you.' This was bad.

I called another number while I waited.

'Ya sas?'

'Elena? It's Kim.'

'Kim. I have been waiting to speak to you. Can you come?'

'Elena, something terrible has happened.'

'So, you know? This is katastrofi. Please come.'

'I can't. I'm at the hospital. I'm waiting for the doctor. Nick says he'll be fine, but I'm so worried.'

'Nick? So, you don't know of Khaled?'

I felt myself grow suddenly colder. 'What has happened to Khaled?'

'Oh, Kim. I am sorry to have to tell you. Khaled, dolofonithike. He has been murdered.'

Chapter 26

It was already 11pm before I got to see Nick. He was lying in bed and looked horribly pale, but smiled when he saw me.

'Well, this wasn't quite the evening we thought it was going to be.'

'You can say that again.'

'It's not quite the evening we thought it was going to be.'

'Don't joke, Nick. I'm worried sick.'

'I can't help it,' he smiled. 'I'm feeling a bit high. They gave me thorough going over, head to toe and front and back. They've washed the wound, but want to operate tonight.'

'Yes, Dr Christoph told me. What are they looking for?'

'I think they just want to check for additional damage.' Nick wasn't telling me everything. 'You look tired. Are you hungry?'

'No, I'm fine,' I lied.

'Have you called Elena?'

'Yes, just a little while ago.'

'That's good. You might need her over the next few days. And my parents too?'

'Not yet, but I will. I hope that it's your father who answers the phone; your mother hates me.'

'She doesn't hate you.'

'She does.'

'She doesn't hate you.'

'She dislikes me intensely. I'm not good enough for you.'

'I know she can be overbearing at times, but she needs to know what's going on.'

'Yes, I'll call.'

'Wait until I'm in surgery. She can't argue about wanting to speak to me then.'

'Where's your phone?'

'They took it. Soaking wet, anyway. All my belongings have been put in a bag, even my shoes. I think they'll be given to the police. You've still got the last disposable?'

'I hid it in the hotel room. Do you want me to get it?'

'No, you should keep hold of that. You might need it.'

Dr Christoph entered the trauma room holding a clipboard.

'Now we go.'

'It's time for surgery,' said Nick. He squeezed my hand and kissed it. 'I'll be back soon.'

I watched the bed as it was wheeled down the corridor and out of sight. The smaller the bed became, the louder the numbers in my head shouted. One, two, three, four, five…

I walked back to the waiting area and sat on the least stained of the chairs to wait my turn as a young woman with three small kids talked rapidly on the payphone. She seemed to be having an argument with whoever was on the other end, while her children raced each other from door to door and climbed over the chairs. I clung on to the blanket I'd been given and closed my eyes trying to ignore their screams and chatter.

After a few minutes, the spiteful counting in my head was more than I could bear, so using the blanket like a cloak, I decided to step outside and get some fresh air.

I thought a short walk around the block would be enough for me to get my head together, so took a left outside the main entrance, walking away from the town. I took long, slow steps and long slow breaths to match. The madness of the early evening had abated and apart from the occasional car, there was no one around.

As I took the next turn, I saw a little girl, about six or seven years old, strolling along the opposite pavement about twenty yards ahead of me. She appeared to be unaccompanied and I opened my mouth to call out, but wondered how appropriate that would be.

The girl was wearing pyjamas and plimsolls, kicking at the scruffy weeds growing up the side of a building. Her untidy plait bounced between her shoulder blades with each kick until her foot disturbed something and she bent to see what it was. I watched, fascinated, as she picked up a small, damaged ball. It was too brightly coloured to be a football, and too flat to be much fun, but the girl's face lit up, delighted to have found a new toy.

She tried bouncing the ball, but it stayed where she dropped it, unresponsive on the pavement. Picking it up, she gently wiped the side of the ball with the sleeve of her pyjama top and threw it upwards, catching it neatly. Her giggle echoed down the street, and as if aware that she'd made too much noise, she looked around and saw me watching her.

We both paused a moment, assessing each other. Recognising another girl who had sneaked out of the hospital, she waved and I waved back. Seemingly happy with her find, the girl turned and skipped back in the direction she had come from.

The young woman was still on the payphone when I re-entered the waiting area. Elena and Janna walked through the double doors.

'Kim.' Elena held her arms open to me.

'No, I don't want a hug.' I immediately felt mean and ungrateful. 'No, I'm sorry. You're being kind and you're the one who need the hug.' I held Elena's shoulders and pressed my cheek against hers. She smelt like summer flowers and too much coffee.

'You went to a party? What happened?'

'I went looking for Aphrodite and Helen. Helen stabbed Nick.'

'Natalie told me of them. Kim, that was a dangerous thing to do.'

'I know it was stupid, but I didn't even think about it at the time. Nick's in surgery. I don't know how long that will be.'

Elena nodded and held up the holdall she was carrying. 'I have brought you things.' She led me to the chairs and undid the zip. She pulled out a package in greaseproof paper which she handed to me and let me look inside the bag.

'What's this?'

'Tomato bread with chicken and red pesto. Eat it. You need it. Here are some cotton pants and a sweater. Clean clothes for you.' I was pleased to see that she was using American words to describe soft trousers and a lightweight top.

'Thank you. I, I don't know what to say.'

'You have already said it.'

'Tell me what happened to Khaled.'

Elena took a deep breath and filled me in as best she could while I ate. 'I have not been told everything, but the police came to visit me this afternoon. Khaled slept at the farm yesterday, but early in the morning was asked to make a delivery. The truck was attacked when it reached its destination and Khaled was found nearby. The police say he was poisoned with a needle.'

'Who else was with him?'

'No one else. He drove the truck alone.'

'That would make me think that this was planned.'

'But why? Perhaps because he knew of the Olympians' hotel.'

The sandwich was lovely, but I had trouble swallowing my mouthful. 'Oh, Elena. It's my fault.'

'How can it be?' Elena's eyes grew large. 'What do you know?'

'I think they killed him to send a message to The Network that they will destroy anyone who gets in the way of the project. Khaled wanted the project stopped because he feared for his wife. I want the project stopped to avenge a friend and look for a little boy. Helen stabbing Nick was a mistake.'

Elena reached out and held my hand. I dropped my head and saw my reflection in a cup of machine coffee that Janna held out to me. I smiled up at her gratefully.

'I hate hospitals,' said Janna. 'Even the vending machines act like patients. They pee into plastic cups, and we're left to make sense of the contents. We have to assume that if it looks all right and smells all right, it must be all right. It never is.'

I took a sip, but tasted nothing.

'You look tired,' said Elena. I was exhausted, but didn't want to admit it.

'I'm OK.'

'You are not,' she said. 'Go and change your clothes. Janna will show you the way.'

I glanced towards the corridor down which Nick had disappeared. Elena must have known I was terrified. Nick always said my eyes gave me away. I looked at Janna, who shrugged.

'OK. I'll be back soon.'

Janna led the way to the ladies' toilets where I scrubbed my face and stuffed the evening gown into the holdall. I changed into Elena's clothes and felt a little cleaner. Outside the toilets, I saw a face I recognised.

'Stay here,' I instructed Janna. I walked towards the doors to talk to the enforcer from the villa. His eyes still had the terrified look they had by the pool, but he'd managed to find clean clothes from somewhere.

'Helen talked to Hera,' he said, confirming my suspicions. 'You are no longer a goddess. I cannot protect you.'

'Am I no longer useful?' The enforcer shook his head. He didn't know. 'Do you have a car? Can you take me to the hotel?'

'I have a car, but the hotel is empty. There is no one there.'

'Where is Hera?'

'I don't know.' The young man looked like he was going to burst into tears in front of me. I grabbed the front of his shirt. 'I swear! I don't know.'

'Where is Helen?'

'You want to go looking for her?' I hadn't heard Janna creep up behind me. 'What the hell for?'

I could feel hot anger well up inside me. 'I'm going to find that evil bitch and rip her head off!'

The scared enforcer nervously watched this exchange as his eyes darted from me to Janna and back again.

'But Kim, Nick was not her target, you were.'

'All the more reason to find her.'

'Kim, no. You must be careful. And you don't know where she is.'

I looked back at the enforcer. 'Do you know?'

He thought for a moment. 'There is somewhere you can go.'

'Then take me there.'

'Kim, no!' Janna tried to grip my arm, but I shook her off.

'Well then, I'm coming, too.' Janna ran with the holdall back to the waiting area, but I followed the enforcer back on to the street. Janna caught up with me as I was getting into his car. I didn't ask what she had told her mother, but explanations would have to wait.

In about ten minutes, we had reached the Parthenon complex, with the Temple of Athena Nike just in view.

'I can't get there,' I complained. 'The complex is protected. It'll be hours before it's open to the public.'

The enforcer stopped the car and turned to shrug. 'You are not public. Someone will be there. I must leave Athens.'

I nodded my understanding. He was scared and desperate to get out of the city. Janna and I watched him drive away.

'We'll have to take a taxi back to the hospital,' she said.

'Look!' I pointed to a flat area, just a little further up the hill. A woman was standing by the side of the road and waited for us to join her. Her pretty deep blue head covering was one I'd recognise anywhere.

'I was not sure that you would know where to come,' she said.

'An enforcer brought me here. You are Gamila, aren't you?'

The woman I'd seen in the café smiled sadly, her face puffy and sore. 'Yes, but you can call me Nike.'

'You have a goddess's name?'

'Our friends in The Network suggested it. I can talk to the enforcers, but I must be careful.'

I glanced at Janna, wondering if I should introduce her, but Janna pointed, her eyes wide. 'You're Khaled's wife!'

'Gamila, I'm very sorry,' I said.

'I know,' she said. 'The police have already spoken to me. I cried many tears, but our marriage was already over before we came to Athens.'

'I'm surprised you're not angry. He died because of me.'

'I am angry. He died because he was asking questions he had no business to ask, much like you. He did not believe that I would leave him when we arrived. People had already come to look for women. Recruiters, they said. Some women went with them, but I did not believe their promises of work and ran to the student encampment to hide. Then I heard that Athena had come to Athens. I asked who that is, and they tell me that she is the face of the resistance.'

'When did you find out I had arrived in Athens?'

'The same day I saw you. The students know of Fireflight, they have tried to recruit from there, but they also know of The Network. I told them I would help them if I could.'

'Why did you not try to contact me before now?' I felt myself becoming frustrated. 'We went to the villa for answers and were attacked.'

If I had been expecting any kind of comfort from Nike, I was to be disappointed. She was also disappointed; she had expected a heroine and my hasty actions had been far from heroic.

'What were you thinking?! You walked straight into the lion's den,' she said bitterly. 'What did you think was going to happen? That was stupid and dangerous.'

'We didn't know what that place was.'

'But instead of reaching out to your friends, you marched in and started asking questions. I was told that Hera had threatened you once before. Did you not believe her? She must have thought that all her birthdays had come at once when you walked in through that door.'

'Hera wasn't even there.'

'She didn't need to be! You would have been safe in Central Athens, but you go to the villa? You have guts, I will grant you that.'

'We had no idea what was going to happen there. They

still have our coats and my bag.'

'Forget about your belongings. All will be destroyed. Your money and your bank cards. What of your passports?'

'In the hotel safe.'

'Fortunate. At least you can still leave Greece.'

'But I still need more information. And now there is nobody for me to ask; the hotel is empty.'

'Of course. As soon as Khaled discovered it, they were making plans to leave. But then the students tell me that a stupid girl attacked you on the street, and the gods could not risk staying there.'

'How will I find Helen now?'

Nike shook her head. 'You won't. I don't know where she has gone, but she has probably fled Athens. And they will try to kill you.'

'I've been told that Helen spoke to Hera. Is she still in Athens?'

'Yes, she and a few others. But they will leave soon, we think perhaps to America to speak with Troy.'

'Troy? I've heard talk of them at the university,' said Janna.

'I always thought this was some stupid conspiracy theory. Is it really true?'

'It's real enough to threaten the lives of the people I love,' I answered.

'So, what do you do about it?'

'The Network identifies the latest project, tries to identify the main players and disrupt the money routes. Hera is clearly one of the main players in this project.'

Nike nodded. 'We think there are four. Hera and Zeus, obviously. Poseidon and one other. We haven't been able to identify who that is.'

Poseidon's name sent a shiver through me. 'Medana told me that was the man who raped her. She made me promise to discover who he is.'

'Medana?'

'The girl who attacked me. Will you and the others do something for me?'

'Of course.'

'Find Medana for me. I need to ask her more questions. And find out where Hera is. If she leaves Athens before I can find her, the boy I'm looking for might still be in danger.'

'You are looking for a boy?'

'Yes, Dion. Son of Simone. I was told he was adopted by a winemaking family. I just want to be sure he is safe.'

'I will ask.'

Janna's phone jangled with sounds of popular Greek music.

'Mama? Ne, OK.' She turned to me. 'Mama says we must come back immediately. The doctor wants to talk to you.'

Nike pointed down the hill. 'Go back the way you came, thirty metres. A car will be waiting.'

I reached out and took her hand. 'Thank you, Nike. Take care.'

'Good luck, Athena.'

A large, sleek black car stood waiting with its rear door open.

'There's our carriage.'

Janna looked at it with suspicion. 'How can you be sure it's safe?'

'Here in Athens I've learned to trust my gut. If it feels unsafe, it probably is. If it's recommended by friends then it's probably OK.'

'The villa wasn't safe.'

'No, it wasn't. And I went anyway.'

'But you don't know that woman. How can you be sure she's a friend?'

'I can't. but when I met you and your mother, I sensed that you were good people. Was I wrong?'

'No!' said Janna, climbing in the car beside me. 'Well... No, you weren't wrong.'

'It's just that...?'

'It's just that I didn't believe any of this, at least not to begin with. It all seemed so dramatic, so ridiculous.'

'To the hospital, please.'

'But I think I believe it now.' I looked across to Janna who sat quietly, looking worried. She turned in her seat suddenly to look directly at me. 'Mama is a kind person. She would do anything you asked. Is she safe?'

I couldn't answer. No one who helped me could be safe. Janna nodded at my silence which told her all she needed to know.

'Then if you need anything, ask me.'

Modern young people; they think they are invulnerable. I remember feeling that way once. I smiled and nodded with what I hoped looked like more confidence than I felt.

Chapter 28

'The Kyria Anderson?' Dr Christoph had changed into blue scrubs and looked pale and tired. 'Please, this way.'

'Can you tell me what happened? My husband was just going into surgery when I left. Is he OK?'

The doctor looked over his shoulder at me, but did not reply. He led me through a semi familiar maze of corridors, but when we reached the entrance to the ward, he turned right and opened the door to what looked like a small waiting room.

'Could you just tell me what's going on?'

'Please.' He held out his hand towards the room, allowing me to walk in ahead of him, before closing the door and sitting at one end of a small and uncomfortable looking sofa. I took the chair opposite.

'Look, less than ten minutes ago, I got a call from a friend asking me to come back here. You said there might be two opportunities for damage. Is that what's happening?'

Dr Christoph sighed and frowned before leaning forward on his knees, clasping his hands in front of him.

'You know that your husband had internal bleeding, yes?'

'Yes. You explained that was a possibility when he was admitted.'

'Yes. In the operating room, your husband Anderson, his blood pressure was down. This was because there was more internal bleeding.' Christoph glanced at the wall clock. It said 1.32. Early morning haze was making the dirty window look misty, prickling a chill against the side of my arm. Noisy bustle echoed in the corridor outside. 'Twenty minutes ago we operated to stop this.' Christoph held my gaze and spoke very gently. 'I am very sorry, but your husband Anderson died before the operation was complete.'

I looked at the clock. It still said 1.32. It had taken no time at all for the doctor to irreparably damage my life.

'But it was only a small knife,' I said and then felt stupid.

'It is not the knife,' said Christoph patiently, 'it is the damage it creates. I hope you understand; we did all that we could.'

My chest suddenly felt very tight and I could hear my breath coming in short gasps. I stood up; too quickly, I realised, as I felt a rush of giddiness.

'I am very sorry,' repeated Christoph.

It was 1.32 when he'd told me. I'd remember that time for the rest of my life, a life that I would now have to face alone. I leant forward and tried to breathe a little more deeply as the room continued to spin. I realised my trousers felt warm and wet.

'Kyria Anderson?'

'I need a glass of water, please. And also a pair of panties, I think.'

Dr Christoph held out his arms to me and I just had time

to think, 'no, I don't want a hug. Why does everybody try to hug me?'

I opened my eyes to find that I was lying on my back in the waiting room, with my feet up on a chair and a dressing was being applied to my jaw.

'Why does my face hurt?'

Elena's face came into view above me. 'You fainted. Your face hit the small table. How are you feeling?'

I didn't know how to answer that question. My face felt very hot and tears burst from me. The nurse on her knees beside me patted my arm and backed away so that Elena could take her place. She helped me up on to a chair and pointed to some hospital pyjamas.

'These are for you. The hospital would like you to stay for a few more hours, to be sure you are all right. You can have a little sedative if you want it.'

'No thank you.' I smiled at the nurse. 'I'm fine.' The nurse raised an eyebrow but said nothing. She must have known that I was very far from fine, but was kind enough not to push the issue.

'They said the police will be here later to talk to you.'

'The police? Oh, yes. Yes, of course.'

Elena smiled her sweet and gentle smile. 'Friends have come to see you.'

'Friends?'

'I will give you a few minutes to change before I send them to you.'

Paper panties had been provided with the hospital

pyjamas. They rustled every time I moved. The door opened slowly and Charles Little walked in.

'Oh, my God! Charles! How did you know where to find me? How did you know I was here?'

Charles stepped forward and took my hands.

'Reg White is also here, we met on the same flight. He says that you and he have been friends since your husband bought him beer. He doesn't drink and gave it back.'

'That's right. He asked for lemon soda instead.' Reg was the railway attendant who was on duty at the time I was kidnapped. He was also the first person I turned to after my release, not wanting Nick to see the state I was in.

'He and I have been talking and it appears that we both received a call from the same person, informing us that you were in danger and that we should fly to Athens immediately.' He sat beside me and continued to hold one of my hands in both of his. 'Kim, I'm so sorry. What happened?'

'I don't really know. Nick was defending me. Helen attacked me.'

'Helen is here? In Athens?'

'Nick stepped in front. He was stabbed in the stomach.'

'In the UK we call that a Penetrating Abdominal Trauma.'

'He seemed fine in the ambulance.'

Charles nodded 'Stab wounds are horribly unpredictable.'

'How can this happen? How can Hermes suffer a knife wound and survive and Nick....?' I couldn't complete the sentence.

'There are many possible reasons,' said Charles. 'Different knives, different blades and attacked in different areas of the body.'

'How did you get here? Who called you? I left a message on your answerphone.'

'Did you? We must have already been on our way. I don't know who called. Tickets had already been arranged and were waiting for us at the airport.'

I was silent for a moment while I processed this information. My heart started to beat a little faster.

'Could that have been my father?'

'We don't know, but his unusual disappearance coincided with a situation that's been troubling me for some time.'

'Oh, what's that?'

Charles squeezed my hand. 'You really don't want to be worrying yourself with my troubles. I came here to be with you.'

'Oh, for God's sake, Charles! Please tell me. Tell me I'm not crazy. Tell me there's a reason for me to be in Athens, otherwise I'll either start turning the lights on and off a hundred times, or curl up in a corner and scream uncontrollably.' Hot tears of frustration splashed on to our clasped hands.

Charles reached into his pocket and pulled out a neatly ironed handkerchief.

'My dear, of course you're not crazy.' When I had calmed down a little, he continued. 'Emily, my daughter, has managed to convince herself that I'm starting to lose my marbles and has decided that it would be best for everyone if I moved in with her.'

'And you don't want to?'

'No, I don't. I know she means well, but she can be terribly bossy and the thought of having to share living space with Mathew and Charlie is more than I can bear.'

'Mathew and Charlie?'

'My son-in-law and grandson. Oh, don't get me wrong, I love them dearly. But I'd really rather not.'

'What makes Emily think that you're losing your marbles?' Charles gave me a gentle smile and squeezed my hand paternally. 'Oh. It's me; my claims of crime and conspiracy. I'm so sorry.'

'No, no, you mustn't think that. But Emily really doesn't believe it.'

I was now worried. Was I a nuisance to Charles? 'What do you think?'

'Well, of course, I believe you. When the investigation ended last year, I felt that the Chief had closed the case with unseemly haste. All the files were sent to archive but something didn't smell right to me, so I decided to do some digging on my own. I requested some of the files back, but was told that they were unavailable. Soon after, I was told that I should start thinking about my retirement.'

'You think information was being kept from you?'

'Almost certainly. And it was a pain in their side to have me there. Emily first made her suggestion at my retirement party, but the next day I received an unexpected gift.'

'Oh, yes?'

'An early morning delivery had been left on my doorstep. It was a brand new laptop with a note warning me to never wear the watch I was presented with.'

A flutter of excitement beat hope like butterfly wings. 'It's possible! That could have come from my dad!'

'I'm afraid I don't know; I've not been able to trace it, but since then Emily has become more vocal in her insistence that I sell up and move to Cambridge.'

The new hope started to fade within me like the light controlled by a dimmer switch. Charles had been an experienced and kind-hearted police officer. He thoroughly deserved his retirement and shouldn't be chasing ghosts with me. 'Cambridge is nice.'

'So is my own kitchen. Emily tries hard, bless her, but she's not as good a cook as her mother was.' Charles wrinkled his nose at the thought. 'It's true, the family home is too big and I should downsize, but I'd rather cook my own meals than have to tolerate her lower fat versions.'

'What does her husband, er, Mathew, think about this?' Charles smiled then. 'I don't think the poor chap has any say in the matter.'

'Do you know anything of the other women from the hospital?'

'A little. Natalie sends her love; we're in regular contact and Harmony is such a lovely little girl. But none of us knows where Sarah is. Natalie visited her flat and it looks like there was a break in. We're all very worried.'

'Sarah sent Nick an email. She's out there somewhere, but being cautious. Now I know why. Who could have broken into her flat?'

'We don't know, and DI Kelly won't tell me anything; it's a police matter now. But I'm pleased to hear that she's alive and well. Natalie and I suspect that whoever broke in was looking to reclaim the paperwork that she was holding. She seems to have changed her mind about sharing it with the police.'

Reg walked in just then. 'That,' he said, jerking a thumb over his shoulder, 'is a lovely looking woman. Almost as lovely as this one.'

I smiled, grateful that he was here. I held out my other hand, which he squeezed gently, before bending to kiss my cheek.

'You've had a rough time of it,' he said, taking the chair opposite. I nodded not knowing what to say. 'It's tough, but y'know, your loved ones, they never really go away. They're here,' he patted his chest. 'Always with you.'

'I have to call Nick's parents.' My voice sounded small and far away.

'We should give you some privacy,' said Charles.

I gripped his arm before he had a chance to stand. 'Don't you dare! I need you here.'

I borrowed Charles' phone. Knowing I was going to make the call that no one wants, I stood up. Thinking that I might feel a little more secure with both feet flat on the floor, I entered the country code followed by Patricia and George's home number.

One ring, two, three...

'Hello?'

Three rings. That was bad; it was an odd number.

'Patricia? It's Kim.'

'Good heavens! Do you know what time it is?' Patricia wasn't pleased at having been woken, but then her voice always sounded a little clipped when she spoke to me. Patricia had been a teacher, she didn't have patience for hysterical, nervous or unfocused children. I could imagine her sitting up in bed with cold cream on her face. 'How's Nick?'

'Actually, not well. that's why I'm calling.' Suddenly, my mouth felt very dry.

'What? Not holiday tummy, again? Let me speak to him.'

'We're in Athens...'

'I know you're in Athens, Kimberly,' she interrupted. 'Nick called me before you left. He's considerate like that.'

'Do you remember the trouble we had ten months ago? It was...'

'I remember that silly conspiracy goose-chase you took Nick on. Have you got him into trouble again?'

'Yes.' There was a moment of silence before I heard George's voice in the background.

'What's going on?'

'Patricia, you need to come to Athens right away.' My voice was cracking and didn't sound like my own.

'But we're going on a cruise in September,' she protested.

'I've bought new suitcases.'

'Patricia, please don't argue. Something's happened and I need you to come to Athens on the next flight.'

'We have no plans for Greece this year. Just give the phone to Nick. I'll speak to him.'

Charles held his hand out for the phone. 'Give it to me.'

I did as I was told and pressed my hands against my ears so that I couldn't hear what Charles was saying. I was breathing incorrectly and could hear myself gasping.

'Oh no. Please, no. Not another panic attack.'

Pressing a hand against the back of my shoulder, Reg steered me away from Charles to the other side of the room.

'Leave it to the professional, love.' He patted the top of his shoulder. 'Here.'

And for the first time since I was a child, I sobbed in the arms of someone older and wiser.

<h1 style="text-align:center">Chapter 29</h1>

Elena invited us back to her apartment for breakfast, but we politely declined. She and Janna needed sleep and I had to wait to speak to the police.

I'd had no sleep at all, so Dr Christoph recommended that I take the sedative previously offered and Reg sat with me while it took effect.

'Close your eyes and have a nap, darlin'. Charles will come back for you when the cops get here.'

'Did you know,' I said, feeling a little drunk, 'I never thought I'd get married. Never in a million years.'

'Didn't you? Pretty woman like you?'

'I know I'm odd, but I've always felt that having other people in my life was an intrusion. The cacophony and confusion they bring is like nails on a chalkboard. I set boundaries. Too many, perhaps. But they're necessary. The panic attacks I get are overwhelming, and I am told, unpleasant to witness.'

'But people need people,' said Reg. 'I knew I needed Dolly from the day we met.'

I yawned. 'Tell me about her.'

'She was a knockout.' Reg wriggled forwards in the chair and rested his head against the back as he remembered. 'I first saw her in the off licence. I popped in to get my beer and smokes and there she was, behind the counter. She was so young and pretty, I asked her if she was old enough to drink. That made her laugh. That was a beautiful sound. It pushed a beam of sunshine into my gloomy life.'

'Gloomy?'

'Yeah. I was in the army. They found me a job, but I couldn't settle. Went from one job to another and never had any money. When I saw Dolly, I knew I'd have to settle on a job if I was going to have a girlfriend.'

'You had a happy marriage?'

'Yeah. We had our ups and downs. All couples do. But we were a match. She got me to quit the booze and cut down on the fags. We were happy. Harmonious, I think is the word.'

'I don't believe that human beings are designed to live well together. Life would be unbearably boring if we did. Existing in a state of controllable disharmony is the best that we can hope for. At least then, if things feel like they're getting out of hand, we'd have to talk to each other.'

I didn't hear what Reg said in reply.

Charles was gently shaking my shoulder when I finally opened my eyes. 'It's eight-thirty, Kim. The police are here. They're in a visitor's room in another corridor.'

I sat up and rubbed my face. Reg let out a loud snore from the chair.

'Here,' said Charles draping his jacket over my shoulders. 'When the police have taken your statement, we can take you back to the hotel.'

I held Charles's arm as we walked slowly to the visitor's room.

'I still feel a bit wobbly.'

'That's probably a mixture of shock and medication. If you feel that you need a break, don't be afraid to say so.'

'Can't you come in with me?'

'I'm afraid not. They won't allow anyone else in the room who might influence your answers. If you don't know the answer, just say you don't know. Don't try and guess anything.'

'They got here pretty quickly.'

'The hospital would have called them. They would have had a duty to do so when... Well, in circumstances like this.' Charles reached forward and knocked on the door. 'Just tell them what you can remember.' He smiled reassuringly as he opened the door for me.

Two police officers rose from the sofa to greet me. The older man, with an impressive moustache, held out his hand.

'I am Detective Michalis of the Hellenic Police, Directorate of Public Security. Please sit.' He was wearing what looked like a dress shirt with epaulets and had a holstered firearm on his right hip. 'This is Senior Constable Gabris. He will be writing your statement.'

The constable, a younger man with closely cropped dark hair, picked up his notepad and smiled kindly. 'My condolences.'

'Thank you.'

'We must provide a translator for you while our investigation continues. This will be Senior Constable Gabris.' The detective shifted uncomfortably on the sofa, a band of unhealthy eating already pushing against his shirt buttons. 'We have already spoken to others. Now we must hear from you. I want you to tell us everything. Start with why you decided to visit the brothel yesterday.'

'We didn't know it was a brothel. At least, we weren't sure. We went there to look for someone. Omorfia Markham. But I met Dr Helen Markham, her mother. She's the one who stabbed Nick.'

'Was that the only reason you went to the brothel?'

'I told you, we didn't know for sure that it was a brothel.'

Detective Michalis repeated his question, this time placing his emphasis on the fourth word. 'Is that the only reason you went to the brothel?'

'Yes.'

'The Doctor Markham and her daughter, why did you meet with them?'

I glanced at the constable and then looked back at the detective. Whatever I said was going to make me sound like a crackpot.

'My husband and I found out that the company they were both working for was conducting illegal fertility drug trials. I wanted to question them about it.'

The detective stared at me for several seconds. 'You have proof of this?'

'We did have. It was stolen.'

'You have proof of this now?'

I looked down at my hands. I'd forgotten one of my father's golden rules. Never print off or retain anything that could be used against you.

'No.'

Detective Michalis raised his eyebrows. 'This proof, your husband had it in his possession?'

'No, it was being looked after by a friend.'

'A friend of your husband's?'

'Sarah. A friend of ours.'

'Where is this friend?'

'I don't know.'

'You do not know where your friend is? The one with the stolen proof?'

I took a couple of deep breaths and willed my heart to slow down. 'We've already explained this to the British police; we stole paperwork from Fireflight. Sarah took it back to her flat, which was broken into. Now she is missing.'

'The proof that you say was stolen, was first stolen by your friend.'

I pressed my lips together to supress the anger that was bubbling inside, from bursting out.

'Look, you already know who stabbed my husband. What are you doing to search for her?'

'We have requested an arrest warrant.'

'And how long will that take?' I couldn't hide my frustration, but it didn't really matter how long it would take them to get an arrest warrant if, as I suspected, Helen had already left Athens.

The detective ignored my question and continued with one of his own. 'Who else was there at the poolside?'

I closed my eyes as I tried to remember. 'Omorfia Markham, Helen's daughter and two bodyguards. I don't know their names.'

'Do you know why the Doctor Markham would attack your husband?'

'She didn't. She attacked me. Nick was protecting me.'

'We already have a report of a woman who threatened you.'

'Yes.'

'And now he is dead.'

I glanced at the constable, who lifted his eyes from his notes to look at me with a serious brown stare.

'He died in the early hours of this morning.'

'But the woman...', continued the detective.

'Her name is Medana.'

'...She died first.'

I was horrified. 'What?'

Senior Constable Gabris nodded. 'It's true. She was found at the university campus late last night.'

My mouth was dry and I felt a little sick. 'What happened to her?'

'We cannot say,' replied Detective Michalis, sternly. 'But she attacked you. She waited for you and jumped from a passageway. You spoke to us and now she is dead.'

'What are you suggesting? Neither Nick or I had anything

to do with her death.'

'I did not say that you did.' But the implication was clear. What boat did I rock to create this crisis? The pain in my jaw started to throb.

'What makes you think that what happened to her and what happened to Nick are connected?' I realised as soon as I asked the question that although these were separate incidents, everything was connected. Everything pointed back to Fireflight.

The officer straightened his back and squared his shoulders. He wrinkled his nose, twitching his moustache.

'I ask the questions. You answer.'

'You know who they are.' I felt my eyes widen with the realisation. This was not the first time the detective had to question someone regarding The Company. 'You know of Fireflight.'

'I ask the questions,' he barked.

I breathed deeply through my nose as I pushed away the numbers in my head. 'You may think the two attacks are connected,' I answered. 'I have no way to know if they are.' I clasped my shaking hands. 'I would like to see my husband, now.'

'The autopsy will be this afternoon,' said the detective, still bristling. 'The er...' he spoke to the constable who provided the correct translation.

'Pathologist.'

'The pathologist will visit here. The mortuary is not open to the public. You will see him tomorrow. His belongings come to us, we will give them to you.'

I stood up and felt my nails dig into my palms. 'I don't care about his belongings! I want to see him before the autopsy.'

The detective turned to the constable and spoke irritably in Greek. The constable rose to his feet, the detective did not.

'I will take you.' Gabris spoke softly. 'You will see him behind the window, not in the room.'

I nodded. 'I understand.'

Charles was waiting on a stiff looking chair, just a little way down the corridor. He said nothing as we left the room, but offered me his arm when he realised we were not walking back the way we had come.

Two corridors and three sets of double doors later, we arrived at a room covered in no entry signs in Greek, Spanish and English.

The constable rapped on the door which was opened by a young woman dressed in a white all-in-one suit. He spoke to her and indicated to me. What he was asking was clearly not usual practice, as she stared at me for a moment before nodding and pointed beyond the door.

We walked another half dozen steps and stopped in front of a large window with blinds drawn down. A moment later the blinds were lifted and the attendant stood on the other side of a gurney with a white paper sheet covering a body.

Constable Gabris glanced at me. 'Ready?'

I nodded. The attendant lifted back the sheet and let it

rest against Nick's chest. I peered at the empty shell that used to be my husband.

'He has an ink smear on his temple.'

Both Charles and the Constable turned to look at me.

'What's that, Kim?'

'An ink stain,' I said to Charles. 'He's always doing that. He uses a fountain pen and is sometimes careless when he replaces the cap. He then scratches his head with his little finger. It's a nervous thing. He doesn't know he's doing it.'

Charles looked across to Constable Gabris, who shrugged.

I tapped on the glass to get the attendant's attention. 'You need to clean the ink stain,' I called. The attendant seemed not to hear and pulled the sheet back over Nick's head. I tapped the glass again.

'Hey! You can't leave him like that. You only need a little cleansing lotion.'

The attendant lowered the blind.

'She's ignoring me! Hey! You can't leave him like that!' I smacked my hands on the window. 'Hey!'

Charles gripped my shoulders and pulled me back a couple of steps. 'Come on, Kim. Let's go.'

'But the ink stain,' I protested. The numbers were starting up again. One, two, three...

'You have to say goodbye, Kim.'

'He wouldn't have wanted me to see him like that.'

'Let's go.'

Charles held his arm around my shoulder and led me, like a child, back to the waiting room.

'No one will ever make chilli for me the same way again.'

Chapter 30

Charles and Reg helped me into a taxi and took me back to the hotel.

'We're staying at the same hotel as you,' said Reg. 'Very fancy.'

'Bookings had already been made for us,' said Charles. 'I'm glad about that. We can be on hand to support you.'

I was grateful that I had friends around me. Already, I could see that I was slowly being adopted. With no family of my own, I was being welcomed into a created one.

'I have no money,' I said. 'My bag was at the villa.'

'Passport? Return flights?' asked Charles.

'In the hotel safe.'

'That's good. You will have to contact your bank, cancel all your cards and request new ones to be sent to you. That may take a couple of days, but you'll have to stay in Athens for a couple more days anyway to... Well, to make arrangements.'

It briefly crossed my mind that even before Nick was stabbed, plans might have been made to keep me in Athens longer than we had intended. I kept that thought to myself.

'You had better fill us in on what you've found out already,' said Charles. 'What can you tell us?'

I relayed my story as best I could and expressed my concern over the boy, Dion.

'After my interview with DI Kelly, I was upset that no one was looking into the disappearance of a young mother and her son. I think they were once at the abandoned hospital. There were rumours that the mother was murdered, but that the boy was safely smuggled to Greece. I came to see if I could find out anything myself. Nick and I found a potential connection online between Fireflight and an investment company called Troy, who own the villa. We went there to ask questions.' I struggled to keep my voice stable. 'That's when we found Helen and Omorfia.'

'Well, I've not heard anything that suggests there's an enquiry going on in the UK.' Charles scratched the top of his head. 'Are you sure he's in Athens?'

'No, I'm not sure, but I do believe he's in Greece.'

In the hotel room, I made Charles and Reg coffee to thank them for being with me. Charles' phone rang and he spent several minutes questioning the caller. When he hung up he turned to smile at Reg and me.

'That was an old contact of mine,' he said. 'I don't have friends in high places any more, but I still have a few friends in low places. She's done a little digging for me and found a few interesting facts.'

'She?' I asked.

'Molly. She owns a café in west London. I busted her a few times for prostitution, many years ago.'

'Molly,' said Reg tapping his chin slowly. 'Not one I

recognise.'

Charles ignored this attempt at humour and continued. 'She thinks that Fireflight probably has an exclusive list of escorts they call for events, like the party at the villa. They may not have anything to do with Fireflight's operations. Molly did manage to connect to your parent's university. The Fireflight Register was operated by a young man called Marcus Alexander. Apparently, he made a pest of himself by distributing pamphlets with conspiracy theory undertones, under the name Max Alex. He had two assistants called Hugo Clearwater and Cezar Edafos. Do any of those names mean anything to you?'

'No, I don't think so... No, wait! Max Alex. I'm sure I heard my mother say that name when I was small.'

'How could you remember something like that?' asked Reg.

'I can remember because my brain doesn't work like everyone else's.'

'But if this Max whoever, and his mates, have an operation on the go, how are you going to stop him?' Reg paused to slurp his coffee. 'I can see it in your face. That's what you want to do, isn't it?'

'Absolutely. I honestly don't know if I can do this. But I do know that I have to try.'

'What are you gonna do?' Reg's voice contained a note of panic that he seemed to be trying to supress. 'I mean,' he shrugged, 'They're invisible. Where would you look?'

'I need to make them visible. The first step is to identify

the main players. I may not be able to fight a whole army, but I might be able to fight one or two at the top. There's an organogram somewhere.'

'A what?'

'Nick had a god's family tree.' I rummaged around the room and found it in the outside pocket of Nick's case.

I spread the diagram over the coffee table and ran my fingers over his handwriting. I pushed down the apple in my throat. 'This tells me who is related to whom, but not all the names here are people. Some are being used as names of drugs. The only name on here that I can be sure is accurate, is my own.'

'What about who Athena is related to?' asked Charles.

I pointed to the top of the diagram. 'That would be Zeus, Athena's father. But I can't prove a connection. I remember when I met Hera previously. She said something very interesting. She said that none of the Olympians are related by blood. Unfortunately, until we can match names and identities, that doesn't help much.'

Reg scratched at his stubble. 'So, who is this Zeus, this Mr Big?'

'My best guess would be Marcus Alexander. If your contact, Charles, found the founding Fireflight members at my parent's university, this means that, if I'm right, either Clearwater or Edafos is Poseidon and the other is Hades.'

'So there's a Poseidon and Hades, too?' sniffed Reg.

'Yes. In the legends, Zeus overthrew the Titans and he and his brothers split up control of the world between them. Zeus took control of the heavens, Poseidon took control of the seas and Hades was given the underworld.'

'That sounds a lot like the way territories are divided by a winning army,' said Reg.

'Well, it was, I suppose. But if I want to find out who Poseidon is, I'll have to take these names to the police and ask them to investigate.'

Reg shook his head firmly. 'No. That's a really dangerous idea. I'm not suggesting the police are crooked,' the expression on his face suggested the opposite, 'but if they run a search on their systems, within hours, Fireflight will know.'

'I don't know who to trust either, Reg. But where else can I go?' I was becoming exasperated and didn't want to take it out on Reg, but those spiteful little numbers were starting up again. 'I have to do something. I can't sit around waiting for answers; my head will explode.'

'There is a simpler option.' We both turned to look at Charles. He stood calmly with his arms folded and his back to the window. The bright mid-morning sun made his neat, grey hair shimmer like silken thread. 'Why don't we just ask Medana's friends at the university if they recognise the names? If we can assume that Max Alex is Zeus and they can identify who might be Poseidon, we'd be two thirds of the way there.'

Reg looked uncertain. 'Are you sure these blokes are going to be the original three from yesteryear? They might have been replaced by younger people.'

Charles nodded. 'You're right. We can't be sure. But if we

don't investigate, we'll never find out.' He looked at me and his composed demeanour quietened my racing brain. 'Let's talk to Medana's friends. We don't have much to offer them in consolation, but we can share what we know.'

'Tomorrow,' insisted Reg. He pointed at me. 'You need sleep. And I need a shower. And I think I heard Charles say that your in-laws are flying in tonight. You'll need to be ready for them.'

'Oh, God.' I dropped my head in my hands. 'I honestly don't think I could cope with them on my own.'

'Meet me in the bar later,' suggested Reg. 'I'll go with you. I've always been a charmer with mothers-in-law.'

At nine o'clock that evening, the streets of Athens were buzzing with people, meeting at bars and restaurants all over the city. While tourists and locals alike were looking forward to an enjoyable evening, Reg and I were in the arrivals hall at Athens International.

I watched the passengers filing through the gate and saw Patricia and George pushing their suitcases on wheels. Both looked shocked and drawn, but both were dressed impeccably. They always insisted on maintaining standards.

Patricia always looked beautifully groomed. She was wearing loose fitting trousers and a silk blouse, her hair, fair like Nick's, neatly swept into a low bun. Patricia was the kind of woman whose age you couldn't guess unless you knew her, and even then you wouldn't say.

We didn't like each other. I suspected that her disapproval of me was borne out of the disappointment that she didn't want to show her son; he could have done better. I agreed, but like Nick once said, you can't choose your family, but you can choose who you marry. And he had chosen me.

George, on the other hand, looked older than his years. I suspected that he was horribly henpecked, but Nick said he was the stabilising force in the family. Nick and I were only children. I quite enjoyed being the centre of my parent's universe, but Nick had said it felt like a burden. When times were good, he couldn't have been more spoiled, but when times were bad, there was no other child to share the ride.

'Hello Kimberly,' said Patricia.

'Hello Kim,' said George. 'How are you, dear?'

'I'm not sure,' I replied, trying to control the tremor in my voice. 'I think I might be unravelling.' Reg kindly put a reassuring hand on my arm.

'Tish and I have been talking on the flight, and we've come up with a plan.'

'I've been told that we will be given a medical death certificate and can then approach the consulate to arrange for Nick to come home.' Patricia lifted her head and attempted a smile, stoic in her distress, as she waited for me to respond. Her eyes looked sore, but she'd be damned if she'd share her tears with me.

'This is Reg,' I said, introducing the stranger they had failed to notice. 'He's a friend of ours. Reg, this is Patricia and George.'

George extended a shaky hand, but Patricia couldn't hide her surprise.

'But we don't know anyone called Reg.'

'No, Patricia. I mean he's a friend of ours. Nick and me.' Patricia immediately corrected herself by giving Reg a gentle, yet watery smile.

'You must forgive me. My mind is not where it should be at present.'

Reg dismissed her apologies and pointed to their bags. 'How about I give you a hand? We've got a taxi waiting outside.' He took the handle of Patricia's suitcase and started wheeling it towards the exits.

'We're staying in the same hotel as Nick,' said Patricia, as if Reg hadn't spoken, 'but we'll go to the hospital first. I'd like to see Nick straight away and then we can call the consulate to request the necessary forms.'

I put my hand to my chest and could feel my heart dancing a Polka. I didn't know how I would cope if Patricia insisted on taking charge. She'd say it was so that I didn't have to worry, but I knew it would be because she was reclaiming her son; taking back what I had stolen from her.

'Everything is already in hand, Patricia.' Think logically, I reminded myself. Emotional thinking overwhelms me.

'Already?' Patricia looked shocked. 'But how can it be? We haven't agreed anything.'

Think logically. 'I'm afraid you'll have to wait until tomorrow to see Nick. The autopsy took place today and the mortuary won't be open until tomorrow morning.'

'Autopsy?' the colour drained from Patricia's face and she gripped George's arm. 'You mean they... they cut him?'

Both Patricia and George stared at me uncomprehending.

'Yes. They had to. I'll insist you get to see him tomorrow.'

'But, but who could possibly have agreed to that? And why would they?' Patricia stared at me, clearly expecting an explanation for the desecration of her son's body.

'The family don't get a say in the matter, the police decide when to perform an autopsy.' I was trying to explain how the process worked, but the look of horror on Patricia's face had not subsided. 'Nick will be returned to us when the pathologist has completed their report. Then we can start making arrangements to take him home.'

Patricia pulled herself up to her full height, although even in flat shoes, I was still taller than her. 'I'm going to the hospital to see my son, Kimberly.'

'The mortuary is closed to the public until tomorrow morning,' I repeated.

'I'm not the public, I'm his mother!' Patricia's face was stern, but her lips trembled uncontrollably.

'I'll call Constable Gabris first thing in the morning.'

'Well, that's just disgraceful! I want to speak to someone. Right now. Who's in charge of this matter?'

'That's me, Patricia.' Our little party came to a halt on the pavement beside a cab that already had the boot open. 'Because I'm his wife.'

PART 3

Chapter 31

Breakfast was a fraught affair. Reg knocked on my door and walked with me to the dining room.

'How are you, love?' he asked. 'How'd you sleep?'

I'd slept fitfully; drifting into disjointed dreams, only to wake crying an hour later. 'OK,' I lied. 'I slept a bit.'

Reg gave me a sideways look, but said nothing. The cut on my jaw was still sore, but Reg and Charles were kind enough not to draw attention to it.

Patricia and George were already at the breakfast table with Charles when we walked in. A layer of dread hung heavy on my shoulders.

I'd once asked Nick why his mother was so mean. Even when she was pretending to be nice, she would pepper her conversation with tiny spikes of spitefulness. One Easter lunch at her house was particularly painful.

'Answer her back,' said Nick. 'Defend yourself. I chose you; she's just going to have to get used to the idea.'

'I know you've spoken to her before,' I said, 'but she's relentless. Why can't we just try to get along? There's no democracy in her house. She runs it like a fiefdom.'

'When people talk about democracy, they think of order and structure. Democracy, when it was new, meant the right to have arguments and debates, the right to have a different opinion. Argue back.'

That was a skill I had yet to master.

Charles smiled up at me. 'Good morning, Kim. Have some coffee. Did you manage to sleep?'

Before I could answer, Patricia responded.

'I honestly don't know how anyone could sleep after what we've been through. My nerves are in shreds. I may never sleep again. Last night my mind kept churning, thinking of all those precious moments in Nick's life.'

I clenched my fists and felt my cheeks burn, but when I looked at Patricia, I noticed how pale she was. It was true. She probably hadn't slept. I didn't bother to mention how I'd spent the small hours with my hands wrapped in tissues, opening and closing the bathroom door. Exactly one hundred times.

'His first steps, his first words,' Patricia continued. 'His school days, university and girlfriends. So many. He was so popular.' I flinched at the little barb that I knew Patricia would insist she never meant.

'His wedding day,' I supplied.

'Oh, yes. What a shame that you didn't get married in church,' sighed Patricia. 'It's always so much more special that way. Of course,' she looked across at George, 'we had our marriage blessed by God.'

I thought our register office wedding was beautiful in its simplicity. I had no idea how to respond to Patricia, but Reg, to my eternal gratitude, stepped in for me.

'My mum and dad had their marriage blessed by God. Didn't stop the pair of them getting drunk and knocking seven shades o' shit out of each other. Wasn't until my mum broke dad's jaw with a rolling pin that they decided to call it quits.'

I looked across at Patricia, who stared, horrified at Reg. Charles remained busy buttering his toast, but was unsuccessfully supressing a smirk.

'Patricia,' he said, 'why don't you let me escort you to the hospital this morning? It can be horribly confusing requesting a taxi in another country.'

Once toast and coffee had been consumed, Charles left with George and Patricia. Reg put down his cup.

'I'd much rather have a nice cup 'o tea,' he said, 'but the tea they got 'ere ain't nothing like wot we got at home.'

'Thanks for speaking up for me.'

'Forget it. All true, anyway. Listen, you wanted to go to the university today?'

'Yes please. You could come with me, if you wouldn't mind?'

'Well, you shouldn't go there on your own. Which one? Where do we start looking?'

'I should phone Elena. Her daughter, Janna, studies at one of the universities. Perhaps she can help. There might be a connecting social media platform.'

'That sounds like a plan.'

I used the disposable phone I had in the hotel room. Elena told me that Janna was in the city and would meet us at a café she went to with her friends.

Reg and I took a tram to Akadimias and alighted opposite the Academy. Janna was waiting for us.

'The café is just a little way along this street,' she said. 'I asked a few questions on the student's intranet page and I got a lot of responses. Fireflight is well known amongst the students. Most of the replies told me I was being paranoid, but one guy got back to me. He was a friend of Medana. He believes you.'

The strong smell of sweet coffee and fried food enveloped us from the door. An unshaven, skinny and nervous young man sat in front of a small cup; his deep brown eyes looked too big for his face.

'This is Leander Regas,' said Janna. 'He studies law. He knew Medana.'

'It is not safe to talk here,' he said. He dropped his eyes to his shaky, nicotine stained fingers. 'But it is not safe anywhere.'

I sat opposite Leander and stretched my hand across the table towards his. 'I'm very sorry for your loss.'

He looked up then, and seemed puzzled, as if he didn't quite understand. He smiled a funny little upside down smile and dropped his head again. He didn't want me to see his eyes.

'We were not...,' he began, 'I mean, she was not my girlfriend.' He blushed. Perhaps he had wished that she would be.

'She was your friend,' I said. 'Tell me about her.'

Reg sat next to me and Janna sat next to Leander. Two heartbroken souls, sitting with their friends.

Leander smiled. 'She was funny. Before last year, before the attack, she was funny. Ana had only grown up with her sisters. Her parents were travellers, she had seen many places, many people, many cultures, but not grown up with other children; only her sisters.'

'Sounds like it coulda been lonely,' said Reg.

Leander lifted his head and smiled again. 'Sometimes. I think so, yes. But Ana was funny. She had not learned how to be polite. I would tell her, "Ana, you should not say such things." But she did not care. Her parents taught her to be brave. What she wanted, she would take. She had fire inside her.'

'Until...,' I prompted, gently.

'Until the spring term.' Leander's smile faded and his eye's darted around the café again. 'People had come to the University.'

'What people?' I interrupted. 'Where were they from?'

'Business people.' Leander shrugged. 'Men and women. They have permission to be there. They visit the study rooms and lectures. They say they are looking for the best students. They will guide their careers. It is...' a frown clouded his face as he searched for the right expression.

'Business sponsorship,' supplied Janna.

Leander nodded. 'But Ana and I, we had heard rumours. We hoped they would not talk to us. Bad things happened to the students who said no.'

'Medana told me that she was attacked at a nightclub in the city.'

'Spring break. The American students, they like Spring Break. We take them to the places we go. We eat and drink and then Ana is missing.' A flash of panic lit Leander's face with the memory. 'No one has seen her. Her friends look for her and then...' His eyes looked beyond me, brimming with tears. If he blinked, I would have seen them stream down his cheeks. 'And then, they found her.'

'She said that the man who attacked her was called Poseidon. Did she say anything about him?'

'She did not know anything to say. A business man. Older than her, younger than her father. The police know this.'

'And what did they say?'

'Nothing. They have nothing to say and nowhere to look.'

'Do you know the name Marcus Alexander?'

'No. Not that name.' Leander kept his eyes averted and spoke softly.

'What about the names Hugo Clearwater or Cezar Edafos?'

Leander shook his head and then paused. 'Clearwater,' he repeated. 'Yes. But not a student, not our university, the American. He was American, at the nightclub.'

I nodded. Already, images were starting to form, but I didn't want to scare Leander with what I was thinking.

'What happened yesterday?' Both Leander and Janna dropped their eyes. 'I'm sorry. I didn't mean for that to sound so blunt.'

Janna shook her head. 'The news was all over campus. A former student, Medana Osman, had been found murdered in the university grounds.'

Leander swallowed. 'I did not see, but they said her throat had been cut.'

Reg winced. 'Gruesome.'

'So sad,' continued Leander. 'When Ana came back to the university, I thought she had returned. But not all of her came back. She gave blood at the hospital. Now Christoph will have to find another to give for the little girl.'

'The little girl?' My mind went back to the girl in pyjamas who had found a damaged ball. 'What little girl is this?'

'Many of us gave blood. Ana too. She was told there was a little girl, a perfect match.'

I got up to leave. 'Thank you for speaking with me, Leander. My condolences.'

'Wait,' said Janna. 'Before you go, Mama has invited you over for dinner tonight. I don't always go back for dinner, but I will tonight if you will come.' She gave me a hard stare and I understood why. She didn't want me asking favours of her mother.

'Sweet of her,' said Reg, 'but it's a no from Charles. He said he's stopping off in the city this evening. Keeping the mother-in-law busy, I expect.'

I glanced at Reg. 'If your mother wouldn't mind just the two of us, we'd be very grateful. I'll pick up a bottle of wine. What would be suitable?'

Janna shrugged. 'Anything with alcohol.'

Leander pushed away his cold coffee. 'My mother made youvetsi. The best in Crete.'

'You come from Crete?' I stared at Leander, who nodded.

'Next time you're there, visit Perdika, a little restaurant in the square. Tell them I sent you. I promise, you'll be served more than you can eat.'

'You were a bit cagey in there,' said Reg, when we were back out on the street. 'What are you thinking?'

'I think that poor Leander knows more than he's saying and is justifiably terrified. Did you see his face when I asked about Marcus Alexander? It seems to me that Clearwater probably is Poseidon, but if he's older than Medana, but younger than her father, he's not the original.'

'And the kid said he was American.'

'Yes, but that's not necessarily so. He could have been a Fireflight member simply speaking with an American accent. Maybe someone who's spent a lot of time in America.'

'So, if Zeus is, what's his name?'

'Marcus Alexander.'

'Alexander, and Clearwater is Poseidon, then the other bloke...'

'Cezar Edafos.'

'...is Hades.'

'It's certainly starting to look that way, even if a few characters have been replaced over the years. Although I'm pretty sure Zeus is still an original.'

'You've got a few more names to add to that family tree of yours,' said Reg. 'Clever idea, that.'

I thought how proud Nick would be to hear that, and almost gasped with the pain that I couldn't tell him.

'Reg, do you mind if we stay on the tram a few more stops? I'd like to stop off at the hospital before going back to the hotel.'

'What do you wanna be back here for?' asked Reg, wrinkling his nose. 'Hospitals always smell funny.'

'I need a word with Dr Christoph,' I said. 'He needs to tell me about that little girl.'

I made my enquiry at the front desk and Reg and I sat drinking machine coffee for almost an hour before Dr Christoph came out to see me.

'You do not have an appointment. What is the matter?' He crossed his arms over his scrubs and looked worried, but I was distracted by the rabbits and flowers on his surgical cap.

'You are a surgeon for children, too?'

'Yes?'

'Including a little girl with a blood disorder?'

'I cannot talk about the patients.'

'Can you talk about Medana Osman?'

At the sound of her name, Christoph glanced over his shoulder and nodded curtly. He led the way through a pair of double doors, along a short corridor and through another door. Large laundry trolleys lined the walls and the smell of detergent and disinfectant wafted through the ceiling vents.

Christoph pushed his cap off and ran a hand through his hair. Maybe one day he'd get to catch up on some sleep, but not today.

'People have come to collect Medana,' he said. 'They did not have the correct papers and I was in surgery. She is still here.'

Reg looked from the doctor to me. 'Who are these people? What do they want with her?'

'They will try again.' I held up a hand to halt Reg's questions. 'Her blood is unique, isn't it? Did you keep samples? If you did, you will need to destroy them, or risk having them stolen. I need you to tell me about her blood. And about the little girl she was helping.'

'I cannot talk about a patient,' repeated Christoph. 'But Medana was special. There is a blood disorder. Thalassemia comes from the parents and affects red blood cells. It is a lifetime condition and needs blood transfusions and medication. Come.' We followed him the length of the laundry corridor and turned back on ourselves through another set of doors. I realised we had approached the mortuary from the other side. 'The public cannot come inside, but you,' he said pointing at me, 'you should see this.'

Christoph bleeped his pass at the door and I followed, leaving Reg outside. He checked against a clipboard on the bench and then approached one of the mortuary drawers. I turned my head as he opened it, but the body was covered. Christoph stood beside me and lifted back the paper cover just enough to expose Medana's right arm. He pointed to puncture marks in her wrist.

'See here? Blood tests.' He pointed to more puncture

marks inside her elbow. 'Here? Blood donation. Donations are tested, checked, who is the best patient. It is never a perfect match. Except with Medana and the little girl. I had never seen anything like that.' He clapped his hands together and aligned his fingers. 'Perfect match.'

'Were they related?'

'No.' Christoph drew an imaginary line between his both index fingers and thumbs. 'Perfect.'

Later that evening, I changed in to a loose fitting pair of linen trousers and a soft blouse. Reg had also smartened up. We met in the hotel reception to journey to Glyfada.

'The reception will call a taxi for you,' said Reg.

'I'm hoping we have a more secure option,' I replied. 'Let's see.'

Outside the building, I let my eyes roam over the carpark and saw the shadow of a Mercedes parked close to the gate. 'That's our car.'

'Our car? That could be anybody's.'

'If the doors open when we approach, it's for us. Fireflight provided cars in Crete to keep an eye on its members, but most of the drivers are already part of The Network.'

'Does Charles know this? I'd like to run it by him first; get him to check out these drivers. It all sounds a bit dodgy to me.'

'I'm sure we'll be safe, but I haven't seen Charles all day. He hasn't been back to the hotel.'

The rear doors of the car opened as we drew near. I climbed in first.

'I still think this is dodgy,' grumbled Reg.

'To Elena's apartment, please,' I called and the car glided forwards into the night.

We arrived in Glyfada a little before eight and Elena immediately held out her arms towards me. She wriggled her fingers until I took hold of her hands and kissed me on both cheeks.

'I am so glad you came. How are you, Kim?'

I didn't know how to answer. 'Um, OK, I think.'

Elena looked into my eyes. 'You have not been sleeping.' She turned to Reg. 'And eating?'

'Only some toast at breakfast,' said the tattletale. 'She skipped lunch.' I hadn't even noticed lunchtime come and go.

'Tonight we fix. You both like moussaka?'

The love and comfort of Elena's family was something she believed could be baked into food. After tasting her béchamel sauce, I almost believed it too. I didn't know if I was being unfaithful by thinking that it was almost better than Nick's, but the tears in my eye's gave me away.

'What have you been doing today?' asked Elena, conversationally.

'I went to the hospital to talk to Christoph.' I spoke without thinking, but Elena was the only person I knew who had intimate knowledge of Greece and whose word I could trust. 'I saw a little girl at the hospital the night Nick was stabbed. She looked like she had snuck out of bed. I'd love to find out who she is.'

Reg smiled. 'Good luck with that. There could be dozens of kids at the hospital.'

'But only one that I know who is ataktos, a naughty girl,' smiled Elena.

'Have another glass of wine,' said Reg topping up her glass.

'I know her mother, we worked together once. Sweet Idyia. She is very sick. A blood disorder. She was such a pretty baby; chubby and smiling. When she became sick her parents, so unhappy and guilty. They have a gene and Idyia needs blood.'

'But she looked like such a happy girl.'

'She is, but not all the time. When she is sick her smile is gone. But her parents are hopeful. She has had new blood and is getting better.'

Reg held the wine bottle towards me. 'A top up, Kim?'

'No more for me, Reg. You'll get me drunk.'

'I've always thought the blush in a lady's cheeks looks prettier when they're tipsy.' He turned his attention back to our kind and lovely host and while they were engaged in a conversation of their own, Janna and I slipped from the table.

Janna's bedroom was neat and tidy with a study space set up in the far corner. Her taste was clearly young and modern, but the fluffy toys on her dressing table betrayed the woman-child before me.

Janna sat at the desk and switched on her PC. 'It's so tiny, not enough space.'

I ignored her complaints; I thought she was very lucky to have a PC in her bedroom. Although Elena's apartment was bright and tasteful, there wasn't very much in the way of luxuries.

Janna looked over her shoulder at me. 'You don't look very sad,' she said, 'about your husband.'

I felt my cheeks flush as the number counting monster screamed in my head. 'I'm too angry to be sad.'

'What do you need?'

'Could you search the internet for a few names? I want to see if they appear on social media. Start with Hugo Clearwater.'

Janna's fingers tapped at the keyboard. 'There are a few. Can you narrow this down?'

'Is there one who works for Fireflight Healthcare, or Troy?'

'Hmm. No, nothing like that.'

'OK, how about Cezar Edafos? Same business.'

'One moment. No, nothing for that name at all.'

'Strange. OK, this is the last one. Try Marcus Alexander or Max Alex.' Janna tapped away on her keyboard.

'Max Alex has a hit. There's no picture and no biography.'

I clenched my fists and felt my nails dig into my palms. 'This is so frustrating! Social media is where most people let their guard down. I was hoping there'd be something.'

'He might be using another name,' suggested Janna.

'Or, just as likely, Marcus Alexander is a false name.'

'Wait a minute.' Janna continued to tap. 'There's a blog.

A very simple one. Let's see what it says.'

'That's like an online diary, isn't it?

'It's a conversation that the user has with the internet. They can post their thoughts and feelings, ideas and updates, whatever they want.'

'What does he say?'

Janna's eyes widened as she read. 'Wow, this guy really doesn't like the modern world. He says he only blogs to reach the young before they are corrupted by the world their parents created. He's saying the police, news agencies and health companies are puppets of a controlled world order.'

'Yes! That sounds like our man. Can you send him a message?'

'There's no contact on here, but I can leave a comment.'

'Say that Athena has something he wants. She'll reveal it tomorrow night.'

'That's all?'

'Yes, that's all.' My fingers went to my throat as I thought about the locket in my jewellery box and the piece of paper within. I hoped that the diagram would be enough leverage to get information about Dion. Someone had gone to great lengths to hide it, disguising a drug formula as a syrup in an autopsy file. It had to be important.

'Kim? Where are you?' Reg put his face around Janna's bedroom door. 'We need to be getting back, love. Charles has sent a text. He wants to meet us in the bar.'

The sleek, black car was waiting for us on the street outside.

'Did you get done what you needed to?' asked Reg as the car pulled away.

'What?'

'You and the girl. Did you get what you want?'

'She was very helpful,' I said.

'Be careful, darlin'. I know you're brave, but looking for information you ain't supposed to have is dangerous.'

I took a long and curious look at my friend. 'Reg, what did you do when you were in the army?'

Reg grinned and shot me a wink. 'Some questions are best left unanswered,' he said.

The hotel bar was dark and quiet. The guests who were looking for nightlife had already left and the three of us had the leather chairs and low tables to ourselves. Charles ordered the drinks and the bartender discreetly moved to the other end of the bar. The dim lights above him cast subtle shadows over the bottles. Charles asked us to sit as he had something important he needed to share.

'I decided to do a little digging on my own,' said Charles. 'I went online and made a few discreet enquiries, suggesting that I was a businessman looking for company.'

'We all do that,' said Reg. 'It comes with age.'

'I asked for a young lady who was used to attending lavish parties. We met for dinner this evening.'

'So that's where you were.' I sat facing the bar. 'We thought you were looking after Patricia.'

Charles took a deep breath and shook his head slowly. 'My God, she's exhausting.'

'Who?' Reg looked up. 'The hottie or Patricia?'

'I meant that Patricia is emotionally exhausting. But the dinner was most productive.'

'I don't think I want to know everything,' I said, 'but you're a free man, Charles. You can do what you like.'

Charles looked at both of us as if we were children being deliberately annoying. 'We talked. I was looking for information.' He indicated me. 'She remembers you.'

'Me? This woman was at the villa?'

'Yes. She says she was working in the Garden Room. You stopped to speak to her on your way outside.'

'Yes, I remember. She thought I was a reporter.'

'She thought the same of me, but was still willing to talk to me. I was hoping to find a young lady who was involved with Fireflight, but to find one who was also at the villa was extraordinarily lucky.'

'What did she say?'

'She said she saw you walk past the windows towards the pool; you did not go back the way you went.'

'That's right. I left Helen in the garden and walked around the building.'

'She said that when she saw you walk away, she thought an argument had taken place, although hadn't heard what was said. She then heard Helen's phone bleep. Helen took a very brief call and then ran back into the villa through another door. She didn't know anything more until the ambulance came. Apparently, the police arrived as the ambulance was leaving.'

'And she told the police all of this?'

'Yes. No one was allowed to leave the villa until everyone had given a statement. I can't be sure, but I'm hopeful that we now know what the police know.'

'That is being hopeful,' said Reg, lifting his soda. 'Who is this hottie? Can you trust her?'

'I won't say her name, but...'

'It's Gamila,' I said. Both Reg and Charles turned to look at me. 'Well, she is, isn't she? When I saw her at the villa, I didn't recognise her. In the café, she was dressed modestly, wore no makeup and had her hair covered. But at the party, she was wearing an expensive gown and glamorous makeup.' I took a large gulp of wine. 'Poor Gamila. When she discovered what had happened at the pool, she must have been terrified knowing that Khaled was asking questions, too. She would only have had a couple of hours to give her statement to the police, then race to the temple to meet me there.'

'But that means that my request for company was intercepted!' Charles was indignant.

'Yes, Charles. I'm afraid it was. But by friends. I trust her;

she's working for The Network as Nike. The information she's provided explains so much.'

'Does it? She couldn't explain why Helen attacked you.'

Reg shrugged. 'Whoever Helen spoke to on the phone gave the order.'

'But we're only assuming that,' I pointed out. 'The enforcer said that she spoke to Hera.'

Charles dropped into a chair that sighed under his weight. 'So, now you don't think so? You said that Helen walked from the garden to the poolside with a mobile phone and told you that you are no longer a goddess.'

'That's what she said. But there are two things that now make me think she was lying. Firstly, the enforcer I spoke to was still protecting me after we left the villa. I don't think the assassination order was given until after I met with Nike. Such an order would presumably come from high up in Fireflight.'

'And the other thing?'

'Nike saw Helen talking on her mobile and then running back into the building. That's when she went to get the needle. I told Helen that I'd found out she'd gone to Hissarlik. That's the place that historians think might have been Troy. I assumed this detour was because she'd tried to fix the mess Aphrodite made when she played Troy and Fireflight off against each other, but now I think that she was reporting what she knew of Fireflight back to Troy, who have an office in Canakkale. They told her I was in Athens.'

'You said she was working for Fireflight,' said Reg

frowning.

'She was,' I answered. 'That doesn't mean she stopped working for Troy.'

Reg nodded. 'So, Helen knew you were there before she arrived. But that still doesn't explain why she would attack you.'

'Fireflight probably instructed her to re-recruit me. That was the purpose of meeting me in the garden, but I knew her secret. I'd figured out that she had developed The Fates compounds. If she had done that while working for Troy and given them to Fireflight, then Aphrodite wasn't the only one playing the two companies off against each other. That also explains why she was so surprised when I found one of the drug diagrams in an autopsy file. She probably hadn't realised that Fireflight had started using the compounds independently. Just imagine the possibilities if Fireflight could weaponise them!'

'Stop, stop!' Reg held up his hands. 'This is getting complicated.' He pinched the bridge of his nose as if he was getting a headache. 'You're going to have to put the pieces together for me.'

I stood and faced the folding doors that led to the hotel garden. I could see my refection clearly in the long glass panels and wondered what Athena was supposed to look like. I closed my eyes as I talked, trying to put my thoughts in order.

'Helen discovers that Aphrodite is in Athens, but before following her here, she flies to Canakkale to report what she knows. They tell her that I'm here. Helen makes sure that we meet at the villa and she tries to bring me back into Fireflight. The Network must have heard of this and sent Nike – that is, Gamila – there to observe. I said no to Helen. Then, I think she received a call, one that told her to report in to Fireflight. I can't be sure that Helen did create The Fates, she wouldn't confirm it. But if she did and I told someone – anyone- what she was doing, she'd be at risk of an assassination order herself. That's why she attacked me.'

Charles shifted in his seat. 'Kim, I admire what you're doing, I really do. But maybe it's time for you to leave Athens.'

I turned to face him. 'No Charles. I think it's time for you and Reg to leave Athens. Nike and I are in extreme danger. Fireflight will try to assassinate me again.'

Chapter 34

Reg had responded with an emphatic 'no' to my insistence that he and Charles return home. Charles diplomatically suggested that we discuss things over breakfast the following morning.

I rose early with a speech already prepared and arrived at the dining room earlier than promised so that I was ready to deliver it.

Patricia and George must have had a similar idea as they were already sitting at the breakfast table when I walked in. George looked up and smiled.

'Hello, Kim. How are you?' He poured me some strong, black coffee.

'I don't know,' I answered truthfully. 'I'm OK, I guess.'

Patricia reached for her orange juice and waited for me to sit and pay attention. She carefully repositioned her glass on the table and pulled some papers from under her plate.

'We'd like you to sign these, please.' She started searching her bag for a pen.

I gasped as I opened the papers. 'Repatriation of the Deceased. Patricia, where did you get this?'

'You don't have to worry about filling in the details; George and I will take care of that.'

'Where did you get this?' I was starting to breathe incorrectly and my hand shook as I reached for my coffee cup. I left the cup alone and put my shaking hand flat on the table. I closed my eyes as the room started to spin.

Patricia placed her pen by my hand. 'It's clear to us that you have certain, well...' she rotated her wrist in the royal wave as she pretended to search for the right word, 'problems coping with formalities, so George and I have talked it over and we think it would be best if you let us take care of everything.'

I opened my eyes slowly, but the room was still moving. 'But you can't take care of everything, can you?'

'Pardon?'

I spoke a little more loudly. 'But you can't take care of everything, can you? The medical death certificate will be given to me. I am Nick's next of kin.'

'I'm his mother!'

I swept my hand across the table and sent Patricia's pen flying off the edge and skittering over the tiled floor. The toddler two tables over giggled, and thinking we were playing a game, tossed her spoon away.

'The medical death certificate will be given to me because I am Nick's next of kin. I am his wife. You can't arrange to take Nick back to the UK without it.' I looked at the papers again. 'I don't know who, or how much you paid to get these forms, but I'm not signing anything over to you.' I tore the forms in half and tossed them on the table.

This time, it was Patricia's turn to gasp and she looked

like I had slapped her. The temptation to do so was great. I rose from my chair and hurried from the room before the tears came.

'Kim,' called George. 'Please come back. Have some breakfast.'

Outside the dining room door, I almost collided with Charles as he exited the lift.

'Ah, Kim. Listen, Reg and I have talked and we think...'

'Fuck off, Charles!' I screamed. 'I'm sick of people telling me to listen to what they think. It's my decision when I leave.'

Charles looked shocked at my profanity, but I was already running for the door.

'The Kyria Anderson?' the quietly spoken voice came from behind the reception desk. I hurriedly brushed the tears from my face but the receptionist was already holding out a tissue. I was grateful to notice that she didn't ask me what the matter was.

'A delivery for you. Sign, please?'

'What's this?'

'One from the police and another.'

'The police?'

'The mother, she tells me that what is addressed to Mrs Anderson is for her. But Mrs Anderson, that is you, is it not?'

I smiled, relieved to have found a friend. Opening the first envelope, I found the medical death certificate and contact information for an International Funeral Director. The second envelope was from my bank, containing my new bank cards.

'Is there an internet café near here?' I asked.

'Yes. Two blocks west. Very good breakfast.'

Thanking the kind and smart receptionist, I ran from the hotel. I slowed my pace when I realised that no one was following me. I took a few breaths and slowed my racing brain.

On entering the internet café, I felt somewhat out of place being the oldest person there. The assistants at the back of the shop were drinking coffee. One rose to greet me as I walked in. It appeared that they hadn't long opened their doors.

The first half of the shop had benches on either side. The posters above displayed pictures from films and what I guessed to be online games. The furthest end of the shop had a patisserie counter on the left and a shop counter on the right.

'I'm going to need a disposable phone and half an hour's time on a PC, please.'

The assistant, a young man in his twenties, nodded at my request.

'And a large coffee.'

I sat at one of the computers and looked up the British Consulate. I unpacked the phone and punched in the number. I had to wait several minutes for the call to be answered but managed to explain what had happened. The person on the other end made an appointment for me to visit later that afternoon. I then made a call to the

International Funeral Director. He was sympathetic, but professional and explained to me what was required of me at the Consulate.

Once the call was ended I sat in front of the PC and, not knowing what else I could do, I dropped my head into my hands and tried not to cry. There was insufficient admin to keep me busy and old memories invaded my mind.

I remembered the day we moved into our house. I'd stood on the front doorstep and counted twenty-four blemishes on the front door. I remembered thinking that would need repainting as quickly as possible.

Nick stood beside me and put his arm around my shoulders. 'Isn't it wonderful? It's all ours.'

And it was wonderful. The blemishes didn't diminish the importance of the moment. That was a momentous day for me; I wasn't just moving in with the man I loved, I was making a decision to go forward with my life in the company of someone else. That was terrifying, but I also knew that it was something I wanted, more than anything else. I'd never been so scared in my life.

We had no money. We moved in with half a loaf of bread and six cans of beans. Deciding to leave beans on toast for the next day, we counted out what change we had on the rough wooden floor in front of the old gas fire. It only came to a few pounds, but there was a cheap fish and chip shop around the corner and Nick was confident that he could get something. He came back with rock and chips, a pickled onion and a can of coke. We split everything 50-50 and raised a toast to our new home and all the wonderful memories we'd make there.

'Here you are.' I looked up to see Charles standing in the sunshine that poured through the windows. 'I asked the receptionist if she knew where you'd gone and she pointed in this direction.'

'Look, Charles, I'm sorry about earlier, but I really don't want to talk about it.'

He reached for a chair and sat beside me. 'You don't have to explain. I told Patricia and George that I had plans for yesterday afternoon and evening and I think that's when they acquired the forms. They were still lying on the breakfast table when I walked in. I asked Patricia what they were and she looked as guilty as a schoolgirl caught smoking in class.'

I smiled at the image. 'I need to visit the Consulate this afternoon, and I need to buy a new purse and bag.'

'Let me come with you. I could do with a break from the terrible twosome.'

'I feel a little guilty leaving them on their own.'

'Don't. You know Patricia would just take over if she was with you. George does try to hold her back, but she's a force to be reckoned with.' Charles eyed my coffee cup. 'I see no evidence of food. Allow me.'

Without waiting for me to protest, he rose and went to the patisserie counter. While on my own, I turned back to the PC and searched for Troy on the internet. I still had no proof of Dion's safety and wasn't sure where to look.

Charles returned with breakfast pastries and placed one

on the table next to me. 'Unfinished business?' he asked.

'Do you remember, in the cab back from the hospital, I told you why Nick and I had come to Greece?'

Charles nodded, crumbs flecked across his chest. 'You were looking for evidence of the safe adoption of a little boy.'

'When Sarah sent her email, she said that Dion had been adopted by a winemaking family. That was why we went to the villa. Troy is one of the biggest producers in the country.'

'But with Fireflight working against you and Sarah in hiding, you have no proof.'

'I've asked friends to look, but it may be that Troy isn't connected.'

'If they're doing business with Fireflight, they're connected. They might not be able to lead you to the boy, but they're still worth another look.'

'This is their American page,' I said. Charles read over my shoulder.

'For over 70 years we have been investing in the future, wherever in the world that may be. We select our partners from a range of industries, all of whom have a proven track record in enhancing the communities in which they work." That sound like a grand way of using a lot of words to not say very much.'

'Let's try the Greek page,' I suggested. There was a search box on Troy's webpage. I typed in Golden Apple. A picture of happy little children blowing dandelion clocks appeared. Text beneath the picture was in Greek.

Charles pointed. 'Can you translate that?'

'Not as well as Nick could, but I can use a translation tool. Here we go. "Troy are happy to announce it is emerging into healthcare investment." The party at the villa was to celebrate a new partnership, but they're not mentioning the name. A friend in The Network thought the payments from Troy to Fireflight had stopped. This makes it look like they've started up again. I don't understand what these payments could be for. When Nick and I looked up Troy before the party, we found they were an investment and business development company. If they are moving into healthcare, and maybe developing their own drugs, wouldn't that make them and Fireflight competitors?'

'Not necessarily,' said Charles. 'Any two companies, even usual competitors, can come together in a mutually beneficial deal. You should see what the Fraud department investigates. Unfortunately, there's no-one in the British police I can call on to help you. I've heard that DI Kelly is already calling both Fireflight and The Network, terrorists.'

'Terrorists? That's extreme.'

'Yes, it is, but if each of your friends has a skill that can be used to your advantage and disrupt the money routes, as you wish to do, then you are at least, political agitators.'

'I'm not sure how I feel about that.'

Charles lifted his eyes to give me a stern look. 'I hope you feel committed. Because if you're not, you're vulnerable.'

Chapter 35

Charles and I rode in the back of a Mercedes to the Consulate buildings.

'Reg told me about these cars. I haven't been able to verify who any of the drivers are.'

'You won't,' I replied. 'But I feel safer in one of these than in a street cab.'

The British Consulate at 1 Plantarchou, was next to the church of St Nicholas and the two buildings could not have been more different. While the church, with its ancient beauty reminded me of a village chapel, the Consulate was an ugly blue and white six storey tower block.

The British coat of arms sat proudly front and centre on the wall facing the street and a guard sat in a tiny grey booth to the left. White painted corrugated fencing stood either side of the blue painted gates. Metal lattice panels were mounted above the fencing and razor wire sat in untidy spirals on top of the panels. The whole image made me think of the unsightly blob of an official stamp on a beautifully hand-crafted letter.

We showed our passports to the guard and were directed where to go. The security officer in one building told us we were in the wrong area and another sent us back the way we had come. Eventually, we found the correct office and Charles was asked to wait outside while I spoke to the official.

Mr Halkias gave me two sets of forms, one in Greek and the other in English. He and I signed both and he told me that the English translation was for me and that I should show it to the International Funeral Director.

'And you are leaving?'

'The day after tomorrow.'

Halkias nodded. 'It is best you speak to the Funeral Director today. You have your husband's passport?' I handed it over for him to see. 'Good. And your flight's arranged?'

'We had return flight tickets. They're in the hotel safe.'

'Yours is good, but the Funeral Director will advise a different ticket for your husband.' Halkias looked at me with a sad little smile. 'He cannot give it at the gate. The hospital will call you before your flight. You must visit to sign forms that allow your husband to leave Greece.' He rose to shake my hand and opened the door for me. 'All is good. Any problems, you call me.'

I thanked him and reunited with Charles in the corridor.

'That was relatively painless,' I said, 'but I need to speak to the International Funeral Director again. Nick might need a different kind of plane ticket.' Charles nodded, but said nothing and I was glad. I didn't think I could cope with any more sympathy.

Although it was already approaching four o'clock, the sun was still fiercely hot as we exited on to the street. Our car slowly rolled into view to stop at the same place it had dropped us less than an hour earlier.

'Did the car have to move?' asked Charles. 'I didn't see it leave as we crossed the street.'

'Maybe an official or traffic cop asked him to move.'

The rear doors swung open as we approached and we bundled in, glad to be out of the heat of the day. I was tugging at my seatbelt as I heard the clunk of a car door.

'What was that?'

Charles frowned. 'What was what?'

'I think I heard the driver's car door shut. They never open their doors. They have to keep their identity secret.'

'Well maybe he had to get out...' Charles' eyes suddenly clouded over. 'Get out the car!' he yelled. 'Now! Get out the car!'

I yanked at the door handle on the pavement side, and almost tripped as Charles pushed me forwards. He followed after and continued to push until we were squashed against the wall of the building opposite.

'What the hell, Charles?'

'Get down!' he screamed. He waved his arms impatiently at passers-by. 'Get down!'

The last part of his command was lost in an earth-shattering boom that lifted the car door that I had opened, into the air and spinning twenty yards down the street. The open driver's door was folded back on itself, neatly wrapped over the side and bonnet of the car. The rear passenger seats were now folded in to the centre of the car and fully aflame.

I lifted my head to see Charles still crouched over with his eyes squeezed tight and his back speckled with glass burning tiny holes into his linen jacket. He mouthed words at me. My vision was blurred and my head felt like I was underwater.

Charles gripped my shoulders and brought me back to the present. 'Kim, are you all right?'

I gripped Charles' arm and tried to regain my balance. 'What the hell happened?'

I stood up to look up and down the pavement. I could see dozens of people running away, a few bystanders with mobile phones to their ears and a few people who were staring at the car as it burned. Any one of them could have been our potential assassin.

I fumbled for my disposable phone and stabbed in Perry's number. 'Perry, someone has tried to kill me, they've blown up my car!'

'Athena, are you injured?'

'No, I'm OK.' I looked at the hand not holding the phone. It was shaking uncontrollably. 'I need you to tell the drivers in Crete. If Fireflight could get to my driver, they could get to yours, too.'

'I will tell them.'

Wailing sirens and flashing lights came skidding to a halt beside me.

A woman in a pale blue uniform ran from a paramedic response car to sit Charles on a low wall. She made him follow her finger with his eyes.

'Can you also put the word out that I'm worried about Nike? I can't risk making contact again in case I put her in danger.'

'Please,' said a police officer, pointing to his cruiser. 'You will come with us.'

'I've also met a young man called Leander Regas, a friend of Medana Osman. He has family in Crete. Do you know anything about them?' I continued to Perry.

'Please,' said the officer, a little more sternly. 'You will come.'

'I'll explain everything as soon as I can. Stay safe.' I pressed buttons to delete the call information on my phone.

'Where are we going?' I called. 'Where's Charles?'

'Your father? Nosokomeio. He is going to the hospital.'

I turned my head to see Charles being bundled into the back of the paramedic's car. The door had barely shut before it sped away.

'The hospital? Oh no, he's not my father.' But the police officers were not interested in the misinterpretation. The driver kept his eyes on the road and the one who spoke to me used calming words as we wound our way through the city.

I turned my phone off when we reached the police station and dropped it in my bag, which was taken from me at a security desk. The police were being a lot more formal with me today than they had been when I complained about Medana.

I allowed my eyes to roam over the wide foyer, with the

public reception desk to the right. The last time I was here, Nick had stood roughly where I was standing. I pressed my lips together to stop them from trembling. An officer walked towards me and indicated that I should follow.

I was shown to a small interview room where a stern looking woman in her forties sat waiting for me. She was wearing a doctor's white coat with a police ID card clipped to the collar. The woman stood and indicated that I should sit in the chair she had just vacated.

'Giatros,' she said, pointing to herself. 'Doctor.'

She pulled a pen from her top pocket and pointed to the top. 'Follow, please.' She then proceeded to take me through the same tests I saw Charles undertake outside the consulate.

'Headache?' asked the doctor.

'No, I'm fine. Where is Charles? Is he OK?'

'Sickness?' she asked.

'No, I haven't felt sick. Can I see Charles?'

'Zalismenos?'

'What?'

The doctor held out her arms and pretended to have difficulty maintaining her balance.

'Dizzy? No, no dizziness. Look, when can I see Charles?'

The doctor pocketed her pen, seemingly satisfied and opened the door. Detective Michalis entered, notepad and a pen in hand. He mumbled thanks to the doctor who closed the door behind her.

Michalis sat at the table opposite me and came straight to the point.

'You are going home when?'

'It's supposed to be the day after tomorrow. Will I have to stay longer?'

'No. You will go.'

'Really? Won't you need me for the investigation?'

Michalis's eyes slid to the recording equipment at the far end of the table. All the buttons were dark. 'No. We investigate, you go.'

'Anyone would think you don't want me here.'

'You go to the Consulate today. For your husband?'

'Yes, Charles came with me.'

'Your friend?'

'Yes, is he all right?'

'He goes to the hospital. Senior Constable Gabris will be there.' Michalis picked up his pen.

'When did you arrive at the Consulate?'

'About 2.45. My appointment was at three.'

'The car came back for you?'

'Yes, about ten to four.'

'You see anybody there?'

'There were several people about, but nothing out of the ordinary.'

'Your friend, he protected you. Are you injured?'

I looked at my hands and ran them through my hair. Apart from the fact that I was still a little shaky, I seemed to be in one piece. 'I think I'm OK.'

'You have the forms?'

'Yes.'

'You give them to the International Funeral Director. They arrange and you and your husband go home. The British police will talk to you there.'

'What for? The bomb went off here.'

'It was an explosion. Not all explosions are caused by bombs.' Michalis's body language suggested that he was trying very hard not to look at the door.

'But it happened right outside the Consulate building! Surely their security will want to talk to me?'

'You talk to the British police.'

I slowly pointed my finger at the detective. 'You think I'm a danger. I'm a pest to you; a political agitator.'
Michalis wrinkled his nose, making his thick moustache wiggle. 'Bad things happen with you. You are...' He struggled for the right expression. He clenched a fist and made an action that looked like he was stabbing his waist.

'A thorn in your side?'

He mumbled something in Greek, which I presumed translated as a pain in the arse. He opened the door for me and gave the briefest of goodbyes.

I collected my bag from the security desk and was told that a car would take me back to the hotel. When I said I wanted to go to the hospital to check on my friend, I was told that the destination was not open to debate, I was being taken back to the hotel. I glanced over my shoulder to see Michalis still standing where I had left him, waiting to see me leave.

In the back of the police car, I turned my phone back on to find two text messages from Perry. 'Nike is well, she is safe' and 'Do not trust Leander Regas, he blames you for Medana'.

These texts gave me three very interesting pieces of information. The first was a relief; Nike was aware of the danger and taking care. The second was reassuring; The Network was communicating efficiently between Athens and Crete if Perry knew of Nike, Leander and Medana. The third sat less comfortably. If Leander blamed me for what happened to Medana, he could have tipped off Fireflight to our conversation the previous day.

Chapter 36

Charles, Reg and George were standing in the hotel foyer when I walked in. They appeared to be in serious conversation, but broke away to deliver smiles as soon as they saw me.

Reg stepped forward with relief written all over his face. 'Glad to see you. Bin to hospital?'

'No, really, I'm OK. I was worried about you, Charles, when they told me you had to go to hospital.'

'Nothing to worry about,' said Charles. 'A few minor marks on my back, but I've had back problems for years.'

'Judging by the state of his jacket and shirt,' said Reg, 'those minor marks will need looking at by a doctor when we get back home. And you should get yourself a hearing test, too.'

Charles bristled. 'My hearing is fine. I didn't experience any ringing.'

'Sometimes that's delayed. I was in the army; there's nothing minor about experiencing an explosion, even if you think you're uninjured. You're getting seen to, or I'm taking you to my quack.'

'It seems that you took the worst of the blast, Charles,' I said, interrupting before an argument could develop. 'But how did you know what was happening?'

'Well, actually, it was more of an implosion; the car folded in on itself. But when you said that you thought the driver had got out, he or she would have needed time to distance themselves before anything happened to the car. And you did say that you thought Fireflight might try again.'

'Try what again?' asked George.

'What did the police say to you?' I asked Charles, sidestepping George's question.

'Garbis seems to have his head screwed on the right way. He asked me when we arrived, when we left, who did we see, etcetera. He also asked me when we were leaving.'

'Michalis asked me the same. The Hellenic police do not want me digging in Athens.'

Reg sniffed. 'Well, as far as I'm concerned, the sooner we get back home, the better.' He waggled a chubby finger between Charles and me. 'You two need to rest up. Any ear ringing, headaches or blurred vision, you come and find me. I'm going outside for an oily rag and then taking a nap before dinner.'

'Kim,' George stopped me as I turned towards the stairs. 'Tish and I are glad you're all right.'

'Thanks, George.'

Charles accompanied me to my door.

'Charles, doesn't it seem unusual how quickly the paramedics and police arrived at the consulate?'

'Well, I'm sure there would be a police presence close to the consulate buildings,' replied Charles, 'but yes. The response was rapid.'

I looked up at Charles. 'That makes me think that they either knew what was going to happen, or suspected that something would happen.'

A frown clouded Charles' face as he thought about this. 'If you were in the UK, it's likely that certain departments of the police would be watching you. You and any associates or eyewitnesses would be questioned separately in the event of any incident.'

I nodded. That was exactly what had happened. 'I'm glad you're here, Charles.'

He squeezed my hand paternally. 'I'll see you later.'

After dinner I feigned tiredness. I went back to my room to change into darker clothes and waited until I thought everyone would be safely in the hotel bar. Leaving my phone and bag in the hotel room, I took only my purse. I crept down the stairs, deliberately avoiding the lifts and walked briskly through the foyer. I put a finger to my lips and the friendly receptionist from yesterday smiled and winked.

I walked briskly to the main street and hailed a cab. I felt nervous of taxis but it dropped me, without incident, near the Presidential Palace, just two streets away from where I met Medana.

The imposing Hotel Fortune sat on the corner between the Presidential Palace and Syntagma Square, a landmark that drew attention from locals and tourists alike, the biggest and most illustrious in Greece with a reputation to uphold. The opulent entrance was a fast track education in the presentation of antiques. The reception desk was quiet, but the concierge smiled at me as I walked in. He said nothing, but pointed me towards the lifts.

My soft shoes slid over the marbled floors and gold mirrors redirected light from the chandeliers to illuminate my path. The strength of history in this building was so strong, I could almost taste it.

I couldn't be sure if my comment on an obscure blog had reached its target. But apparently it had: an enforcer was waiting for me at the lifts. Dressed all in black and with the bearing of a bodyguard, he moved his arms from behind his back and held out an electronic wand. I opened my arms to be scanned. Satisfied, he entered one of the lifts and escorted me to the eighth floor.

We alighted at the rooftop restaurant and bar. The open sided room permitted uninterrupted views of the Acropolis, Lycabettus Hill and Parliament buildings. Athens came alive at night and the city lights were putting on a show.

I followed the enforcer between the empty tables and discreet waiting staff politely pretended not to see us as they continued to clear away the remains of dinner service. I was led to the far left corner where the bar twinkled with multi-coloured stars, bouncing off the bottles. Zeus sat waiting at the end of the bar, dressed in a loose fitting black shirt and trousers, his black gloves and balaclava mask neatly in place.

'It's good to see you, Athena. Please sit. Can I get you a drink?'

I was ready to rage against the man before me, but

remembered my manners. I'd promised myself, I wasn't going to lose control.

'No thank you. I'm keeping a clear head tonight.' Both the bartender and the enforcer departed at my response. 'Are the other gods listening in?'

'No. we can keep this a private conversation. I assume that's what you wanted?'

'Yes. Thank you.'

The man in black leaned back on his bar stool against the dark wooden slats. He looked perfectly at home in these magnificent surroundings. 'You've come home to Greece. I've been looking forward to seeing you again.'

'Have you? You've got a funny way of showing it. The murder of my husband, three other assassinations and two attempts on my life.'

'I was sorry to hear of your husband. The incident at the villa was not authorised.'

'The incident?! Is that what you're calling it?' I was starting to shake, my rage barely beneath the surface. 'Someone authorised it and I've been told that it was Hera.'

'Hera does not have the authority to make decisions against you.'

'Well, she has. And you seem to lack the authority to keep her under control.'

Zeus stiffened at my response. I was pushing my luck in the way I was talking to him. 'You leave Hera to me,' he said. 'You said you have something I want.'

'Helen appears to have fled Athens. I have her locket,

which contains a diagram I stole from the abandoned hospital. I'll return it in exchange for information.'

Zeus shrugged, unimpressed. 'Whatever you think you have, we already own.'

'I know that. But does Troy know everything you have? Now that they are investing in Healthcare, won't they want to know what this is? Won't the police?'

Zeus leaned forward slightly. 'Are you trying to blackmail me? You really are an extraordinary woman, Athena. Anybody else would be consumed with grief; but you? You're threatening me.'

'I'm too angry to be grief stricken. I'm raising an army.'

Zeus laughed. 'An army! You mean the dad's army you've managed to create here in Athens?'

'Don't underestimate your enemy,' I warned. 'I'm stronger than I look.'

Zeus nodded. 'I believe you are. What do you want?'

'First I want information about the children; Eric, Harmony and Dion. I want to know what your plans are for them.'

'We have no plans for any of these children. Their futures are entirely in their own hands.'

'I don't believe you.'

'Athena, believe what you like. You won't stop our operations. You won't derail our plans. Our future is assured. Unfortunately, yours is a little more uncertain. There is only so much I can do to protect you. Continue on this path and you will face the wrath of the other gods.'

'That brings us to the other thing I want to know. Are you really protecting me? Why is that? Are you my birth father? Presumably, you've had my blood tested.'

'I have, and it appears that you are one of mine, yes.'

'One of yours?' I raised my eyebrows at Zeus, but he didn't elaborate. 'Did Mother know?'

'She didn't say anything to me, but I'm sure she must have suspected.'

'Did you know, when you set fire to the lab she was working in?'

Zeus dropped his head. 'Actually, no. Not until you were brought to the abandoned house, but I don't expect you to believe me.'

I didn't. I was only ten when Mother died and she wasn't that much older than I am now.

'Why did you have Gaia assassinated?'

'I didn't. Ares was meant to reclaim her, not assassinate her.' So, Helen's guess was right; Marie knew something about Ares that she shouldn't.

'What judgement did you make against Ares? You're the Archon, right?'

'There is no judgement against Ares.'

'But you came to the hospital to judge Ares for killing Gaia.'

'I went to the hospital to look for Simone and her child.'

'But now you are in Athens, so you must believe that he is in Greece.'

'I am in Athens for business. I have no interest in the

child.'

'Why do you want me in Fireflight?'

'You have something else I want.'

'The aegis? The shield of protection that Zeus gave to Athena. At the hospital, Helen told me that one of your projects involved trying to export paternal protection to the foetus. Is that connected? Explain it to me.'

Zeus fingered the stem of the wine glass next to him. I guessed he was weighing up how much he should tell me. He slowly swirled the red velvet within before he spoke.

'The experiment was to isolate protective material from the father, create an injectable compound and administer to the mother. The foetus would absorb the protection, resulting in a stronger or unique child.'

'And it worked...' I started cautiously.

Zeus opened his hands towards me. 'The proof is sitting before me.'

'...But not as well as you hoped. If all was well, why would you need me?'

Zeus shifted in his seat. 'Come to Fireflight. My protection is limited outside, but I can protect you from within.'

'I've finally realised that no one can protect me. Not even you. These procedures and projects, whatever their purpose, are knotted together in a tangle like Ariadne's yarn. But I will unravel them. I will find a loose end and tug until every project you have is exposed. Even if it's the death of me.'

'I promise my protection as your father.'

'No!' The squeal burst from me before I could stop it. I held up a shaky hand. 'You are not my father. I already have a father.' I pointed a finger at Zeus as I slid from my seat and started backing away. 'You, you're nothing more to me than my sperm donor.'

I walked briskly towards the lifts and the waiting enforcer, biting hard on my lip to stop myself from crying. Zeus did not follow.

I took a cab directly back to the hotel and snuck back to my room. I lay awake for most of the night, my brain whirring. The purpose of Fireflight's latest project was to reclaim the women that Tony Brownlow had freed. I understood why; each of us had unique traits that would be useful to Fireflight, but if I was needed, why would one of the gods order my assassination? Was it so that no one else could use the aegis? And what the hell was that anyway? Or was someone trying to kill me because I was disrupting their operations?

Time was running out for me in Athens; the police didn't want me here and I was putting others in danger. I only had one full day left. I decided to make the most of it.

I only had a few changes of clean clothes left and was starting to feel anxious about the cleanliness of my suitcase, but pushed these insecurities to the back of my mind as I showered the next morning. I had to stay focused.

I left the hotel early, before breakfast and went back to the internet café a couple of blocks away. I connected to a PC in the hope that I could find a way to contact Sarah. The best way I could think of was to hack Nick's email. I briefly wondered if he'd mind.

I stared at the empty box asking for his password. I was sure I'd seen him use my name before. I tried that without success.

'God, Nick. What am I supposed to do? Tell me what to do.' I dropped my head into my hands and tried not to cry.

'There's no need to get upset,' he would say. 'All problems have a solution. Clear your mind and it will come to you.'

I thought back to when we were in an internet café just a few days ago. I took a breath, closed my eyes and watched his fingers on the keyboard. I tried ilovekim. It worked! I hoped I'd be able to send an email to Sarah, but it looked like she had already sent one to Nick. She had sent an attachment. I hovered the cursor over the icon for several seconds, then with a nervous glance over my shoulder, I clicked on it.

Autopsy of Participant, Gaia. Performed by Chiron.

Oh, my God! This couldn't possibly be a legal document. And who was Chiron? Wasn't he a centaur? Weren't centaurs originally the heralds of chaos?

I couldn't bring myself to read all the details, but it spoke of the drugs in her body, some I recognised. There was Clotho, Lachesis and Atropos. These were the compounds that Helen had told me about in the villa garden. I skipped to Chiron's findings at the end.

'Examination of tissue and blood work show expected results for Clotho and Lachesis, but not Atropos. Atropos blood levels in living subject were below expected levels until the introduction of the antagonist. Low levels of Atropos are detected in tissue samples, but only minimal traces of antagonist can be found.'

These findings seemed to back up what Helen had told me. Marie had not experienced the possible detrimental effects of Atropos until she had been given the antagonist. Atropos had then killed it off.

I needed to get this information out into the open. I needed to get this to The Network. I rose from my seat to request a USB, then thought better of it. My father's warning came back to me. Never retain anything that can be used against you.

I sat back down and pondered what to do. I had an idea. I didn't know if this would work, but I could try. I brought up Troy's internet page. I looked for a 'Contact Us' option and clicked on it. A contact box opened into which I could type a message. I couldn't attach the report, but I could copy and paste the notes at the end. This I did and sent the message before I could talk myself out of it.

I then went back and deleted all trace of the report. I hastily connected to an email provider and created a new account. I gave it the name iamathena and sent it to Sarah before deleting Nick's account.

'I'm sorry, darling,' I whispered. 'I just hope my plan works.'

Chapter 37

I re-entered the hotel just after nine and bumped into Reg outside the dining room.

'I've been looking for you,' he smiled. 'You've missed breakfast again. Where did you go?'

'Reg, I've been doing some thinking. Can I talk to you privately? I think Charles should be in on this too.'

A frown clouded Reg's face but he remained calm. 'Righto. Why don't you take a seat outside and I'll go find him?'

I sat at one of the tables in the outside eating area. Nick and I had enjoyed dinner here under electric stars before... well, before I'd opened a massive can of worms. I ordered enough coffee for three and soon, Reg and Charles walked out to join me, with anxious expressions.

Charles pulled out the chair opposite me. 'What is it, Kim? Are you sure you're all right?'

I was far from all right, and I didn't know how to tell them, but Reg and Charles had become dear friends and I felt I owed it to them to share what I'd discovered.

'I snuck out of here last night and went to visit Zeus at the Olympian's hotel.' The sentence came out in a rush and I expected Reg and Charles to admonish me, but both sat with open mouths waiting for me to continue. 'I have something he wants. The aegis.'

'Well tell him he ain't getting it, whatever it is,' responded Reg. 'He'll have to go through us first.'

'The aegis is the shield of protection that Zeus gave to Athena,' I explained. 'I'm not sure what it is, but I presume it's something in my blood. That's why he wants me in Fireflight.'

'You can't possibly be thinking about this,' said Charles. 'Please tell me you won't go.'

'I won't go. But I do need to find out what the aegis is. When I met Zeus, I asked him to explain it to me. He described it as a protection from the father that's injected into the mother to enhance the foetus. That's why he was at the hospital looking for Simone and Dion; he must have wondered if Dion has it, too.'

'That sounds well dodgy.' Reg nodded his thanks to the waiter who brought the coffee and we remained silent until he left the table.

'Most protections, even vaccinations, have limited lifespans,' I said. 'But this is something different, something unique. And dangerous enough that one of the gods would kill me for it.'

Charles pushed his cup away. 'They can't kill you if they need you. What's the point of that?'

'I was thinking about that last night with Zeus,' I said. 'And then it hit me. He offered me his protection as my father.'

'Wot's that supposed to mean? He ain't no father to you.'

'That's when I realised. Hera, or whoever ordered my assassination, doesn't know that Zeus is my father.'

'But Zeus is Athena's father,' said Charles. 'We're familiar with the Olympian's family tree.'

'Yes, but they don't know that Marcus Alexander is my biological father.' I tapped the centre of my chest. 'None of the Olympians can be related.'

'Why is that?' asked Reg. 'Maybe if they're asked to bump someone off, it's less difficult?'

'Perhaps.' I sipped my coffee. 'But maybe also because if they're playing with genetic material, there's less cause for concern if the players are unrelated.'

Charles leaned forward on the table. 'That might narrow things down a bit. Who does know that you're related?'

'Well, Zeus, obviously. I think Hephaestus knows, or at least he might suspect. He investigated my mother last year. This may mean that Hermes knows.'

'You can't trust anyone,' said Charles, rubbing his chin, 'but it's my guess that we're looking for someone else in the god's family tree.'

'Zeus said that I should leave Hera to him. He'll be watching her carefully. But what if it wasn't her who ordered the assassination? The enforcer said it was, but he could have been lying. It also could be that the person on the other end of Helen's phone called themselves Hera.'

'Is there anyone you can ask?'

'Not that I can think of without putting them in danger.

Sarah's made contact again. I was going to reveal my conversation with Zeus, but she had information of her own. She sent an attachment of Gaia's autopsy report.'

Reg blew a puff of air through his lips and wrinkled his nose. 'I bet that made for interesting reading.'

'I doubt that it has any legal validity, but I leaked the comments to Troy.'

'Do you think that was wise?' asked Charles. 'Fireflight might trace that back to you.'

'They might,' I agreed, 'but they already know that I intend to stop them. I've not been secretive about that.'

'What about you being here?' Reg couldn't help looking around him. 'They might come to the hotel.'

'Possible, but unlikely.' I shook my head. 'Too public, too many witnesses. What Ares did at the coffee shop was unusual. And unauthorised, apparently.'

'What do you want to do now?' asked Charles.

'I need to reach out to the rest of The Network. But I'm not sure how.'

Reg laid his arm on the table and held out his hand towards me. 'What can we do to help?'

I took his hand and reached for Charles' too. 'You already are helping. You are friends and you believe me. I couldn't ask for anything more.'

I made a call just before noon.

'Ne?'

'Janna? It's Kim. I'm just calling to say goodbye. We fly home tomorrow.'

'Mama wants to see you, but we didn't know how to contact you. Do you have plans for lunch?'

'I'd love to meet for lunch. Is everything OK?'

'A package arrived for you at our apartment this morning,' Janna's tone sounded slightly accusatory, 'but we don't know where it has come from.'

'For me? I'm sure if it was important, it would have come to the hotel.'

'That's what makes me nervous. Will you meet us at the café in front of the gardens? One o'clock?'

'Yes, of course. I'll be there.'

When I told Charles about the call, he insisted on coming with me. 'Reg might want to come too. He'll only pout otherwise.'

I sat with Reg and Charles facing the door. My hands wouldn't stay still.

Charles placed a calming hand over mine. 'If it was anything potentially dangerous, I don't think Elena would risk driving with it into the city.'

'I'll take a look at it when they get here,' insisted Reg. 'If I think it's suspect, I'll call the police.' He pointed his finger at me. 'And you get the hell out of here.'

'I won't leave you behind, Reg.'

'You'll do as I tell yer.'

When Elena and Janna walked in, I breathed out, not realising that I'd been holding my breath. The three of us stood to welcome our friends.

Janna took the package from her mother and held it out

to me, but Reg took hold of it. We sat as he inspected the large manila envelope.

'Well, my spidy-sense ain't tingling.' He turned the package over in his hands. 'It feels like paperwork. No marks to say where it's come from. Flaps ain't been interfered with. This was hand-delivered.'

'Perhaps I should go into the park and open it alone,' I suggested.

Reg shook his head. 'No way you're gonna be alone for this one, love.'

Laying the envelope flat on the table, I peeled back the largest flap. I reached in and pulled out the papers. At first, I couldn't make out what they were. Most looked official with a crest in the top right corner. Then, as I scanned over the pages, I recognised a name in amongst the Greek text.

'Dion! These papers are about Dion.'

Elena took the first page from me, her eyes scanning over the text. 'These are court documents showing the adoption of a boy called Dion Eastman.'

I snatched the page back to see for myself. 'Do they say who adopted him?'

Elena pointed to thick black squares on the page. 'Someone does not want you to see everything.'

Charles took the page and inspected the text. He ran his fingers over the surface of the page. 'Someone has photocopied these pages and then used a marker pen to obscure certain details.' He flipped the page over. 'Look. You can see where the blackout shows through the paper.'

'Why would anyone do that?' complained Reg. 'That's like offering you a donut and scrapping off the sprinkles.'

'We should get this back to the UK and see if we can find Sarah,' continued Charles. 'She'd know what to do with this.'

Janna's eyes lit up. 'I can help you with the translation.'

'I'll investigate where the paper came from,' said Charles. I banged my hand down on to the table top, making my palm sting. Everyone turned to look at me.

'My father warned me to never copy or retain anything that could be used against me.' I felt mean, raining on their parade, but I had to be firm. 'Sarah is experiencing enough trouble looking after what she has. These photocopies must stay in Greece. I came to Athens to look for evidence of Dion's safety, but knowing who his new family is, might put him in danger. I'll have to be content with what we have.'

I gathered the paperwork together and put it back in the envelope and handed it back to Janna. 'Keep this safe for me, but tell no one you have it.' Janna nodded solemnly.

I held Elena's hands as I kissed her goodbye. 'Take care, Elena. Tell Senior Constable Gabris, thank you.'

Charles sent coffee and sandwiches to my room at dinnertime, but I only drank the coffee. In the room, everything looked so temporary. Most of the time I liked that. Everything that could be changed and renewed would be fresh and clean.

Nick didn't much care for temporary options. He said hotel rooms made him feel pressured to keep moving.

Usually, he didn't bother to unpack. He rummaged in his case for the things he wanted and complained that I had failed to remind him of what he had failed to pack. I took his toothbrush and toothpaste from the bathroom and let my eyes roam to ensure that we weren't leaving anything behind.

I stared at the contents of Nick's case and mentally scolded him for being so untidy. My case was a lesson in ordered neatness. Every item was folded and wrapped within the folds of another, not only to save space, but to save time when unpacking and choosing what to wear.

Nick's case was a chaos of piles. A pile of shirts sat next to a pile of shorts, which sat next to a pile of socks, next to a pile of pants. Sorting in piles was as neat as Nick could be. I no longer offered to pack his case for him. It was only today that I had to. It struck me as silly to think that unpacking makes life less of a temporary journey.

I watched my tears as they dropped from the end of my nose, on to a cotton shirt and soaked through the thin fabric. I picked it up and inhaled him.

'God, Nick. Why did you have to leave me?' I cuddled his shirt tight in bed and cried until I slept.

I woke early and showered and dressed, but ignored the rumblings in my tummy and let breakfast time pass until Reg came to fetch me at 9.30. My thoughts were interrupted by a gentle tap on the door. I hurriedly brushed the tears away and called out, 'Just coming.'

Reg took Nick's case and I wheeled mine to the lift and

down to reception. A taxi took us to the hospital and waited while Reg and I were shown to the Administration Office behind reception. Dr Christoph was waiting for us.

'There are two forms for you to sign,' he explained. 'One releases your husband from us to the International Funeral Director and the other confirms his security to travel.'

'Will I see him going on to the plane?'

Reg wrapped an arm around my shoulder. 'You wouldn't want to, love.'

'No,' said Christoph. 'It is discreet.'

I signed quickly, without allowing myself to think about it. 'Thank you, doctor. For everything.'

Christoph took my hand and smiled gently. 'Be well, Mrs Anderson.'

Back in the taxi, Reg held my hand. 'You didn't come down for breakfast again this morning.'

'Definitely not this morning. How was Patricia?'

'Pretty much as you'd expect; difficult and emotional. George was calmer. Charles has more patience than me. He's escorting them to the airport.'

'Poor Charles. Poor George.'

'Be nice to Patricia when we get there; she's had a rough ride.'

I kept my mouth shut for the rest of the journey. I had no idea how I was going to respond to Patricia.

Chapter 38

'Oh, there you are,' Patricia straightened as we approached. 'Finally. Perhaps we can get a move on now. Where's Nick?'

'The hospital transport is following us. They'll ensure he is boarded. I've just signed the forms.'

'Yes, thank you for that, Kimberly. I'm asking where he will be.'

'I don't know where he'll be. Probably in the lower levels of the plane.'

Patricia gave a little smile and continued to talk to me like a child. 'That's where the cargo goes.'

'Were you expecting first class?'

'I'd expect better than the lower levels. I'd expect a little respect.' Patricia's voice was rising in both pitch and volume. 'I'd expect you to know what's happening with our son and to have arranged this appropriately.'

George put his hand on Patricia's arm and spoke gently. 'Now, Tish. Kim's doing everything she can. We don't know that we could have done more.'

'We would have behaved more kindly. We would have these details arranged. I don't think she's doing enough.' Tears were forming in Patricia's eyes and the frustration she felt with me could not be contained any longer. 'I don't think you've handled this at all well,' she said to me. 'It's been an absolute nightmare. You've ignored our feelings and withheld your own.'

'Tish...'

'Oh, shut up, George. It needs to be said. Why? Why have you ignored us? Why have you been so insular, so cold? Don't you have any feelings at all?'

'I can't deal with this,' I whispered. My breathing was ragged and my own tears threatened to spill.

'Let's check in our luggage and get a cup of coffee,' suggested Charles. 'We have time before the flight.'

'I don't want any coffee,' said Patricia, her voice still shrill. 'I want to know why Kimberly has remained indifferent, especially as it's been obvious that George and I haven't been coping well.'

'I can't deal with this.' I pressed my hand against my pounding heart. 'I want to go to Crete.'

'Can't deal with what? Honest emotion? And now you want to run away!'

'Fuck you, Patricia!' My tears burst forth and my cheeks burned. I'd supressed my emotions but now the lid had flown off. 'When I said, "I can't deal with this," I wasn't trying to fob you off. I really mean, I can't deal with this, I don't know how. I don't have the words to tell you how I'm feeling. That doesn't mean I don't feel anything. Sometimes if you ask someone how they feel and they say "I don't know," that is an honest answer. So please, do me an enormous favour and don't bother telling me how you're not coping. I am barely surviving my own misery. I can't handle yours as well.'

Patricia stared at me, horrified.

'Really! What a performance! Well, if that's how you feel, perhaps we should cut ties now. George and I will arrange the funeral and we need never see each other again.'

'Tish! Kim's still his wife.' George's attempt at placation fell on deaf ears.

'You know what, Patricia, I'm sick of tiptoeing around you.' I thrust Nick's paperwork towards George. 'I'll arrange the funeral and send you an invitation.' I grabbed the handle of my case and started wheeling it towards the information desk. I needed to change my flight. 'You can sulk at home until then. I'm going to Crete!'

I used my disposable phone to make a quick call to Perdika and Perry assured me that he'd be delighted to see me.

Perhaps Patricia was right, I was running away, but I still had unanswered questions and knew I couldn't face returning to the UK without some closure.

Less than an hour after boarding the plane, I landed in Heraklion. Perry and his mother, Sofika, stood waiting in the arrival hall. The expressions on their faces told me that they already knew about Nick. Sofika held out her arms and again, just like I had with Charles and Reg, I experienced a sense of family. The welcome was bittersweet, but Crete felt like home.

'Kokaliaris,' said Sofika, holding my face in her hands.

'Kourasmenos.'

'Mama says you need food and sleep,' said Perry. 'Come. You'll have lunch with us.'

'Being in my company has become a dangerous pastime,' I warned. 'Someone is after me.'

Perry nodded. 'News reached us of your friend's death and then that of your husband. And the explosion outside the Consulate was on the evening news. They say it was caused by unhappy political demonstrators.'

Perry led the way towards the exits, his lanky body dipping to the left with each stride. I'd forgotten he walked with a limp. He looked young and fragile. I suddenly stopped. Perry and Sofika turned to look at me with surprise in their eyes. I bit my lip and felt it tremble as I tried to put awkward words in order.

'Am I doing the right thing? Is it worth it? Should I give up?'

Perry and Sofika looked at each other before Sofika frowned and waggled a stern finger in my direction. Her voice was soft, but it was clear I was being told off.

'You should never give up,' translated Perry. 'We did not create a resistance in the war to give up our freedoms to corporate greed. You are doing the right thing. Yes, it is dangerous, but the right thing often is.'

'But, I'm not just worried about Fireflight. I'm also worried about Troy. They have a financial interest still ongoing.'

Perry shook his head. 'Kiki tells me the payments have

stopped again. I don't know what you did, but it worked.'

'It's just that...' I squeezed my eyes shut so that I wouldn't cry. 'I don't think I can forgive myself for what happened to Nick. I couldn't bear it if anything happened to you, too.'

Perry grinned. 'But we are not alone. You have an army, Athena. You have The Network.'

There was little lunchtime trade at Perdika and Perry was able to cope with the customers alone, while Sofika loaded their private table at the rear with enough Meze to feed twenty. After I had eaten and Sofika was satisfied I couldn't manage another bite, Perry and I retired to the comfortable chairs in the coffee lounge to speak privately.

'I heard that you had a meeting with Zeus,' said Perry, with more than a hint of admiration in his voice. 'That must have been an interesting conversation.'

'He wants me in Fireflight.' I leant back against the soft chair and felt very tired. 'Someone in the Olympian group wants me assassinated; Zeus offered me his protection as my father.'

'But none of the Olympians can be related.'

'That's what we've been told. The gods can't risk familial relationships in their group; the gene pool is too shallow and the risk of genetic abnormality is too high. That's why they need the female participants.'

Perry sat forward with his elbows on his knees and rested his chin on his fists. 'But what if,' he frowned as he put his thoughts in order. 'What if they experimented? What if they tried and were successful?'

'You mean if they chose to break the rules?' Perry nodded. 'Then the gods, and the procedure, must have been chosen very carefully. And only certain Olympians would have known.'

Perry shrugged. 'Yes, unless...'

'Unless what?'

'Unless they forgot about being gods and remembered that they are human.'

'You're talking about Zeus and Metis? I know that Mother was his girlfriend while they were at university, but she was already looking for a way out. Mother and Dad married when she found out she was pregnant.'

Perry nodded as he absorbed this information. 'That makes me think that maybe the pregnancy changed your mother's mind about Zeus, or maybe she had two boyfriends and could fall from the arms of one into the arms of another.'

That was an uncomfortable thought.

'I can't imagine that my mother would do such a thing.' But I realised as I spoke, I didn't really know her. 'Mother and Dad must have discussed what they would do at some point between university and work.' That made any possibility sound a little more reasonable, but I dropped my head with the unhappy realisation that I could no longer ask them.

Perry asked a question that I had not yet asked myself. 'If Zeus is offering you protection, could he know who from?'

I took a moment to think about that. 'It's possible, but

even if he suspects, I don't think he can be sure, or why not just eliminate the threat? No, I think he and I both know that whoever is doing this, doesn't know that Zeus is my biological father.'

'You have a list of suspects?'

'Yes; too long to mention.'

'Who among them have you angered the most?'

I laughed humourlessly. 'Pick anyone you like. Ares wasn't pleased to see me, but it was Gaia she assassinated. I still haven't managed to figure out why. Zeus told me that was unauthorised. Helen suggested that Gaia might have known something about Ares she shouldn't. You wouldn't know what that was, I suppose?'

Perry thought about that, frowning. 'Helen was Eileithyia,' he said.

'Yes. So?'

'Eileithyia and Ares are brother and sister. Or in the legends they were. What is the relationship between Helen and New Ares?'

'I don't know. This is news to me. Ares has disappeared in the UK and Helen has disappeared in Greece. If they are sisters, we now know why. If Gaia had found out, would that have been enough of a reason to get her killed?'

'How would she have found out?'

'Perhaps Helen told her, although I think that's unlikely. Unless...'

Perry leaned a little closer. 'Unless what?'

'Unless Helen told Ares that Gaia knew. If the

assassination was unauthorised, perhaps Helen and Ares had another reason to get rid of Gaia.'

Perry nodded. 'Maybe. But what about the threat to you?'

'I don't think this is enough cause for Ares to want to kill me; I didn't even know.'

'Then we are looking for someone else. Perhaps someone unexpected, someone you did not know you had angered.' Perry's choice of words made me think back to Medana.

'There was one thing. We were on our way to the Olympian's hotel, when I was ambushed by Medana. She was furious, and justifiably, I think.'

'Yes, the student who was assassinated at the university.'

'That's right. You know the story, don't you? She was assaulted last year and wanted me to find out who he was.'

Perry nodded. 'I investigated Leander Regas. He blames you for the attack.'

'So did Medana.'

'Did she give you any clues?'

'She only knew her rapist as Poseidon, that was the only clue she could give me.'

'Poseidon? But Athena, he is your enemy!'

I massaged away the tiredness in my neck. 'I must have hundreds of enemies by now.'

'No, I mean Poseidon is the enemy of Athena. In the legends, they fought for Athens and Athena won. Poseidon never forgave her. We should find out who this person is.'

I paused my massage and sat up a little straighter. 'So, you think my digging into Medana's story brought me to

Poseidon's attention?'

'For sure.'

'My friend, Charles, discovered a name, but we thought the threat came from Helen or Hera. We were under the assumption that she spoke to a woman.'

Perry parted his hands as he made a suggestion. 'She could have spoken to a man who told her the order came from Hera.'

'How does an assassination order work?'

'We think that all the Olympians need to be in agreement before an assassination can be ordered. But we also think it is Zeus who has the final say. If he is offering you protection, then he would not approve the assassination of his daughter.' I wasn't so sure. Zeus needed me, but that didn't make me indispensable.

'Did you tell anyone what Poseidon's real name might be?'

'No, I mean, we can't be sure if the name is current or an original...' I closed my eyes and smacked my forehead. 'Yes, I did tell someone! Stupid! I asked Leander if he recognised the names Charles had uncovered. Hugo Clearwater. Leander said that was a man at the American university.'

A huge smile spread across Perry's face. 'I think perhaps the Hellenic Police would be interested to hear that name.'

'Yes,' I said, thinking of Senior Constable Gabris. 'But there are still a few things I don't understand. The relationship between Troy and Fireflight is still unclear. Troy might be aware of Fireflight's illegal activities, but the way they behaved after I leaked information suggests that they'd back off if anything they were involved in became public knowledge. It must cost Fireflight huge amounts of money to do what they want. If they're getting their financing from Troy, then what are Troy getting in return?'

Perry shrugged again, but continued to smile. 'Another conversation for the Hellenic Police, I think. If they know of Fireflight, they will know of Troy.'

I tried to share Perry's upbeat demeanour. 'I hope so,' I replied. 'I hope so.'

Chapter 39

That night, in the tiny box room above the restaurant, I looked out towards the coast. As the fiery sun dipped below the horizon, the sea responded sending fingers of steaming light upwards with a silent hiss.

I slept with a peace I hadn't experienced in over two weeks, but as the early morning sun expanded to fill the room, my dread grew with it. It was time for me to go home and face the reality of my life.

Perry made me coffee as his mother slept, and pulled a package from the fridge.

'Sandwiches,' he said. 'Mama made for the journey.'

I took them gratefully. 'Tell her thank you. For everything.'

I stared out of the car window as Perry drove me through the pretty streets of the old town. Crete had a charm I knew I was going to miss back in the UK. I watched as the shops and apartments became more modern and touristy as we approached Heraklion International.

'I'm going to miss you,' I said as I hugged Perry goodbye. 'I owe you more than I say.'

'We are never far away,' said Perry. 'Nowhere is more than a day away from anywhere else. Take care, Athena.'

I landed at Gatwick just before 10am UK time, and spotted the detectives standing just the other side of passport control. They were just two very ordinary men in ordinary clothes, talking to each other, but their shoulders stiffened and their eyes narrowed as soon as they saw me.

'You're not under arrest. At present,' said the eldest. 'But DCI Gardner and DI Kelly would like a word.'

I was taken directly to the police station, hot and sweaty from the flight and desperate for a shower and a cup of tea. I was not going to be offered either.

DCI Gardner sat upright in his chair. I guessed him to be in his late forties, his fair, sandy hair fading to grey at the temples. His wedding band winked at me from across the table and his clear blue eyes appraised me steadily as he maintained a calm and neutral expression. Could I trust him? Probably, but he showed no concern for my wellbeing as Charles had done when we first met. Gardner was a good guy, but not a friend.

'Thank you for coming,' he said, as if I had a choice in the matter. 'I'm sorry for your loss. Your co-operation under the circumstances is appreciated.'

Kelly folded her hands on the table in front of her. She pretended to look bored, but the shine in her eyes told me otherwise.

'We keep on meeting, don't we, Mrs Anderson?'

'We do, DI Kelly. And what is it that summons me today?'

'Paperwork has been sent to us.' Kelly slid a sheet, protected by a plastic cover, across the table towards me. This was a transcript of the conversation I'd had with Detective Michalis following the explosion at the Consulate.

'Would you care to put us in the picture?'

'What exactly do you need to know?'

'Perhaps you could start with why you were at the British Consulate in the first place?'

I looked at DCI Gardner and wondered if perhaps Kelly was simply making a joke in bad taste. 'My husband was stabbed in Athens and I went there to pick up the forms I needed to bring him back to the UK.'

'Is that the only reason?' asked Gardner.

'Yes, of course.' I could hear anger creeping into my voice.

'Really?' responded Kelly. 'Because we're given to understand that you are part of a clandestine movement designed to provoke and disrupt the activities of an illegal drugs trial operation. The British police and government do not operate with agents provocateurs.'

'I'm not a provocateur.'

'Then what are you?' DI Kelly looked as if she could smell something nasty as her eyes ran over me. 'A political agitator, a spy, or a terrorist?'

'If the British police really believed I was any of those things, I wouldn't be here explaining myself to you.'

'You certainly wouldn't,' agreed Gardner. 'And this wouldn't be the friendly chat it is at present. You need to stop with this ridiculous fantasy, Mrs Anderson. There is no conspiracy. Stop playing these silly spy games and leave the police work to the police.'

'And stop wasting our time,' said Kelly.

I felt myself start to tremble with rage and had to speak slowly to keep control. 'If there was no conspiracy, this conversation wouldn't be necessary.' I looked at Kelly. 'You don't think that you're wasting your time; I can smell your ruthless ambition from here. Who, exactly, asked you to interview me again?'

'Chief Superintendent Maxwell.' Kelly rose an inch in her chair, happy to boast about her boss.

'Wow. You gave that up easily.'

Gardner squared his shoulders and spoke sternly. 'It's him you have embarrassed, making a minor incident an international concern.'

'And what is his interest in my adventures?'

'I'm not at liberty to say...'

'So, you don't know, then,' I interrupted. 'Allow me to tell you what I think. I think that the British police are perfectly aware that Fireflight are operating in the UK. CS Maxwell shut down the investigation last year to save political embarrassment between the UK and Greece. Now I've kicked the hornets' nest, the police are obliged to investigate these issues at a time when they'd rather not. CS Maxwell has asked you to interview me to make sure that you know everything the Greek police know. How am I doing so far?'

'We're perfectly confident we know what the Greek police know.' DI Kelly lifted her chin, a move that made her look like a boastful child. 'We have an excellent relationship.'

'Excellent? Then you won't need to keep me any longer.

There'll be nothing more I can tell you.'

Kelly leaned forward across the table and narrowed her eyes at me. 'We're going to be watching you very carefully, Mrs Anderson. Very carefully.'

I kept my hands in my lap and leaned towards DI Kelly. We were nose to nose and I was close enough to smell her perfume; both sweet and sharp, mirroring the two sides of her personality.

'I'm easy to find, DI Kelly. Just follow the chaos.'

I was allowed to make my own way back home, but I was sure, the police weren't very far behind.

I dropped my keys into the bowl and dragged my case through to the tiny utility room at the back of the house. If Patricia had taken Nick's case from the airport, I'd probably never see any of its contents again. I hurriedly shoved most of my clothes into the washing machine and added extra detergent. If Nick were here, he'd be sorting through the mail and listening to the phone messages while I did this.

When the washing machine started its regular rumble, I walked slowly back through the empty hallway. I was unprepared for how physical this felt. It was if I'd lost an arm or leg; something was missing that I couldn't replace.

The answerphone light on the hallway phone was blinking. I pressed the play button.

'Our records show that you were involved in an accident. For comprehensive insurance advice...' delete. On to the next message. An automated voice.

'Thank you for your online purchase. Your credit card will

be charged four hundred and ninety-two pounds and seventy-two pence.' Where the hell did they get these figures? 'If this is incorrect, please press one to speak to an operator or five to cancel your order.' Delete. Next message.

'Hello Kim, it's Natalie. Hope you don't mind, but I asked Charles for your home number, I haven't been able to get you on your mobile.'

Yeah, sorry about that, but I've been kind of busy, what with my husband dying, and all.

'I'd really love to get back in touch and discuss our next steps; how we're going to bring down Fireflight and expose the government officials who knew all along.' Delete. Next message, please. I'm sorry Natalie, but I honestly don't have the strength.

'Hello, darling. It's me.'

Nick? Oh, my God! Nick!

'Hopefully I'll be through the door first and can delete this message before you hear it, and you'll be in the utility room putting the first load in the washing machine while I'm sorting through the mail. But if you're listening to this... well, then we both know the operation didn't go quite as planned.'

'You can say that again.'

'It didn't go quite as planned. I know your sense of humour, remember?'

A short laugh burst from me and I held my hand over my mouth to keep other noises contained while I listened to his voice.

'I'm borrowing Dr Christoph's phone and God knows how many rules he's breaking by letting me use it, so I'll be brief. He's explained to me the dangers of the operation and the CT scan doesn't look good. I'm running on adrenaline, but the outcome is uncertain.' He paused for breath. 'Christ, this hurts. I've been thinking of an old poem. I can't remember all the words, but if I don't make it home, be bold but modest in your grieving, there is a change but not a leaving. Listen for my footfall in your heart.' Nick took another breath. 'If things don't go our way, promise me three things.'

'Anything.'

'Firstly, don't let mum bully you or take over. She's highly strung and the way she copes is to take charge. Just give her time, she'll come around. Secondly, and this is important, don't retreat inside yourself. Our friends love you and it'll upset and worry them if you do. If you're invited somewhere, then go. You need to eat more than baked potatoes and beans on toast.'

'But that's all I can cook.'

'And thirdly, delete this message.'

'No way! I need this.'

'You don't need it and persuading yourself that you do will add to your anxiety. So, here goes. Three, two, one, delete. You didn't, did you?'

'No, I didn't. I couldn't.'

'Well, make sure you do. And soon. Goodbye darling. I love you.'

And then he was gone. I grabbed the phone and jabbed at the buttons. I needed to replay the message, or at least a bit of it.

'...soon. Goodbye darling. I love you.'

One more time. Please.

'Goodbye darling. I love you.'

I leant against the wall and collapsed into a seating position. It was all my fault. I was the one who had wanted to go to Athens. I was the one who refused to come home. I dropped my head into my hands and cried.

Chapter 40

The following weeks were taken up with funeral arrangements and I was glad of the distraction. March was drawing to a close and already, the early crocuses that had bravely bloomed first, were fading in the lawns, with daffodils dominating the flowerbeds.

Patricia left frequent messages on the answerphone to help with the arrangements, reminding me of Nick's favourite flowers and who his friends were. Despite our argument at the airport, she obviously wasn't ready to let go.

I'm sure Patricia would have insisted on a full church funeral with very dear friends, whom I had never met, but I decided on a simple cremation. It's true I probably couldn't have coped with larger crowds.

When the day arrived, Reg stood on my doorstep looking more dapper than I had ever seen him. Patricia and George sat stiffly in the limo in black overcoats, their sensible Volvo parked a little way down the road. The attendants standing by the flower-laden hearse politely bowed their heads as Reg and I climbed aboard and we slowly set off.

April showers had not yet started and a weak sun was trying to make itself felt. I remembered another time I had sat in the back of a black car on my way to a frightening event. It was our wedding day. Dad was more nervous than me. He'd arranged for a black cab to take us to the register office.

'You look beautiful, darling.'

'Thanks, Dad.'

'Your mother would be very pleased. She was always very proud of you, you know.'

'She was?'

'Of course, even though you were terribly independent, even as a little girl.'

'I can't even remember her that way. I remember doing a lot of things for myself at a young age.'

'You were the first in your class to knot your school tie on your own,' boasted Dad. 'And tying your shoe laces was a piece of cake. You were seven when you boiled your first egg. You were ever so cross when it came out hard. Like a rock, it was.'

'It seems strange that she'd let me boil an egg at that young age. You were the one who helped me.'

'Frequently, you would push your mother away and say "I can do it, I can do it". But she was never far; always watching from a little distance.'

'She didn't mind my stubbornness?'

'Darling, she encouraged it. Your mother didn't just give birth to you, she watched you grow and mentored your development. Nobody really wants to think about this, but parenting is basically teaching your children how to survive life without you.' Dad lent over to kiss my cheek. 'And you are living proof of a job well done.'

Nick's work colleagues stood nervously, sharing cigarettes and sad smiles with a couple of his old uni friends. Charles and Natalie came too.

I took Reg's arm as we followed the coffin with Patricia and George close behind and everyone else filed in silently behind them. I had requested a Church of England vicar to take the service, just to please Patricia, but asked him to open the lectern to anyone who wanted to say a few words. I had the honour of going first.

I stumbled forwards, notepaper in hand, intending to convey my love and gratitude for having Nick in my life. The words fell from the page like raindrops on a windowpane and I crumpled the paper in my fingers. I looked up to see Natalie and Charles smiling encouragement and Patricia with an I-knew-you'd-mess-this-up look on her face.

'I just wanted to say,' I started, 'I just wanted to say... well, just that, um,' I took another breath. 'I want to tell you that it was never lost on me how lucky I was to be married to Nick.' You don't have to be polite, I reminded myself. Just say what you think. 'I don't know if Heaven exists. I'm sure that Nick thought it unlikely,' I risked a sideways glance at the vicar, but he seemed unconcerned. There probably wasn't much he hadn't heard. 'But I'm also sure that if I'd asked him, he'd say that on balance, the unknown possibilities for the use of outer space make it more of a probability than not. And that is what made Nick my anchor, my safe place, because if you have a mind that shows you a view of the world that you know is different from the one everyone else sees, you need a translator; someone who will bridge the gap between how you see the world and how the world sees itself. I don't think that he intended to rescue me, but he did – from the first panic attack he witnessed at a friend's housewarming, to every shaky moment since.

'I've no idea why Nick married me. There were prettier, more intelligent women, more suitable women. But there were possibilities in each of us that the other saw. Like the possibility of Heaven, the fact that it's invisible doesn't make it impossible and the world is full of possibility.' I looked out at everyone looking back at me; at Charles and Natalie, 'The possibilities of kindness,' at his friends, 'the possibilities of fairness,' and at his parents, 'the possibilities of love. Nick taught me to be brave, because it is by embracing those possibilities that we become stronger.'

I stepped down and rather than returning to my seat, I kept walking and headed for a side door. An attendant stood guard, and looked surprised, but opened the door for me. I walked out on to a covered pathway where the brisk wind flapped at my coat. I sat on a low wall and waited for my breathing and heart rate to slow.

A shadow momentarily blocked the sun and Reg sat on the wall beside me. I hadn't expected anyone to follow me outside, but Reg didn't behave as if this was anything unusual. He remained silent as he took a small pouch from his pocket and started rolling himself a cigarette. I watched him in his simple task until he sparked his lighter and huffed a blue cloud into the space above our heads. I watched the smoke swirl and thought it a metaphor about the fleeting nature of life. I looked back at Reg, and still he didn't speak, but held out his arms in invitation. I fell against his shoulder and sobbed and sobbed.

Over the following days I left messages on Patricia and George's answerphone saying that if they wanted any of Nick's things, they only had to let me know, but I didn't receive any response.

I sorted through his clothes and got rid of the things with holes and the things that were damaged. I wrote to the dentist and visited the bank and called his employer. The university sent a letter of condolence to me and an invitation to Nick for a new course on the same day.

In unguarded moments, I'd still hear his voice.

'Why are you crying?'

Stupidly, I'd respond. 'Why do you think I'm crying? You left me.'

'Calm your mind. Remember the old poem, listen for my footfall in your heart.'

'Oh, shut up. You're gone. You left me.'

'I am still with you. Listen for my footfall...'

'Shut up, shut up, shut up! You left me you bastard! I know it wasn't your fault, but you left me. I hate you!'

'I love you.'

'I love you too. And I hate you. And I miss you.' And then I would try and drown his voice in tears and sub-standard gin with not enough tonic.

There are supposed to be five emotional stages to grief; denial, anger, bargaining, depression and acceptance. But they are unkind and disobedient and pay no attention to the order in which they should appear. The thing people often forget to tell you is that two or more can gang up and attack you at once.

Charles tried calling the following week. I watched my new mobile jiggle on the dining table as it vibrated. With a swift swipe left or right, I could make the noise stop, but I didn't want it to stop, I wanted the caller to go away.

Charles left a message, but I didn't retrieve it. I didn't want his messages. I didn't want his sympathy. I wanted my husband back and no one could give me that. He tried again the next day, and the next.

'Oh, for Christ's sake, Charles. Take the hint.' I had another drink and found my gin bottle half empty.

The day after that, I got up early to empty the cupboards of Nick's favourite foods. I had two boxes of shredded wheat, four boxes of extra-strong tea bags and two packets of chocolate digestives. I had no idea what I was supposed to do with them. Then the doorbell rang.

'Piss off,' I muttered. The neighbours could go screw themselves. It rang again.

'Kim? I know you're in there. Your wheelie bins are full and smell of lemons.'

'Go away Reg. I'm not answering the door.'

'Do you really want the neighbours to see me bending over to yell through your letterbox? It ain't pretty.'

I stood in the hallway to yell back at the door. 'I don't give a stuff what the neighbours think.'

'I know that's not true. Not if you're spraying the wheelie bins with air freshener.'

I opened the door. 'It's citrus disinfectant, actually.'

Reg held up a supermarket carrier bag. 'I brought you a present. Thought I'd drop it off on my way into work.'

I turned and marched back to the kitchen. 'I don't want any presents.'

'You're getting it anyway.' Reg followed me and eyed the glasses on the draining board. 'Especially if all you had for breakfast was paracetamol and coffee.'

'Would you like a cup of tea?'

'Sure.'

I flipped the kettle on. 'You can take the whole box of extra strong if you like. I only drink regular tea and coffee.'

'And gin, apparently.'

'God! What is this? Charles can't get me on the phone, so he's sent you round to spy on me?'

'I don't drink. I can smell it in your house; gin, furniture polish and lemons.'

'So he has sent you to spy on me.'

'He doesn't know I'm here. He called me 'cause he's worried. I'm worried, too.'

'Why? You're not my Dad. I'm not anything to you.'

'You're our friend, Kim. And we've got every right to be worried, if all you're eating is shredded wheat and chocolate biscuits.'

'Have one. Take the pack. These were Nick's favourite.'

'Kim...' he reached for my hand, but I shook him off.

'Don't. Don't you dare be pitying. And, for God's sake don't tell me you know how I feel.'

I sulkily put two cups on the kitchen counter.

Reg spoke gently. 'How are you, Kim. I mean, really? I do know what it's like to lose someone you love.'

I almost screamed with frustration. 'You have no idea what it's like – I'm drowning! I'm at sea and lost my anchor. I've got nothing left, except for a spiteful mother-in-law who wishes I was dead instead of her son. I wish that, too.'

'Don't you fucking dare tell me I don't know what it's like!' Reg's face was pink and his fists clenched the supermarket bag. 'I had no proper life until I met Dolly and nearly lost myself when she died. She wasn't just my anchor; she was my North Star. The only thing that stops me going back to the drink is knowing Dolly wouldn't like it.'

'But I have no one,' I shouted back.

'You have your Dad.'

'But he's not here! Why hasn't he made contact? I need him now.'

'Maybe revealing himself would put you both in danger. He's still out there.'

'But I have no one with me. I have no family.'

Reg angrily jabbed a finger at his own chest. 'I've got no family. You think you're the only sad screw-up around here? Dolly and me, we wanted kids, but they never came. All I've got now is you and Charles.'

I thought Charles was luckier than us. He had a child and grandchild, but he had also experienced grief.

'Charles lost his wife, too,' I whispered.

'Yeah, I know.' Reg spoke gently. 'His Jenny; he told me about her. But he's got a daughter. When his wife died they had each other, they had to pull together.'

I looked at Reg and suddenly felt very selfish. I had experienced something of Charles's situation myself. I remember when my father had sat with me in the living room, held my hands and explained that Mother had gone and it was just us, now. He promised to take good care of me, just like Mother would have wanted. We'd be all right. We had each other. I didn't understand. Gone? Gone where?

But Dad couldn't explain.

Reg lifted the bag and placed it on the countertop. 'In the micro, full power, three minutes.' He nervously ran his hands down the front of his trousers. 'I don't know what Charles wants,' he said softly, 'but he's a friend and when friends reach out to you, you don't turn away.' He left me there in the kitchen and saw himself out.

I waited several seconds before I felt brave enough to look inside the bag. It was a plastic takeaway box, refilled with something homemade. Lifting a corner of the lid, I took a cautious sniff. It was unmistakably chilli. I laughed in spite of my misery. Would it be unfaithful of me to enjoy it?

I didn't want it, but that lunchtime, I made myself eat it, salting it with my own tears. It was the only hot meal I had that day.

Chapter 41

Letters arrived with the logo of the local support team of social services in the corner. I kept them in a neat pile on the hallway table where they silently yelled at me. I guessed that they wanted to know what to do regarding Marie's dying wish. I was pretending that if I didn't open the envelopes, I wouldn't have to make a decision.

My phone rang again.

'Hello?'

'Hello Kim.'

'What is it, Charles? I'm actually quite busy.'

'Doing what? Reorganising your hallway closet?' My mind drifted to the half bottle of Beefeater's I had at the back of the glassware cabinet. 'Social Services have asked to speak with you.'

'What's it about?'

'You know bloody well what it's about. You've not responded to their correspondence, so a contact there looked me up. I've taken the liberty of making an appointment for you.'

'But, Charles...'

'Be at the council offices at 10 o'clock tomorrow morning. You won't have to be alone; I'll meet you there. It's decision time, Kim.'

I listened to the dialling tone for several seconds before I hung up. I turned and stared at myself in the hallway mirror. The woman who stared back at me had aged horribly over the past three weeks. My hair was dry and wiry. My skin looked like a grey, un-ironed bedsheet.

I felt like a failure. I was battling an unseen army, both within and without, and failing miserably. Fireflight would fix what I had done and I had no more cupboards to organise.

The following morning, I dressed as if going to work. I drank strong coffee and resisted the urge to add a shot of brandy to it.

The social worker was an older woman with a kind and sympathetic face. She introduced herself as Trudy and showed no surprise when I asked Charles to join us in the meeting room.

'I've been told of your recent upset, Kim,' she said, offering us seats around a small coffee table. 'My condolences.'

'Thank you.'

Trudy picked up a cardboard folder from the table. 'I understand that it was Ms King's dying wish that you care for her son, Eric.'

'That's right. I can't for the life of me imagine why.'

'Probably because she knew that if anything happened to her you'd go out of your way to discover the truth.'

Charles and I glanced at each other, wondering what she

knew, but Trudy didn't explain her perceptiveness.

'The current situation is due to change,' she continued. 'Eric was found an emergency placement and his foster parents have other children waiting, so alternative arrangements must be made.' Trudy shuffled some paperwork on her knees. 'Are you agreeable to fostering Eric?'

I looked across to Charles hoping for a sign, but this was a decision I had to make on my own.

Trudy coughed discreetly. 'I should mention, Eric's current foster parents have described him as a disagreeable and discontented child. He demands constant attention but seems reluctant to respond to his foster mother's face or voice.'

That sounded like a perfect description.

'Yes,' I said. 'I'll do it. But I'm going to need help.' Trudy nodded kindly. 'I was once described as a disagreeable child,' I continued. 'That was because the grown-ups around me didn't bother explaining anything.'

Charles smiled. 'Young children don't really have the capacity to understand what's going on around them.'

'That's true of most children,' I replied, 'but I think we can all agree, Eric is far from ordinary. Has he been tested for advanced IQ?' Trudy shrugged and shook her head. 'Then I think he should be. And to supplement my income, I'm going to rent out Nick's office, it'll make a great room. The spare bedroom will be for Eric.'

'Everyone in your household will have to undergo the

proper police checks,' said Trudy.

'I can vouch for this one,' I said, pointing to Charles. 'But go ahead. Charles is the most honest and decent man I know. I elect him to be my sponsor.'

Charles raised his eyebrows, but was kind enough not to reveal that this was a surprise.

Trudy handed me some forms. 'I'm afraid there is a lot of paperwork and one of our team will want to visit your house to conduct safety checks, but this is excellent news. I can start making arrangements straight away.'

'How long does this usually take?' asked Charles.

'Typically, about 20 weeks. After the initial assessment, you'll meet a panel and be assigned a social worker who will guide you through the process. As I hold Eric's case file, that will probably be me.'

'Both of us?' I reached out for Charles's arm. 'I mean, we're not, um, in a relationship.'

'Yes,' smiled Trudy. 'Both of you.'

Outside the offices, Charles offered me a lift back home. 'So, I'm moving in with you then?'

'I'm sorry to have dropped that on you, Charles. Would you like to?'

'Yes, of course. You're a better option than Emily.'

'I hope that wasn't too much of a shock.'

'You always manage to surprise me, Kim. What made you change your mind about fostering Eric?'

'Actually, I'd already decided when the letters from Social Services started arriving. But Eric and I do have a few things in common. We've both lost our mothers, I think it's likely that we both see the world a little differently than others and nobody explains things to children. I think that's a mistake.'

'But most children can't understand adult problems. They deserve to be protected.'

'I agree,' I said, 'but I think because nobody bothered to explain anything to me, I grew up asking the kinds of questions other children didn't ask.'

'Were you happy at school?' asked Charles.

'God, no! My parents made the mistake of sending me to a state primary school thinking that it would give me a more rounded view of life. Consequently, I got beaten up fairly regularly. I was the only child in the school who called her parents Mother and Daddy.'

'Did you have a good education?'
I had to think about that. 'I'm sure everybody did the best they could. I just never understood what anyone expected from me.'

Charles nodded. 'My parents weren't really parents. They were academics who had children. I was expected to go on to study law. They were terribly disappointed when I joined the force.'

Two weeks later, Charles had put his house up for sale and most of his furniture was in storage. He arrived on a Tuesday morning with three large cardboard boxes, two suitcases, a pot plant and a set of professional chef's cleavers.

He set a box down on what used to be Nick's desk. 'Do you like Chinese food? I've developed a taste for it.'

'I like any food I don't have to cook. The kitchen can be your domain, Charles. It's just that, um, I...'

'You can't cope with mess. I understand. I like order; everything has to have its proper place.' He glanced at my uncertain face. 'Are you sure you don't mind giving up Nick's office? I could stay with Emily while I look for a flat.'

'No, of course not,' I lied. 'It's nice to know that it'll be used and occupied. You can redecorate it, if you like.'

'Actually, I quite like the wallpaper.'

'Nick chose that.'

'Let me live with it for a while. I promise I'll give you plenty of notice before I start making messes. Have you been polishing? I can smell lemons.'

'Yes, I do that when I'm anxious.'

Charles rummaged in the box and pulled out the biggest teapot I'd ever seen and then produced two matching cups.

'How about I make us both a nice cup of tea?'

Twenty weeks later.

Trudy and Eric had been frequent visitors over the previous few weeks, but at last the day came when he could stay. Trudy said it would be for a three-month trial period, but I had already mentally decided that it would be for as long as Eric wanted.

'I'm afraid he's tired and irritable from the journey,' said Trudy as she carried Eric through the front door. 'Perhaps we should try putting him down for a nap.'

I led the way to the refurbished spare room and Trudy lay Eric in his cot. Eric immediately rolled over on to his front and wriggled himself up into a sitting position and continued to scream. He shook his tiny fists and yelled until his face turned purple.

'This is the issue his foster carers told me about,' shouted Trudy above the din. 'It's not uncommon for foster children to have screaming fits, but Eric's are quite extreme.'

'Why is he having temper tantrums?' I yelled.

'Young children under ten months are incapable of temper tantrums. This is just a screaming fit.'

It looked like a tantrum to me. 'Are you sure?'

'Kim, I've been working with children for over 25 years. I'm sure.' Trudy moved forward and lifted Eric from his cot.

'We'll check his nappy and offer him a drink,' she said. 'There's likely to be a specific reason for his discomfort.'

Eric wriggled and squirmed at Trudy's touch and refused to lie still on his mat as she checked his nappy.

'Hmm. That's strange. He's not dirty or wet. Perhaps some water.' But Eric didn't want his water cup. Trudy sat Eric back in his cot.

'Why are you doing that?' I yelled.

'Young children don't understand why they are feeling frustrated. When he sees that nothing is the matter, the frustration will stop.'

Eric appeared to disagree. His screaming grew louder. I stood up and held my arms out to Eric, but Trudy held up her hand.

'You should ignore the noise and wait for the screaming to pass.'

I looked at Eric. Big, fat tears were dripping from his chin. Exhaustion was slowly taking over, but the frustration had not abated. Trudy's sensible voice turned to white noise as I lifted Eric from the cot and sat him on the floor. I sat with him and pointed a stern finger under his nose.

'Stop!' Much to my surprise, he did. He lifted his pink and blotchy face to stare at me, his pouting bottom lip still quivering. I picked up a small fluffy duck and held it out to him. He looked at it and then back at me. He didn't want to play.

Trudy continued to speak, but I heard little of what she was saying. Eric and I had a communication of our own.

Grown-ups had been deciding what was best for him since his mother died, but none of the faces that had offered him love and comfort was the one he wanted. Eric didn't have the words to say how he was feeling, but I knew exactly. He was angry. And had every right to be.

Trudy hid her surprise well. 'I'm told that you're planning a little holiday at the seaside.'

'Yes, just a few days in Norfolk. We're leaving in a couple of weeks.'

'You've given the address and contact numbers to the office?'

'Oh, yes. Everyone's been very kind.'

Trudy seemed to be of the opinion that it was far too soon to be planning a holiday. 'Well don't forget to take your information pack with you and call if there are any problems.'

Eric rubbed his eyes and I picked him up. 'I think we'll be just fine.' I lay him down in the cot and he closed his eyes for a nap.

Charles and I celebrated Eric's homecoming with a takeaway.

'How come,' said Charles, licking ketchup from his thumb, 'that whatever celebratory meal you could have chosen...' he sucked vinegar and grease from a finger, 'it had to be fish and chips?'

I piled chips into a buttered roll and added ketchup.

'Because,' I mumbled taking the first blissful bite, 'the food that means most to you is often that which brings back favourite memories. One of mine is of eating fish and chips with Nick on the seafront. It was one of our first dates.'

I glanced across to Eric, who was holding a chip in his chubby fist and studying it as if he wasn't sure what to do with it.

'He doesn't seem too keen, does he?' commented Charles. 'Perhaps he'd prefer something a little more organic.'

I nodded. 'Good quality brain food will no doubt assist his progress, but we won't be the only ones watching him grow up.'

'You think The Company is interested in him already?'

'I'm sure they are. It would be naïve to think otherwise.'

'Are you considering moving?' Charles couldn't help glancing at the windows.

'To where?' I asked. 'And take several pairs of eyes with us?'

'Well, I don't suppose that was what Marie wanted,' agreed Charles.

'I'm going back, Charles.'

'Back where?'

'To Athens. There's unfinished business to attend to.'

Charles put down his fork. 'What the hell are you talking about?' He indicated Eric. 'The only business you need to worry about is him. You had to leave; Poseidon could have tried again.'

'That's what I mean,' I said, wiping my mouth with a paper napkin. 'He's not finished. Nothing is. I'll have to go back and end things myself.'

Charles looked at me in horror. 'Are you mad?! Poseidon will kill you. And if he doesn't, your only hope will be if Zeus recruits you.'

I shook my head as I remembered my conversation with Zeus. 'I think it's more than that. If I have the aegis, the gods will want to know if others have it too. They could turn their attention to the children.'

'For God's sake, Kim! Leave it to the police. You said yourself that both the Greek and British police know of Fireflight. You've done enough by bringing them out into the open. I don't know DCI Gardner, but I think he's right. Leave it to them.'

'I can't, Charles. I know you think I'm crazy, but I haven't been able to think of anything else since Nick died. I want to see if I can find evidence of the aegis in the UK and Greece. If so, then I'll have something with which to confront Zeus.'

'I think you're moving too fast.' Charles's eyes darted to the windows. 'If you're right, UK Fireflight will be onto you soon enough.'

I clasped my hands in front of me as I rested my elbows on the table. 'It's a risk, yes. But I can't sit still. It's just as dangerous to do nothing.'

'Well, promise me you'll wait at least until after our holiday,' replied Charles. 'I think Eric has had enough excitement for a while. At least we should be able to relax a bit in Norfolk.' He tickled Eric's cheek. 'We're going to the seaside!'

I asked the neighbours if they would be willing to wheel my bins to the kerb on the second week of August and they agreed.

'Are you sure you want to do this?' asked Charles as he loaded Eric's bag into the boot of his car. 'You can change your mind.'

I looked at Eric asleep in his car seat, waiting to be put in the car. 'I'm sure. This is a significant life change, isn't it? Welcoming a baby.'

'You've been through enough significant life changes over the last couple of years,' said Charles. 'But I hardly think Patricia and George, I mean...'

'Yes, I know. Eric isn't Nick's child. Whenever he touched on the subject of us having children, I'd put him off. I always thought we had time. I regret that now, but I was never sure I wanted children. I couldn't imagine myself as a mother.'

'You are now. And a good one. You're sensible and fair and you maintain a structured routine.'

'Yes, but that's more for my benefit than Eric's.'

'It benefits you both. It's almost as if Eric is content because he knows where he stands with you.'

'Or maybe he already has the measure of us,' I replied, picking up the car seat. 'Thanks for the car seat, by the way. I'd forgotten to buy one.'

'What car seat?' Charles stood up and straightened his back.

'Eric's car seat. It arrived last week while you were out.'

'I thought you bought that. I'm sorry, Kim, but I didn't

buy it.'

'Then where did it come from?' I looked from Eric to Charles and back again. Who else knew I was fostering Eric?

'A kind benefactor?' suggested Charles.

The drive to Norfolk was relatively straightforward, bar one set of roadworks and we arrived in Dereham at lunchtime. Eric woke for a bottle and a snack at about 12 o'clock and was awake and alert as we drew up outside Patricia and George's neat little bungalow.

'Don't you want to check into the hotel first?' asked Charles. 'What if Patricia slams the door in your face?'

'Then I'll have to accept that she wants nothing to do with either of us. We'll drive on to Sheringham and Eric can still have a holiday at the seaside.'

'I'll stand by the car. Then we can make a quick getaway.'

'You chicken!'

'Too right, I am.'

I held Eric tightly in my arms and with just a quick glance back at Charles, rang the doorbell. Patricia opened the door and her enquiring expression soured like vinegar poured into milk.

'What are you doing here?'

'We're on our way to the coast on holiday and stopped here to introduce you to Eric.'

Patricia stared from me to Eric and back again. 'Who is he?'

'He's Marie's baby. Be careful of your hair, he likes to grab.'

Patricia's eyes widened and she leant forward slightly to whisper. 'The one in the newspapers? The one who was shot?'

'Who is it?' called George. His familiar frame emerged from the living room. I felt my heart jump as it was obvious where Nick had inherited his height and bearing. 'Kim? Good Heavens! And a baby!'

'Hello George. This is Eric. Eric, this is Grandpa George.'

Patricia lifted her nose and crossed her arms. 'Well, I hardly think that's appropriate.'

George ignored her to reach over and lift Eric from me. It had obviously been a while since he'd held a little boy in his arms and I saw his eyes water as they observed each other. Eric giggled, showing off his two new teeth.

'Curious little fellow, isn't he? Well, don't just stand there, come in, come in. Is that Charles by the car? Tish, put the kettle on; little Eric has come to visit.'

KL Skinner

Karen is an avid reader and has been writing short stories for as long as she can remember. Unfortunately, Karen found that a lot of what she was reading lacked emotional drama and suspense so started to write for herself.

Karen has been a member of the Hertford Writers' circle for the last 14 years and has contributed to their anthologies. She has two short story collections, as well as other short stories online. This is Karen's second novel, part of a series. The next instalment is due for completion next year.

Karen is married and lives in Essex.

Photograph by David P Macdonald
davidpmacdonald.com

klskinnerauthor.com

Select Bibliography

Pandora's Jar
– Natalie Haynes, 2020, Pan Macmillan

Athens, A History of the World's First Democracy
– Thomas N Mitchell, 2019, Yale University Press

Laws, by Plato
– Benjamin Jowett, 2012, Digital Edition

A Theatre For Dreamers
– Polly Samson, 2020, Bloomsbury Circus

Eurydice Street, A Place in Athens
– Sofka Zinovieff, 2005, Granta Books